"Sir, we have incoming bogies crossing the inner marker. Savage One is in the lead," came the voice of one of the infantry squads on his command channel. Savage One—that was Kroff. Roderick checked his chronometer; she was a little later than expected, but other than that she had matched his predictions.

"You're going down, sir," said Kroff. To emphasize her point she throttled power to her *Violator*'s drill. It whirred menacingly at him as she moved forward.

Roderick signaled his own unit. "Fire for effect on target Alpha One."

She closed the gap at the top of the flattened hill to almost within striking distance when suddenly puffs of white went off everywhere around the two of them. Artillery. *His* artillery. His battle computer recorded damage as he backed the *Rifleman* away from her. Kroff lunged her *Violator* forward as she realized that the barrage was coming down on both of them. Their battle computers logged the damage as the top of the hill was enveloped in white.

He heard her 'Mech but couldn't see it. His sensors told him the story. Things had gone just as planned. "Cease fire," he ordered. It took two minutes for the powder to clear enough for him to see the *Violator* lying flat on its front torso in front of him. It had shut down as she leapt at him.

"Are you okay, Leutnant?"

"You stinking bastard," she replied. "You dropped artillery on both of us."

"Damn it," she spat. "No one would bring down an artillery barrage on themselves."

"Apparently they would."

MECHWARRIOR
DARK AGE

FIRE
AT WILL

A BATTLETECH™ NOVEL

Blaine Lee Pardoe

RoC

A ROC BOOK

ROC
Published by New American Library, a division of
Penguin Group (USA) Inc., 375 Hudson Street,
New York, New York 10014, USA
Penguin Group (Canada), 90 Eglinton Avenue East, Suite 700, Toronto,
Ontario M4P 2Y3, Canada (a division of Pearson Penguin Canada Inc.)
Penguin Books Ltd., 80 Strand, London WC2R 0RL, England
Penguin Ireland, 25 St. Stephen's Green, Dublin 2,
Ireland (a division of Penguin Books Ltd.)
Penguin Group (Australia), 250 Camberwell Road, Camberwell, Victoria 3124,
Australia (a division of Pearson Australia Group Pty. Ltd.)
Penguin Books India Pvt. Ltd., 11 Community Centre, Panchsheel Park,
New Delhi - 110 017, India
Penguin Group (NZ), 67 Apollo Drive, Rosedale, North Shore 0745,
Auckland, New Zealand (a division of Pearson New Zealand Ltd.)
Penguin Books (South Africa) (Pty.) Ltd., 24 Sturdee Avenue,
Rosebank, Johannesburg 2196, South Africa

Penguin Books Ltd., Registered Offices:
80 Strand, London WC2R 0RL, England

First published by Roc, an imprint of New American Library,
a division of Penguin Group (USA) Inc.

First Printing, October 2007
10 9 8 7 6 5 4 3 2 1

Copyright © WizKids, Inc., 2007
All rights reserved

R̅O̅C̅ REGISTERED TRADEMARK—MARCA REGISTRADA

Printed in the United States of America

To my family—Cyndi, Alex and Victoria

ACKNOWLEDGMENTS

My thanks to Jean Armstrong, Tim King and Andy Parks and a spectacular weekend at the Lafayette Foundation in Colorado. My gentle nod to Central Michigan University—my alma mater—as well as Ernst & Young LLP, a constant source of good personalities and potential characters.

Special thanks to Sharon, the unsung hero who corralled the writers of the BattleTech/MechWarrior universe. Without her it wouldn't be possible to bring you some of these stories or any of these characters.

BOOK I

A Matter of When, Not If

"Hard pressed on my right. My center is yielding. Impossible to maneuver. Situation excellent. I am attacking."

—French General Ferdinand Foch, The Great War, Terra, early twentieth century

Algorab
Republic of the Sphere
Eight Months Earlier

"**S**omebody want to tell me what in the hell is going on?" asked Hauptmann Roderick Frost as his Clan-manufactured *Rifleman IIC* jogged along the dirt road, kicking up a massive cloud of dust that floated behind him. There was a hint of rain on the horizon, dark purple storm clouds billowing up, now and then flaring with a white burst of lightning.

"I got a message from our Republic liaison, Hauptmann. Sounded like something was going on—not exactly the training script we agreed to."

Roderick checked his long-range sensors. He was picking up some anomalous readings to the north that kept appearing and disappearing. Could be the storm, but he had to admit that was wishful thinking. "Chancy, what exactly do you mean?"

"She said something about a raiding force. It should be part of the joint exercise, but I thought we had agreed to a different set of objectives."

We did. "Ice Wind to Ramrod," he said into the comm-link. "Colonel, I am picking up unexpected readings in your area. Is that our Republic opponent?"

The crackle of static sounded loud. Jamming. *Shit.* "Ice Wind . . . Jade Falcons. Republic forces . . . and routed. Need to fall back to . . . Hill twenty-nine. Repeat, concentrate on Hill twenty-nine." Colonel Quentin's voice was filled with panic. If they were facing Jade Falcons, panic was appropriate. *Damn!* He had been raised on his grandfather's stories of facing the Jade Falcons on Somerset; even a chance that they really were on-planet tightened his nerves to the breaking point. He wondered if he was genetically programmed to hate what they represented.

He pulled his attention back to the situation and checked the map. *Hill 29?* Roderick shook his head. Drew Quentin's lack of tactical knowledge was showing. Quentin had received his commission based on political connections; this situation called for true military understanding. Hill 29 was a small, exposed hill surrounded by other hills of approximately the same height. *We get onto that hill, they'll flank us and pummel us on the open ground.* "Ramrod, come in. Recommend we fall back to sector one-five. The swamps and forest are better ground for us against the Falcons."

He got no response on the channel but the jamming static. Colonel Quentin's Identify Friend or Foe transponder faded from the tactical display—meaning he was either completely jammed or dead. *If the CO is down or incapacitated, I'm the ranking officer. It's my call.* He switched to the Lyran command frequency. "Rangers, we need to get a handle on this situation. Concentrate at the following coordinates." He stabbed in the location so that it would appear on the general tactical map.

"Sir, what about the command lance?" Forrester asked.

"You have your orders," he said, angling his massive *Rifleman* in a running arc to get a better bearing on the signals racing toward him. "On my authority, execute." If he was still alive, Colonel Quentin would show up to take over running this disaster. *In the meantime, this is* my *disaster. . . .*

Prologue

The Royal Stables and Arena
Tharkad, Lyran Commonwealth
10 November 3136

Trillian Steiner pulled on the hooks to tug her tall riding boot into place. She would have to have her boots cleaned today. They had watered the indoor arena to knock down the dust, and that, combined with the usual barn debris, guaranteed that they would *need* cleaning.

The royal stables and exercise arena had been a sanctuary for her and members of her family for years. The press didn't come here, and the massive domed facility kept out the often bitterly cold Tharkad weather. It was posh, isolated, free from prying eyes and ears. The steeplechase facilities were the epitome of opulence, a luxury few outside House Steiner would even imagine. Trillian loved coming here, choosing her ride from one of the two dozen or so Thoroughbreds in the stable. Here she was not the personal adviser to the archon: on the back of a horse, she was simply another rider, testing her will against the will of the horse.

In the massive arena, she seemed insignificant, and there was something about that feeling that pleased her. From an early age she had been in the limelight. The press hounded her like a pack of wolves, taking pictures everywhere she went. There was no private life except in this place. There was no place else she could simply be herself. Thanks to the press, the whole population of the Lyran Commonwealth thought they knew her. When she dated, they ferreted out the man's background; they knew where they went and what they ate. Her choice of clothing set trends.

They don't know me at all. She approached the horse she had chosen for today, a deep brown animal standing seventeen hands tall, and stroked his long neck. *I'm not sure I know myself that well anymore.*

Unlike her riding partner, she preferred to saddle her own horse. She mounted, tossing her long slender leg over the pommel. Shifting slightly in the English saddle, she glanced at the door to the barn and saw the members of the security detail watching her with just a hint more than professional interest. There were more of them than usual in the stables today, but she understood.

As soon as she cleared the door under the massive dome, she wound her way into the artificially created countryside. Lush green grasses and dense clusters of trees and brush were separated by the occasional low stone or wood fence. A low, shallow wash crossed the field. More than twenty acres of domed land provided plenty of space to ride. "All right, Big Ben, let's see what you've got today. Trot, trot!" As if he were as anxious as she to start moving, Ben broke into a trot. After a few seconds Trillian leaned forward and tightened her stance to canter, ducking low under a limb.

Trillian smiled. For a moment she could forget about her job and even the rest of the Inner Sphere. Here, if for only a minute or two, she was free from obligations, her duty, her family name, the people who admired her and those who hated her. She enjoyed the sweet smell of the air as she turned Big Ben around a low clump of cedar trees. In the distance, on a slow rise, she saw her riding partner. Riding a large white mare named Golden Charm was Melissa Steiner, archon of the Lyran Commonwealth and her cousin. At the moment, she looked more like a practicing dressage rider than the leader of a Great House. She raised her riding crop and touched her helmet at the sight of Trillian. Trillian angled Big Ben toward her superior and came to a stop a respectful distance away.

"You chose Ben today? I'm surprised, after he threw you last time," Melissa said.

Trillian said nothing for a second. She hadn't told Melissa about Big Ben throwing her. *Does she have people watching me?* She knew the answer to that question and regretted even thinking it—of course she had people watching her. One did not remain archon of the Commonwealth without monitoring people in positions of authority. "I can't let him get away with that. If he tosses me and I don't ride him again, he'll think he's in charge."

The archon gave her a warm smile. "It's good to see you, Trillian."

"And you, Your Highness." They had been friends their entire lives, even though the archon was a few years older. She automatically glanced around, looking for the guards who would be shadowing the archon, even in here. The ventilation system pushed a warm breeze through the air. Outside the dome, the snow had stopped.

"You can drop the formality, Trillian," Melissa chided her, angling her own steed in a slow walk to the right. "You know that—we're not at court."

"Old habits die hard." She smirked. She liked giving her cousin a hard time occasionally. The two had been raised like sisters after the death of Trillian's parents in that horrible accident. Unconsciously, she reached up and touched the symbol that hung on the necklace she wore under her skintight top. It was a Cameron star—a symbol of the old Star League. The necklace had been a gift from her father to her mother. Touching it somehow relaxed her.

"Yes," Melissa agreed. "Old habits for nations die hard as well, and that's what I want to talk about." There was a tone in her voice that Trillian recognized, and she knew her cousin was choosing her words carefully.

"You've piqued my curiosity."

Melissa Steiner tossed her a quick grin, and then her expression became serious again. "The collapse of The Republic and the formation of 'Fortress Republic' places the Lyran Commonwealth at risk. Simply stated, I want to avert that risk."

They had spoken before of the risks posed by the demise of The Republic, and had grimly noted that the list was long. "You're afraid that other nations will see us as weak if we don't join in feasting on the corpse of The Republic." Trillian was just restating the concerns Melissa had shared since reports of the consolidation of Fortress Republic. The Republic worlds outside the Fortress had been left to fend for themselves, and the other governments were greedily devouring them.

The archon nodded once. "With the Jade Falcons sitting in Skye, there is little that I can reclaim from The Republic, even if that were my inclination. Even the little Marik-doms are carving out parcels of the old Republic. You're the family historian, Trillian—you know what happens when we are seen as weak."

"We are attacked."

Melissa Steiner's face seemed to narrow at the word. "Yes. There have been exceptions, of course—the Fourth Succession War was sparked by Hanse Davion on behalf of our combined realms. But even during the Jihad—when we did not act aggressively, our neighbors tried to take advantage of our apparently passive behavior."

Trillian could have debated the issue. The Jihad-period attack against the Commonwealth that had been perceived as House Marik aggression was proven to be the Word of Blake's doing. But arguing such points with her cousin never accomplished anything, so she held her tongue. Anyway, Trillian agreed with her cousin's general conclusion. "I agree with you on that point."

"Good," Melissa replied, shifting with her horse. "For weeks now I have been considering how to deal with this state of affairs, and I've decided to implement a policy change, one that will require your special talents."

"Yes?"

"We will not wait for our inferiors to attack us and force us to react. We will take an aggressive stance. We will strike at those nations that we know will one day come for us, those who have shown a historical pattern of attacking our realm. The exarch's Fortress Republic plan has both long- and short-term dangers. Rather than feed on the carcasses of the isolated worlds left outside Fortress Republic, we will move first to ensure that our borders remain safe." Her voice was stern, and Trillian knew there would be no compromise—no wavering.

The mention of Fortress Republic always affected Trillian. She believed in the ideals of Devlin Stone, and the implementation of the Fortress tested her belief. She could see the brilliance of the plan, but also the very real risks. She knew that Melissa was firmly focused on the long-term implications of the exarch's plan. In the archon's words, "We are not going to take rash action that will incur the wrath of the exarch when he or his successors finally emerge." Melissa knew that the consolidation of The Republic's borders would allow The Republic to rebuild, rearm and one day pose a deadly threat.

Trillian thought for a moment. She thought she knew the target of this new policy. Over the centuries, there was one House that had proven itself to be a dangerous foe time and time again. "House Marik?"

"At first," the archon replied. That left room for interpretation.

Big Ben tugged at his reins with a toss of his head, straining to move. *A good horse is meant to be ridden—they hate to stand idle.* "The former Free Worlds League nations are not a serious threat to us, Melissa. Anson Marik is the most dangerous of their rulers only because he seems to have the greatest ambition. The Duchy of Tamarind-Abby is governed by an old man apparently stuck in the last century. The rest of the former League worlds are broken into little fiefdoms all run by pretenders to the captain-generalcy.

"In fact, you've said that Jessica Marik would ultimately come out on top—not Anson."

Melissa tightened her reins. "I believe Jessica stands the *best chance* of reuniting the League—all things being equal. I have a strong belief in female rulers." She arched her eyebrows sardonically. "All things are not remaining equal. Anson is a threat on my border now, and keeping him destabilized or even crippled fits my long-term plans."

"I understand," Trillian replied. She did understand. Melissa Steiner was not looking a year or two out into the future. She was looking down the road decades into the future, an ability Trillian admired in her cousin. "It is hard to see the little kingdoms of the former Free Worlds League as a threat right now, especially for the ordinary citizen."

The archon smiled grimly. "These tiny nations will come across our border. The ordinary men and women of the Commonwealth remember previous invasions. Our enemies have struck at us again and again. Whenever they do, we lose worlds, our defenses are caught off guard and we are forced to step back."

"And then we reclaim those worlds."

A nod was her response. "I have no desire to fall into the traps of the past, Trillian. I propose going after the Free Worlds League—hit them before they get the chance to hit us. Pummel them hard . . . but not hard enough to inspire them to unite under one banner, just hard enough that they do not pose a threat to the Commonwealth again in my lifetime." She urged her horse to a trot and Trillian did the same.

The archon had hit upon the key to conducting such an operation; Melissa always understood the delicate line you had to walk in employing military assets. The last thing anyone wanted was for one of the Mariks to reunite the Free Worlds League. "We will need to convince our people that this is a worthy cause. The Lyran nation does not start wars—we end them," Trillian cautioned.

The archon's eyes narrowed. "With the Mariks, it is a matter of when they will strike at us—not if. But if our people need convincing, I trust that you can provide them with a just reason. Given enough time, we will find the threats needed to persuade our people that such a war is just. History is replete with such cases. You will find a cause and make it stick."

And there was the twist. It was classic Melissa, ever the grand strategist. The hard part—the details—that was Trillian's job . . . and she loved it. Yes, circumstances and the media could be manipulated. It was all a matter of crafting the right story and making sure that it was told properly and often. *She's playing to either my strength or my ego.* In the end, it didn't matter to Trillian.

"If we start this war, it will prove to the other nations that we are not to be trifled with. That's actually the easy part. But there are 'domestic challenges' who will try to take advantage of the situation while our attention is on the war."

"Domestic challenges" was the code phrase they attached to Duke Vedet Brewster of Hesperus II. Trillian referred to him as Duke Vedet, assigning his royal title to his first name as was the custom in Skye. It was an awkward tradition that she pained herself to master.

At the mention of the duke, the archon pushed

Golden Charm to a canter, then to a gallop. She hit the shallow ford for the stream before Trillian had swung Big Ben into line to follow her. The splash of the cool water surprised Trillian as she reached the opposite bank, where the archon had stopped and turned.

"I have only a few options with the duke. You were the one who pointed that out to me, Trillian. I can sit back and let him cause trouble on his own, or I can control the trouble he causes. I have thought long and hard about this. I want Vedet Brewster to be given the opportunity to lead this invasion."

Trillian said nothing. Duke Vedet had proven to be ambitious. He had recently loaned a WarShip to Jasek Kelswa-Steiner's Stormhammers for use against the Jade Falcons in the Skye region. Providing such an awesome weapon to a unit that had only recently pledged itself to House Steiner was not only outside his authority; it was a calculated risk. Trillian kept a close eye on his activities, and so far there was nothing treasonous in his actions—but it was certain that he was seeking a broader role for himself than just running Defiance Industries on Hesperus II. The duke wanted political power. There was no doubt in either of their minds that his efforts were focused on the throne itself.

Which was what made the archon's plan so incredible.

"You would put military units under the control of a businessman with ambitions as large as his?"

Archon Steiner smiled. "I control the military. I know he's tried to seed some loyal officers into the ranks, but I have arranged a string of seemingly unrelated transfers to account for most of them. The invasion plan will be mine, and I will keep him in check by controlling the military."

"What if he crushes the Free Worlds League, or even just key parts of it—which you have to admit is a very real possibility? He could come out of this a hero in the eyes of the people. He will gain experience in managing large-scale military operations, and might earn the loyalty of key military leaders in the process."

"That won't happen."

Trillian stared at Melissa in silence, waiting for her to continue.

"If the duke tries to use this as a step upward, he will fail. He has a protégé, Bernard Nordhoff, who appears to have impressive ambitions of his own. We can use him as one way to check Brewster.

"Ultimately, however, he will fail because *you* will ensure that he is unable to turn anything that he accomplishes into political capital. Running a corporation doesn't prepare you for the complexity of managing a large-scale military operation—you know that." She trotted Golden Charm again, and it took Trillian a few moments to catch up. "He's out of his league, pun intended. Men like Brewster have such egos they don't know when they're in over their heads. Your job is to make sure he faces that reality."

"It is still risky, leaving him alone out in the field." Trillian spoke somberly.

"Which is why you'll be there as my adviser," Melissa replied.

Trillian knew her face betrayed her shock. She had served as the public adviser to the archon for years. She had undergone extensive training in the Diplomatic Corps and possessed strong negotiation skills. Recently, Melissa had begun sending her to hot spots as the archon's envoy. But this—this assignment was much larger. She was going to ride herd on a military invasion and try to keep its nominal leader on a leash.

"Melissa, you are asking a great deal."

"More than you know," the archon answered, a slightly ominous tone coloring her voice. "Part of what I want to accomplish with the Marik-Stewart Commonwealth is to give them something to think about other than coming after us or enlarging their holdings in what remains of The Republic. They need a new worry, one to keep Anson Marik off balance, keep all of our would-be enemies at bay."

Her cousin paused, turned her horse slightly, then continued. "You are going to open diplomatic relations with Clan Wolf through the Wolves in Exile. I want you to bargain with the Wolves to strike at the border between what used to be The Republic and the Marik-Stewart Commonwealth."

The Wolves. She felt her face flush with anxiety. Making a deal with the Wolves was a scenario that she had discussed with the archon months ago, an idea mentioned in passing as part of another conversation. Obviously, Melissa had thought it over and embraced the concept of dealing with the Clan splinter that had lived in the Lyran Commonwealth for generations. *I almost pity Anson Marik. . . .* "Melissa, bargaining with the Wolves is—"

"You will meet with Patrik Fetladral," Melissa interrupted, "the leader of the Wolves in Exile, and use him to feel out Clan Wolf. Using the Wolves in Exile gives us a certain degree of deniability if word leaks out about any discussion between House Steiner and Clan Wolf. I know that Clan Wolf entered into a similar agreement with Clan Hell's Horses years ago, so I think we have the precedent we need to gain their help. Get the audience with Fetladral, and I will close the negotiations. With the Wolves hitting them from the front of the weakened Republic and our forces under Vedet hitting them from our border, Anson Marik is held in check."

"You are practically guaranteeing success to Duke Vedet."

She shook her head. "No, Trillian. I am guaranteeing success to the Lyran Commonwealth. You will guarantee that the success of this war is reflected on my administration. You will be my personal envoy, fully empowered even to command military units if that is what you need."

"What you are asking—"

The archon cut her off again. "What I am asking is for you to be my eyes and ears at the front, Trillian. You are to ensure that the duke doesn't get all the credit for this invasion, and that he doesn't succeed in anything that might catapult him into more power. At the same time, I'm counting on you to negotiate the peace for this incursion. You, above all people, know that we can't leave the Duchy and the Marik-Stewart Commonwealth in total shambles. It's a fine line between leaving them a significantly reduced threat and ripe for unification." The archon broke into a canter and headed for a low fieldstone wall. She jumped it with ease. Trillian stared at her from a distance and carefully considered what her cousin was telling her.

I have to find a way to ensure that any success that Duke Vedet achieves is reflected on House Steiner— not on him personally. It was possible. In fact, she could already think of one officer, Roderick Frost, who would be able to help her with that goal. *Convincing him to help will be difficult, but he's perfect for helping me sway public opinion to the Steiners rather than the duke. It's all a matter of timing.*

At the same time, I have to negotiate with Clan Wolf, a very dangerous proposition. Her mind grappled with the possibilities. Yes, this was all achievable, but it was like juggling hand grenades; with each catch or toss, one was likely to explode. What was at risk was not just the safety of the Lyran people along the border but the future of the Commonwealth.

She stared at Melissa, now far ahead of her on the other side of the wall. *She's asking a lot of me. I only hope I don't fail her.* She brought Big Ben to a canter and headed to the wall. He hesitated at the last moment, but she tightened her leg and calf muscles and pushed him on, despite his fear. Ben leapt forward and she remained stiff, almost rigid, in the saddle, leaning forward slightly.

"It looked as if he was going to balk," the archon commented as she rode up beside her.

"He tried," she replied. "He simply needed some persuading."

"I know I'm asking a great deal from you in the coming months, Trillian," the archon said. "But I also know that you are up to the task. You are one of the few people I can trust with this assignment. You have always acted with House Steiner's interests, and the interests of the Lyran people, first. I trust you to do what is right—and what is necessary."

"I will need a great deal of leeway with the military. We need to ensure that they make up part of the plan designed to keep Duke Vedet overtaxed. And I recommend we keep him in the dark about our dealings with Clan Wolf. Politically, that information in his hands in advance of their involvement, regardless of what we negotiate, is too risky."

"I concur. Even I know that it is easy to start wars. Ending them is where the real skill comes into play. This war will have to end just right, or it will spawn wars for generations to come."

"I am going to reach out to Roderick," Trillian proposed. "I think if I leverage him properly, he can be an asset."

The archon cocked her eyebrow in surprise. "Roderick? You know how he is about family affairs."

Trillian smiled. "Yes. At the same time, you know that he was not to blame for that raid. And his grandfather, our great-uncle, was a great military leader, and a very good archon himself."

"He's always turned his back on the family."

"No one has ever given him a chance to come to terms with his heritage on his own."

"Agreed, then. I've always liked Roderick, ever since we were kids. The only thing that has held him back is his hereditary stubbornness and himself. Anything else?"

"You know Klaus Wehner, on my staff? He will act as my liaison with the military high command. Finally, I want the authority to alter the military plans on the fly to meet objectives as I deem appropriate."

"If it will keep the duke in check, you have all the authority you need."

Trillian paused. "This plan of yours has a lot of moving parts."

"You won't let me down, Trillian," Melissa said as she cantered off. Trillian barely caught her final words. "If you fail, then everything is lost."

Trillian felt a chill run down her spine. The archon was not exaggerating.

1

Trillian knew that the public couldn't fully appreciate the intricacies of diplomacy and negotiations. Talks with any government were a delicate balancing act, like walking a tightrope. Critics of the government couldn't figure out why both sides wouldn't just sit down and talk, but it was never that easy. Diplomacy required getting to know each other, developing trust, learning the boundaries of each person involved in the talks and of each government. Some of it was posturing—some of it was bravado. The average citizen rarely understood where the words ended and the bullets began.

In an important symbolic gesture of respect, she had traveled to Arc-Royal to meet with Patrik Fetladral and deliver the archon's proposal for leveraging the Wolves in the Lyran Commonwealth's planned military operation. He had invited her to go bow hunting, and was surprised by her skill. Like so many others, he initially had been deceived by her appearance. *Like other men, he was so caught up with how I looked that he didn't wonder if I had had any training.* Trillian took pride in the fact that she was much more than just a beautiful spokesperson for the Commonwealth. *My looks are just another weapon in the arsenal. . . .*

Now the Wolves were ready to talk, but they established their parameters before discussions started. Patrik Fetladral of the exiled Wolves had committed to replying to the archon's proposal by 15 January. Before that day, his WarShip arrived in the Tharkad system under the guise of a scheduled diplomatic mission. Though the Wolf visit had been announced, the military commanders were edgy with a Wolf WarShip so near Tharkad.

The room where the Lyran and Wolf leaders met was comfortable but not opulent, situated far from the formal ceremonies. The banner of the Lyran Commonwealth hung behind Melissa Steiner, the upthrust blue-mailed fist, symbol of the realm, contrasting nicely with her deep maroon dress. Trillian considered her leader and hid a smile; Melissa too used her looks to beguile those who considered themselves somehow superior.

Three Wolf warriors sat facing her, their own banner serving as a backdrop behind Patrik. The Wolf leader wore dress leathers and a simply styled shirt. Outside of this room, he could have been mistaken for a common laborer. In this chamber of the palace, he clearly represented great power.

His broad nose and massive muscular frame provided a physical reminder of just how dangerous Clan Wolf could be, regardless of the form in which it appeared. Many in the Inner Sphere considered the Wolves in Exile a tame pack, domesticated by years of contact with the Lyran Commonwealth. Trillian and Melissa did not make that mistake. The main body of Clan Wolf had spent decades wedged between Clan Jade Falcon, their bitter enemies, and the powerful Ghost Bears of the Rasalhague Dominion. They had long sought an efficient avenue to expand their territory, and Trillian's cousin offered them that chance. It was a risky gamble, even when the negotiations were conducted with the less-alien Exiles. Trillian attempted an analogy to caution her cousin, saying, "A wolf in a cage is dangerous. It is even more dangerous when set free."

Melissa restated the proposal that Trillian had delivered on Arc-Royal weeks earlier. Patrik Fetladral's face showed no reaction. It was as if his features were carved from granite. For a few moments he said nothing. "I presented your proposal to the Clan leadership. What you are proposing does not appeal to us," he finally responded. "At least in its present form."

"I believe we are asking no more than the contract Clan Wolf made with Clan Hell's Horses, to bid for possession of three worlds on the border with the Ghost Bears. It gave them a tiny occupation zone and gave you a buffer against the Bears. In a similar way, it is to our mutual benefit to ensure that House Marik remains in a strategically weakened state. You would be gaining worlds, and we would form that buffer."

He sliced his hand through the air to cut her off. "Wolves will never fight under another banner, Archon. Turning over our troops to you would not be efficient. Your commanders would not know how to use us effectively, and my commanders would not follow your orders. The Wolves fight for themselves."

Melissa did not have Fetladral's poker face. Her cheeks hinted pink with embarrassment. Trillian could easily have jumped in and clarified the Lyran position, to gracefully give some ground. But she knew it was important to let the archon handle it. *Melissa knows she asked too much. Let's see how she backs away from this without losing face.*

"I see your point, Khan Fetladral," the archon replied, buying herself some time. "I had not fully considered my proposal from your Clan's perspective."

"No offense is taken, Archon," Fetladral replied. "The Wolf Khan and I have discussed parameters for your proposal, and I have authorization to bid on their behalf for participation in such a military operation."

"Bid?"

Trillian interjected. "The Clans rarely decide matters using diplomacy. In this case, I believe the Khan is suggesting their system of bidding in lieu of diplomatic talks." Fetladral acknowledged her point with a single nod, which Trillian returned. She understood the Clan mentality; in the same way, she could understand the military mind-set without being a military leader.

"I see," Melissa replied. "Then you have me at a disadvantage. I am unsure where to begin, Khan Fetladral."

A narrow smile suggested that he enjoyed having her on a battlefield of his choosing. "You have already bid, Archon, in your original proposal. I will now offer a counterbid on behalf of the Wolves. Your plan intrigues us, and so we bid for the Wolves to attack worlds of our choosing along the border between the Marik-Stewart Commonwealth and the former Republic worlds."

The archon mulled over his words. "Without proper coordination, our troops may fire on each other inadvertently."

"You wish to bid the sharing of your military plans and timetable with us then, *quiaff*?"

Melissa made eye contact with Trillian, and Trillian saw that she grasped the inherent problem. Handing the Wolves, even as allies, the plans of any military strike against the former members of the Free Worlds League was risky. Their honor might prevent them from sharing the plans, but sometimes even the most honorable warriors chose to interpret things to the best advantage of their Clan. "I am not prepared to place such a bid just yet," the archon said. "I wish a few minutes to confer with my aide."

The Wolf warrior leaned back in his chair. "Of course." The archon rose and Trillian followed. They walked into an outer chamber and then to a small room across from where Fetladral sat. Trillian closed the door behind them and activated the white-noise generator to ensure that their words would not wander. Even in the palace, she suspected there were those who would want to know what was being discussed.

"Trillian, I am not comfortable handing this man, even as an ally, our detailed war plans. Not to mention the fact that we haven't actually settled on a plan yet." Trillian thought for a moment. There were more than seventy different plans and scenarios that had been drawn up over the years for striking at the Free Worlds League. The military commanders were narrowing down their choices, but it would be some time before the final options were selected for review.

"Archon, I would suggest that we choose our wording carefully," she said. "We do not have to share everything with him, only our military operations planned against the Marik-Stewart Commonwealth. We shall omit any operations in space that the Wolves would never reach. This limits our exposure dramatically, if we can get them to agree to sharing the same information."

Melissa considered her cousin's words. "There are some things we can offer the Wolves, as well."

Trillian was puzzled, but Melissa ignored her confused expression. "I can offer some aid to the Wolves against their old enemies, the Jade Falcons."

She doesn't understand them, even after all these years. "Melissa, I don't think the Wolves will accept such an offer."

"Let us see," she said, opening the door and crossing back to the Clansmen. Trillian followed close behind. Khan Fetladral waited patiently, sipping from his glass of ice-cold water.

"I bid to provide you with our plans and timetables in the field of operations where the Wolves would be expected to strike. This will help us avoid unfortunate incidents. Likewise, I would want to know the plans of your warriors in that same theater."

"Agreed," the Wolf warrior replied, shifting his

bulky frame. "However, I caution you. You must accept that Clan warriors tend not to map out detailed strategies in the same way as House militaries. Our plans tend to be more general and flexible to the opportunities of war. As such, I would accept your bid with the understanding that we will provide you with our plans at the time we begin to engage in operations. Remember that the Wolves fight for themselves, in their own command, taking what they earn in battle."

Trillian understood clearly. Fetladral was not just saying that the Wolves would not fight under the name or banner of the Lyran Commonwealth. He was also clearly stating that what they won in battle was their own. This was a slippery slope. She glanced at Melissa and saw that the archon also understood.

"I agree, as long as the Wolves, at least for the duration of this conflict, do not find themselves facing our forces in battle," she added.

"The Wolves accept your bid. We have no quarrel with the Lyran people, nor do we anticipate any in the immediate future."

"I can offer more," Melissa began.

For the first time since his arrival, Fetladral looked uncomfortable. "I have placed no other bids on the table, Archon. Your offer of something additional is not necessary."

"While I understand no further offer is necessary for the formality of bidding, I feel that an offer between *friends* is important."

"I will hear what you have to say." Fetladral leaned back into the thick pads of the leather chair.

"It is no secret that Clan Wolf and Clan Jade Falcons are not friends. In fact, one might call you enemies."

The khan shook his head. "Not enemies, Archon. We are competitors. We vie for the same ultimate goal."

Trillian paused. The goal of all Clans was to seize Terra. The Clan that took Terra would become the ilClan, and would unite the other Clans under their banner. It was the driving force in what led to the Clan invasion. It was what pitted the Clan factions against each other.

"I stand corrected. Even so, I can do much in the region of Skye to distract the Jade Falcons," Melissa Steiner said carefully.

His head shaking became more pronounced. "We are Clan. We do not need help in dealing with the Jade Falcons."

"Of course not," she replied. "Simply consider this something that friends do for friends."

He studied her face. Trillian remembered that stare—she had endured it on Arc-Royal when they had first met. Fetladral was trying to discern the archon's motive; he did not want to diminish the honor his people would win by dealing with the Jade Falcons themselves. Honor was everything with the Clans . . . and definitely with the Wolves.

"Is that your bid?"

"It is," Melissa said.

"I cannot accept it. I suggest a modification. Though we will not accept any assistance or interference in our relationship with Clan Jade Falcon, we would review copies of any plans you make for operations against the Falcons."

The archon did not react immediately. Her silence lasted for a full minute and made the air seem charged with tension. Trillian found herself fidgeting in her seat.

"I accept your counterbid," she said.

"Is there anything more that you would add, Archon? *Quineg?*"

Her eyes darted to Trillian. There was no objection that she could offer. Trillian was surprised by the response of the Wolf Khan. He had managed to find a nice compromise to the slight breach of etiquette that Melissa's offer had presented, and it told her something else. The Wolves were up to something more than simply sending troops against the Marik-Stewart Commonwealth. While they wanted to deal with the Jade Falcons in their own course, they wanted to know what Melissa had planned for them. *There is more going on here than any of us realize. I will have to compliment her when this is over for opening that door, if only a crack.*

Trillian shook her head slightly, and the archon took another moment of contemplation. When Melissa spoke her voice was crisp and clear. "I find no other reason to continue this bidding."

Fetladral rose to his feet. Trillian and the archon did as well. "Then I accept your bid. Well bargained and done, Archon Steiner." He shot a quick glance at Trillian. "You have been advised well." He offered no handshake, but none was necessary. This was a Wolf warrior. His word was more binding than any paper contract or agreement. Melissa appeared to not notice what others would have considered an insult to her station. Trillian had prepared her well.

Melissa smiled. "I trust my kin."

"As do I," Fetladral replied. "Clan warriors are all brothers and sisters."

As they watched Fetladral stride out through the massive doors, Trillian let go a long sigh of relief. Bargaining was always tricky. Bargaining with the Clans was infinitely more complex. She looked at Melissa, who seemed unimpressed by the significance of the meeting. *She hides her emotions better than I do.*

Trillian waited for her cousin to speak first.

"That went as expected," Melissa finally commented.

"I agree."

"The Wolves are hiding something," the archon added.

"I was thinking the same thing."

"Have we made a mistake?"

Now is not the time to have second thoughts. Then

Trillian realized that Melissa was making a rhetorical comment. "No."

"Good," she said, putting her hand on Trillian's shoulder. "We've taken the first step on a long road. The next step is harder. It's time to light Duke Vedet's fuse."

2

Maria's Elegy
Hesperus II
Lyran Commonwealth
24 March 3137

The inner chambers of the Brewster estate were splendid, and created a stark contrast to the planet outside. Marble, flowered tapestries, bronze statues—all offered an elegant distinction from the harsh world beyond the walls of the estate.

Hesperus II's atmosphere was thin and mostly toxic, except in certain deep chasms. Her land masses were lined with mineral-rich mountains and deep, practically impenetrable valleys. The planet was inhospitable, and yet possessed a great treasure: the largest BattleMech and munitions factory in the Inner Sphere. Her vast quantities of radioactive materials and metals offered the necessary raw materials for forging the machines of war. For centuries, Hesperus II and Defiance Industries had been the failed target of numerous large-scale military operations mounted by various nations.

On Trillian's last visit, during the crisis of the Jade Falcon invasion of the Isle of Skye, she had been impressed by her tour of the factories. Nestled deep underground and impractical, if not impossible, to seize, the Defiance factories had been the source of the duke's family's influence for generations. This trip had a different quality, though it was equally stressful. She was here to offer Duke Vedet Brewster a chance to do something great in the name of the Commonwealth, to lead a military strike against an ages-old enemy.

Making this offer presented great risks. The duke was ambitious, and ambition left unchanneled could pose a threat even to the reigning archon. Trillian's job was to direct Duke Vedet's ambition in a way that would benefit her cousin as much as the Commonwealth. Vedet was a crafty businessman, though. He would constantly challenge her—she knew that going in, just as she knew he would seek a way to turn this opportunity into something more. Therein lay the true risk.

When he entered the room, she thought he seemed taller than she remembered. His ebony skin provided a nice contrast to his light-colored suit. His head was shaved bald, a new style for him. She suspected it was a hint at his vanity—she remembered him sporting a few wisps of gray the last time they met. Vedet's entrance into the room seemed to charge the air. He took two large steps and grasped her hand, raising it to his lips. Always the charmer. "Trillian Steiner. I must admit I had not planned on your visit. This is a pleasant surprise."

"Duke Vedet, a pleasure to see you again. I come bearing greetings from the archon."

Behind him followed a shorter man with thick, curly black hair. He wore a colonel's uniform, crisply pressed. His uniform was adorned with few medals, and those he wore were not for combat operations. His pale skin was marked only by the hint of a five o'clock shadow. Trillian guessed that he probably *always* had a five o'clock shadow.

Vedet waved his hand at the officer. "I present Colonel Bernard Nordhoff of the Lyran Commonwealth

Armed Forces. He is my aide-de-camp and liaison with the military. When you own the largest arms production facility in the Inner Sphere, a man like him is invaluable."

Colonel Nordhoff stood at attention and clicked his heels in salute, bowing his head slightly. Trillian gave him a thin smile. "A pleasure to meet you, Colonel." She extended her hand, and he shook it firmly.

"The pleasure," Nordhoff said with a heavy Germanic accent, "is all mine."

She turned to her own escort. "This is Colonel Klaus Wehner," she said. Klaus stood at attention and snapped his heels together as Nordhoff had done, only he seemed much more comfortable and relaxed in his stance. That was one of the things she most liked about him. Klaus had been with her for three years, and had proven himself to be very flexible and a quick thinker. "Like you, Duke Vedet, I find having a liaison to the military to be quite useful." Klaus gave her a smile in response to the praise.

Having dispensed with the niceties, Trillian turned to Duke Vedet and stared into his piercing, dark brown eyes. "The archon has sent me to ask for your assistance as a loyal member of the realm. It is a matter involving the security of the Lyran Commonwealth and the future of our state." She cast a glance at Colonel Nordhoff over the shoulder of the duke. *Does he want the colonel to hear what is said?*

Vedet Brewster followed her gaze. "Perhaps our aides can leave us alone for a few minutes?" He gestured to Colonel Nordhoff with his hand, shooing him away. Trillian gave Klaus a nod. Nothing further was said until the door closed behind them.

The duke folded his massive arms across his chest and stood looking down at Trillian. She was taller than most members of the Steiner family, but was still much shorter than Brewster. "I don't usually get visits from members of your family *unless they want something*."

"Then the purpose of my visit will come as no surprise to you. As I said, I am here to ask a favor for the archon."

"I would have thought that my recent public statements against her policies had discouraged her from sending such an attractive spokesperson." The compliment rolled easily off his tongue.

He recently had been critical of Melissa for not taking more direct action to secure the Lyran Commonwealth's borders, given the wars that seemed to be erupting all around them. Critique by a lone duke was not worthy of the archon's wrath, but it did catch her attention. "The archon may not agree with your comments regarding her leadership, but she does know you to be loyal to the Commonwealth. She also understands that you recognize the same threats she sees. It is those threats that bind together all of us who are loyal to the Commonwealth, and that are the impetus for my being here."

"I assume that our enemies are preparing for war?" Vedet replied.

"Aren't they always?"

"I assumed that Melissa was going to continue our policy of nonaggression until our borders were violated." His words practically dripped with contempt. "I stand by my statement that the archon is essentially inviting our enemies to strike at us."

"Policies change," Trillian countered. "There is a new threat from an old enemy. The former Free Worlds states along our borders are rearming, and we have to assume that they are planning a military operation against the Commonwealth."

Her words seemed to catch him off guard, if only for a second. Then he regained his composure. "I knew it. I was right then, when I said that the archon and her policies were placing our people at risk."

Trillian was allowing him to say, "I told you so," but she wouldn't let him go any further. *He just likes others to admit that he's right.* "Things are not quite as they seem, Duke Vedet. The archon currently is preparing to head up a military operation aimed at quashing this attack before it gets off the ground."

"Why tell me?"

Trillian waited for a moment, until she was sure the duke was focused on what she was going to say next. "The archon knows that you are ambitious beyond the success of your business empire. She also knows that you are loyal to the realm, even if you don't agree with its current leader. She recognizes your ability to lead and your desire to secure the realm against adventurism. Based on those assumptions, Archon Melissa Steiner extends to you an offer to command the military operation against the Free Worlds League nations."

He was stunned for a moment. "She wants me to take command?"

"Yes. This threat is serious, and she wants a commander who she can be confident will act in the best interests of the Commonwealth."

The duke stared at her, trying to read her face for more information. "Commanding an invasion force requires skills I don't have. The amount of political knowledge alone that would be necessary is staggering." The duke seemed a little surprised to have admitted this out loud.

"I will be going in with the troops," she said. "The archon has granted me a broad range of authority on this operation. Plainly put, it is my job to tell you when to stop advancing and to negotiate a peace."

"We're not going to simply conquer the Duchy of Tamarind-Abbey and the Marik-Stewart Commonwealth?"

"Not in the traditional sense. Right now, working from the facts we have been able to gain, it appears that both of these governments are preparing to attack. Intelligence reports indicate that the Duchy of Tamarind-Abbey has begun a very aggressive recruitment campaign and has pumped up the garrisons on their borders, good indications that they plan to use those worlds as staging areas for an offensive operation."

The duke began to slowly pace. He crossed his arms and stared at the floor in thought. "What of the Marik-Stewart Commonwealth?"

"We think Anson Marik is preparing for something much larger. Not only is he stepping up his military spending and setting up staging areas on the border, but he has created a new regimental force, one that we can only assume is to be used against us, the Silver Hawk Irregulars."

The mention of the unit made the duke's eyes widen in excitement. The Silver Hawk Irregulars had been employed most often against the Lyran Commonwealth.

The Silver Hawk Irregulars were legendary by the end of the Third Succession War. Historically considered zealots and raised from local populations, the Irregulars were originally formed as a counter to a perceived abuse of power by the captain-general. Over the centuries the Irregulars had proven themselves in battle many times, but they fell to the same fate as many other storied units during the Jihad; they were utterly destroyed. If Anson Marik had rebuilt the Irregulars, it wouldn't take much to extrapolate a reason to go to war with him.

All it would take was politicians and spinmasters—and Trillian took no pride in being one of the latter. While no intelligence agency knew for sure where Anson planned to use the Silver Hawk Irregulars or if they were to be deployed for offensive or defensive purposes, they easily could be used by the media as a reason to justify a war with the Marik-Stewart Commonwealth. *Stir up some of those old fears and hatreds and the Lyran people will practically demand a strike.* The same could be done with the Duchy's reinforcing its borders. Carefully worded speeches and propaganda would convince everyone that this was all a prelude to a coordinated strike by an old enemy.

Trillian gritted her teeth. There was no advantage to telling the duke the truth, that the archon was making a preemptive attack. *I don't want him in a position to use the truth against the archon if he doesn't play along.*

Brewster's pacing accelerated slightly as he began to talk. "Don't take this the wrong way, Lady Steiner, but this offer seems out of character for the archon in terms of her relations with me. My years of negotiating deals have taught me to be cautious. I want some assurances that this is not a ploy on the part of the archon to set me up for failure."

Trillian smiled. "While I am not inside my cousin's mind, I can say this—she is not plotting against you. To paraphrase the old quote, it is better to keep your allies close and your rivals closer." This assurance was not a lie. Trillian usually avoided lying because she believed she was bad at it. Instead, she preferred working with partial truths and, when possible, simply supporting the assumptions others believed to be true. *I will have to accept my share of guilt however this turns out. I don't need to compound my problems by lying.* "As I said, I will be on the front as well. I am not willing to gamble my life to put you at risk. My role is to negotiate peace when the time comes, and serve as your liaison as necessary."

Her answer seemed to soothe the duke's concerns. "Anson Marik rekindling our old fears by bringing the Silver Hawk Irregulars back to life makes sense. It's a classic move on his part. But Fontaine Marik . . . he's an old man. My political advisers say his best days are long behind him. While his claim to the House Marik bloodline is strongest, I just have a hard time seeing him working with Anson on a combined military operation."

"I have been told," she said with complete honesty, "that the Duchy fears reprisals from us should Anson strike alone." That tidbit from the Lyran Intelligence Corps was true. "We cannot ignore this risk."

Stopping behind a high-backed chair, the duke rested his hands on the top rail. "You don't seem concerned that I have never led a military operation before."

"We're not, really. You'll have the support of a very experienced command staff, and you'll be working from a number of plans for this kind of operation that have been in place for decades. We're able to give you flexibility in putting together your immediate support staff. You won't be a figurehead, but you don't need to reinvent the wheel.

"If you agree to head up this operation, I will have Colonel Wehner provide you with complete details as soon as they have been determined. The primary option we are looking at now is aimed at striking a crippling blow to the two Free Worlds fiefdoms on the border. We want them each to keep a few worlds, but ultimately be too weak to pose a serious threat for a long time."

Brewster moved smoothly from behind the chair to stand in front of her, dominating the space between them. "You know, Lady Steiner," he said, his voice low and seductive, "when the dust settles, those who win this little war will be in a position to carve out a portion of the conquered worlds for themselves. You could have a place at the head of such a holding."

He's testing my loyalties—albeit in a particularly limp fashion. "I serve at the bidding of the archon."

"Don't we all?" He flashed a broad smile. "I was not implying otherwise. I simply suspect that you are someone to watch."

She studied him intently. She had refused his bait and now he was lying, but she knew she had to let it go.

"Time is tight, Duke Vedet. Our meeting face-to-face was necessary given the security requirements of this situation, but I must depart immediately. I have to move to the border myself, and the archon will be expecting an answer from you. I realize that this seems rushed, but I would need to know whether you plan to accept this offer." Time, she had found, was a powerful bargaining chip.

He wet his lips. "Please inform the archon that I am honored to lead this assault. It will be one for the history books."

"These are your orders," she said, handing him a folded set of papers.

"It appears we are *both* going to be leaving shortly," he said, as he stared at the papers. "I hope time will be an ally for both of us."

Duke Vedet and Colonel Nordhoff watched as their visitors' DropShip departed.

"You accepted the offer, sir?"

"Of course I did," Vedet snapped. "This is the perfect opportunity for me—no, for *us*."

"I analyzed her voice-stress patterns and compared tone readings from her previous visit. She was holding something back, but unless she's so polished that she can bluff our sensors, then she was not lying."

"Trillian is very good, but if the archon thinks that by saddling me with her cousin she'll keep me in check, she is making a grave mistake. Though Lady Steiner is formidable and skilled, her cousin is putting her in a game in which even she is in over her head. Even if she steps up to the tempo of this dance, a war zone is a dangerous place."

"You are planning to kill her?"

Vedet shook his head wearily. "Bernard, you misunderstand me. After all I have done for you and your family, I would expect you to make a better effort. I am not a killer—that is not my style. I am simply saying that combat is a strange, unpredictable situation. Accidents can happen if one is inexperienced and does not know how to behave."

Duke Vedet smiled, and it was not a pretty sight. "We will not manufacture the right situation. But if it occurs naturally, I know I can count on you to do the right thing."

3

The Yasha cut power to its two massive lift fans and dropped quickly, kicking them back on at the last possible moment. The buglike VTOL was only a few meters above the ground, throwing up a wild storm of dust and debris that almost obscured Trillian's view. The forward weapons array fired a low-power burst of lasers, catching the stunned *Griffin* on its side. The lasers were tuned for practice and only peeled paint, scoring points in the exercise rather than inflicting real damage.

The *Griffin* swung away, exposing its rear to a squad of Gnome battlearmor. Their shots mostly went wide, but a few found their mark—enough to log additional damage to the *Griffin*. The Yasha's fans tilted the VTOL radically forward and it headed up the hillside. Watching from the bunker, Trillian was impressed by the pilot's skill.

Then the *Rifleman IIC* emerged.

Just standing there, the BattleMech was impressive—three stories tall and bristling with enough firepower to devastate conventional opponents. As it strode to the top of the hill, it was obvious it was the king of the battlefield. Based on its utilitarian lines and form, Trillian guessed it was a Clan design. From the amount of fresh green and gray paint applied to replacement armor, it was obvious the machine had endured a lot of damage recently. The Yasha saw it looming and attempted to bank, revving the fans hard in an attempt to gain some altitude.

A Demon wheeled antitank vehicle fired a barrage at the *Rifleman*; some of the shots went wide, but others hit. The simulated damage was minimal, however, and the *Rifleman* shrugged it off. It was after the VTOL. In a half dozen strides, it moved down the hill and caught the Yasha, whose attempt to flee proved too little, too late. The *Rifleman IIC* fired a targeted burst of autocannon fire combined with pulse laser at the Yasha. The underpowered shots and dummy warheads pummeled the VTOL. Its battlecomputer registered devastating damage and it dropped low; this time the pilot barely maintained control as the computer simulated real damage. The pilot popped the tiny landing prods out just as the Yasha touched the ground. The power to the turbofans died and the billows of dirt and dust quickly settled.

The camo-painted *Rifleman* turned toward several squads of infantry that fired and then tried to scatter. It pursued them over the far edge of the hill, dropping down the other side and out of line of sight.

"That was Roderick, wasn't it?" Trillian asked, lowering her enhanced binoculars.

Klaus Wehner nodded. "It was, Lady Steiner."

"I'm surprised they are letting him back in the field again so soon after all of the press coverage." Wehner did not require an explanation of her reference to the incident on Algorab. Anyone who followed the news knew what had happened there. While the ordinary man and woman in the Commonwealth sympathized with Roderick Frost and what had happened to him—

the ordinary man or woman did not control the military legal system. His steadfast insistence on protecting the men and women with whom he served at the price of his own reputation and career was the stuff of legend. There was talk of holomovies, but Frost had shunned the idea of profiting from the situation, making him even more popular with the average citizen.

After what had occurred on Algorab, it was necessary to subject Frost to a court-martial. In most such cases, the disciplinary action would have been a formality and the officer would have been discharged. But Frost had been hung out to dry pretty dramatically by upper command; the situation was too widely covered in the news, and Frost had been portrayed as too skilled a soldier for the military to simply dismiss him without suffering embarrassment itself.

Someone had to pay the price for the failure of the Lyran Commonwealth Armed Forces on Algorab, and Roderick had been set up to take the fall. Frost provided his own defense, walking away with a suspended sentence and his rank reduced to leutnant. The press controlled by those who had set him up told the public that the debacle on Algorab was his fault. Only the independent news services hinted that he had been made a scapegoat.

Because she had access to the trial transcripts and the after-action reports, Trillian knew that he had not performed well on Algorab—he had performed brilliantly. If not for his actions, many more men and women would be dead. He had turned an untenable situation into a merely ugly situation and saved lives. She knew a truth that no one outside a very small circle of people would ever see.

"From what I have been able to gather, not too many commanders want him around."

"Ma'am?"

She smiled. "He's fine where he is, Klaus." She looked off two kilometers distant as the Yasha poked its head up for a moment above the emerald crest of the hill. "For now, anyway." She tucked the binoculars away and motioned for her aide to join her. She ran her fingers across the pendant of the necklace she wore. She was usually able to suppress this nervous habit. She knew she rubbed the necklace when she was forcing herself out of her comfort zone. Involving Roderick in her plans had its risks—primarily, that he would refuse to join her. Stubbornness was a family trait that she fully understood and had to respect. "Let's go see what the general staff has cooked up for dealing with the Free Worlds League."

The conference room was nestled in the center of Boelcke Base, reinforced from every sort of attack, even nuclear. The base was part of the chain of Lyran worlds and facilities along their border with the Free Worlds League. She surveyed the room. It was a sophisticated command center complete with a holographic "sand table" for outlining operations. It was the best computers and gear that could be provided— by the lowest bidder.

As three more officers entered the room, she wondered for a moment how many of them would soon be dead. Her jaw set. *No.* She couldn't afford to think that way. She looked away from the men and her eyes caught on the upright mailed fist symbol of the Lyran Commonwealth. Her jaw relaxed. Melissa was right. If they didn't start this war, if they didn't strike at the Free Worlds states along the border, that fist-flag would be lost. One of the flags of the Free Worlds League would be there instead. The men she had seen enter, they would be dead or prisoners of war. *We are doing this for the right reason . . . we are protecting our people from an age-old threat.*

General Heinrick braced himself on his hands and leaned over the display table as if he were embracing it. "If I could have your attention, please. I'd like to go over the conclusions my team in the strategic planning section have arrived at and what the archon has agreed to, in principle." The officers in the room moved to stand around the table. Klaus Wehner moved to her right side, right where he belonged.

"Lady Steiner, my esteemed colleagues, I present to you Operation Hammerfall." There was a dramatic ring to his voice, and a sense of pride. The lights dimmed slightly, adding to the effect.

Above the table a map of the border between the Lyran Commonwealth and the Free Worlds League flickered to life. The Lyran worlds were highlighted in a regal blue color. Those of the Marik-Stewart Commonwealth appeared in purple. Those of the Duchy of Tamarind-Abbey appeared in orange. The worlds that the Jade Falcons had seized in the former Duchy of Skye were brilliant green. The worlds of the Republic's Prefecture VIII were a dark gray. Trillian saw them with a tinge of sadness. Left alone to fend for themselves outside the invisible wall of Fortress Republic, these vestiges of Devlin Stone's dream seemed doomed.

General Heinrick's voice dominated the room. "Hammerfall calls for a first wave to punch through the gap of planets between the Duchy of Tamarind-Abbey and the Marik-Stewart Commonwealth." Arrows appeared on the map over the former Free Worlds planets colored black: not owned by either government. "This should prevent them from coordinating their efforts and massing their forces. At the same time, we will hit the borders of both worlds. Our deepest strike will go to Helm in the Marik-Stewart holdings." Additional arrows appeared. While the border of Tamarind-Abbey took some hits, the drives into the Marik-Stewart Commonwealth were deep, like ugly stab wounds.

The general paused to allow those in the room to study the map, letting the image rotate slowly above the holographic table. "The Lyran Intelligence Corps places the Silver Hawk Irregulars on three worlds, all of which are targeted in the first wave—Concord, Danais and Bondurant. If Anson Marik's plan is to use that unit to strike into Lyran space, we will crush it right at the start of this fight."

Trillian couldn't prevent her brow from wrinkling at his words. Military commanders always seemed to speak with such bravado, and things rarely worked out as planned. Anson Marik was no fool. While the Lyran Commonwealth Armed Forces had drawn up numerous plans of attack, Marik surely had done the same thing. The Silver Hawk Irregulars must have cost him a great deal to create; he wouldn't just hang them out there to be smashed at the beginning of the war. She wondered if General Heinrick really believed what he said, or simply stated it out of belief that his conviction would make it so.

She cleared her throat. "The archon asked that we present options for a demonstration of sorts against the Jade Falcons in Skye. What are your plans there, General?"

He poked at the holographic controls and a few more arrows appeared. "It's a little tricky, what you and the archon handed us, Lady Steiner. Hitting the Jade Falcons directly could cause repercussions that, frankly, could cripple Hammerfall completely. Instead, we plan to hit them where they are not. We are going to strike at three Skye worlds that the Jade Falcons *haven't* taken yet. The intent here, from a strategic sense, is to control those worlds and deny them to the Falcons. If they want to take them, they will be starting a war with us."

The names of the worlds were highlighted as the arrows reached out to them. New Kyoto, Algorab and Vindemiatrix. It was a good move. It honored their commitment to Clan Wolf without sparking a direct confrontation with the Falcons. "Those moves are to be treated as contingency plans and to be launched at my discretion. Include several variations, General." She was counting on Vedet's ignoring the plans for these strikes. On paper they seemed unrelated to the objectives of Hammerfall, but it was Vedet's reserves who were allocated as the resource for this element of the strategy. Played at the proper time, she could use this part of the plan to keep the duke off balance.

"As you wish, milady," the steely-eyed general responded. "To continue, the second-wave strikes are where Hammerfall shifts. We will drive right into the core of the Marik-Stewart Commonwealth," he said as he activated the long arrows illustrating the second wave. The drives were impressive on the map. Indeed, if the operation went as planned, Anson Marik would find his holdings cut almost in two.

"Our forces in the wedge between the Duchy and the Commonwealth will punch deeper and swing around, cutting off Tamarind, and our forces will rendezvous on Tamarind itself. The defenses of the world are formidable, but they will be surrounded, taking hits from all sides. Crush them there, and the Duchy is out of the fight." He toggled a control that showed the arrows merging on Tamarind. It was alone, cut off, poised for destruction. She almost pitied Fontaine Marik, the duke who ruled Tamarind-Abbey. He was an old man and might not survive the surprises the Lyran command had in store. If his government was captured or capitulated, the entire Duchy would be left weak and isolated—ripe for the picking.

"The last wave," General Heinrick continued, activating the final assault arrows, "will isolate the world of Marik. It will be cut off, left weak along its border with the old Republic. We can then shift our resources from the Duchy to mop up the worlds that are cut off." His voice rang with confidence.

Trillian studied the map. It was an impressive strategy, she had to admit. The Lyran borders would be safe for generations if the plan worked as laid out. And this plan didn't take into account the agreement with Clan Wolf. General Heinrick and Duke Vedet couldn't factor them into the plan, but she could. *They will pounce on the Marik-Stewart Commonwealth. The remains will not be isolated, they will be devoured.*

The general waited a full minute before speaking again. "Lady Steiner, I understand that this plan requires your endorsement before it can be sent to the new . . . operational commander." That probably wasn't what he or anyone else on the command staff wanted to call Duke Vedet Brewster. In their eyes, he'd be nothing but a political interloper—and a politician leading professional soldiers was not going to play at all well with command. But that was for her cousin Melissa to smooth over.

"How will you cope with the lack of HPG communications?" Trillian asked.

"Ah." He rubbed his hands together briskly. "We've been working on that. Simply put, we plan to seize several working stations. Bondurant has one, and is targeted in the first wave. So does Shasta. We are hitting Millungera for the same reason."

Wehner spoke up. "Sir, Millungera does not have a functioning hyperpulse generator."

The general gave him a coy grin. "They will by the time we land. ComStar apparently has come up with a way to restore HPGs. It's a slow and cumbersome process, and they are trying to keep their repair schedule under wraps, but our intelligence people indicate that the Millungera station is at the top of the list.

"Combined with a healthy number of contracts with commercial JumpShips that we can use as a pony-express system, allowing us to shuffle troops and information between the two target Marik realms, we believe we will be able to cope with the time lag in communications."

"I agree with this proposal," Trillian said, casting a glance at Klaus. He stabbed furiously at his noteputer, but paused to give her a reassuring nod. "I do have some minor suggestions—not in target worlds, but in units. We're going to form a new unit that will be involved in this operation—under my personal command."

The general bristled. Trillian could practically watch the hair on his flattop stiffen even more. "Lady Steiner, forming a new unit takes time and planning. Getting them operational and then adjusting the logistics of Hammerfall to incorporate your changes will be difficult." He chose his words carefully, and she recognized that.

"General, I appreciate your position. I do understand what this request means, and I hope you can accept that it is necessary."

He bowed his head stiffly, attempting to hide the angry flush that rose to his face. "I understand. Arrangements will be made."

"You and your staff have done an excellent job, General. Duke Vedet and I will do our best to make sure that Hammerfall lives up to its name."

=== 4 ===

LCAF Staging Base Boelcke
Cavanaugh II
Bolan Military Province, Lyran Commonwealth
18 May 3137

General Bernard Nordhoff studied the hard copy of
Operation Hammerfall, including details of the troops
being deployed, time schedules and all the other minu-
tiae that went into a successful invasion plan. Nordhoff's rank was new, a perk of being "the duke's
man"—a phrase he had already learned to hate. It
was a temporary field promotion, but he was as proud
of it as if he had earned it under fire.

The plan summary included a noteputer and five
data cubes containing modules of the necessary drill-
down data. Duke Vedet pretended to give his attention to the stack of work on his desk, but repeatedly
found himself staring at Nordhoff as he meticulously
reviewed the summary and read each of the modules.
Nordhoff said nothing as he read, which only fueled
the duke's impatience. He glared at his aide, to no
avail.

After an hour, the duke broke the silence. "Well,
Bernard," he demanded. "What do you think of the
operational plans?"

Nordhoff scrubbed his face with his hand and set down the noteputer. "Sir, the briefing from Trillian Steiner and the command staff was quite thorough, and I told you then that I believed Hammerfall was an impressive, complex operation."

"But now you've seen the details," he said, pointing his long finger at the data cubes. "Now what do you think?"

General Nordhoff shifted in his seat. Vedet Brewster considered fidgeting a sign of incompetence, and scowled at his underling.

"Sir, I've only been looking at this for an hour or so, and have only been able to skim the summaries. The number of details is staggering. As you well know, up to now I've only worked on operations of a significantly smaller scale—raids or defensive actions. I need time to absorb all this."

By a supreme effort, Vedet managed to not say what he was thinking, that the promotion to general apparently was not enough for Nordhoff, and that he wanted more before he would choose to be useful. "Tell me, Bernard, what do you need in order to be able to tell me what you think?"

"A larger staff. To stay on top of an operation of this scale, we are going to need more people working under us. I can tell you this—from what I've read so far, I think Trillian was telling the truth. The archon does not appear to be setting you up to fail. This operation obviously has been in the planning stages for years. But the real challenge to your success will be in the details, and to wade through all of this and find those risks, I am going to need bodies."

"I find it hard to believe that you're willing to admit this is too much for you," the duke said scathingly. "Maybe I should bring in some of the operations folks from Defiance to assist."

Nordhoff frowned, but Vedet was encouraged to see that he didn't lose his temper. "Duke Vedet, with all due respect, corporate people, even those who work in the defense industry, are not equipped to understand this kind of operation. As I suggested during the burn-in, we will need some good officers under us, but we want to make sure that we don't duplicate the efforts of the general staff. The last thing we need in an operation on this scale is redundancy and obfuscation."

"But in your opinion, this is not a trap set for me by the archon?"

The general shook his head. "No, sir. This seems legitimate from top to bottom. If this is an elaborate trap of some sort, I can't see it. And in fact, some aspects of this plan are downright brilliant. Seizing HPG stations will both cripple our opposition and give us a higher level of communications access."

"ComStar—bah!" The duke waved his hand as if to dismiss the words. "They want to play corporation, but all they did was hamstring themselves. The loss of HPG communications has almost bankrupted them, and now, suddenly, they've found a way to reactivate some HPG stations. Fairly convenient, don't you think?"

Nordhoff nodded, because he knew that was what Vedet wanted. And it was in his best interests to do what Vedet wanted—and had been for many years.

Nordhoff's father and grandfather both had been senior managers at Defiance Industries. Bernard had worked there himself during the summers when he was a teen. He had shown some talent for engineering and the duke had chosen to show an interest in him. Vedet Brewster had sponsored his application, along with those of other children of loyal employees, to the premier military training ground, the Nagelring Academy. The duke knew that at some point, contacts within the military, people who owed their careers to him, would be important in his own ascension.

Bernard was one of his first protégés, and Vedet had done quite a bit to pave his path to power. The duke had made sure that he was introduced in the right circles, negotiated to get him assignments that would accelerate his promotions. It had proven to be a good investment. Nordhoff had risen to the rank of colonel quite rapidly—and at least partially on his own merit. Now he was a general—a promotion entirely to the credit of Duke Vedet.

Duke Vedet hoped the general appreciated the depth of loyalty he owed to his patron. *You owe me, Bernard . . . for everything you are.*

"All right, then, pull together the staff I will need," he ordered. "I have a number of reassignments for you to issue as well." He handed a data cube to his subordinate.

Bernard stared at the cube for a moment, then inserted it into his noteputer. He studied the screen. "You're forming a new unit?"

Brewster smiled. "Yes. They are going to form the core of the First Hesperus Guards. If Trillian Steiner can form a unit under her direct control, so can I. I want people around me whom I can trust. You, of all people, know that I demand loyalty above all else."

General Nordhoff rose uneasily to his feet. "Sir, if I understood your ultimate goals for this operation, it would be easier for me to ensure that there are no challenges to those goals in the Hammerfall details."

Duke Vedet stared at his general for a long moment. This was a matter of trust. He needed Bernard to be successful in his new role; at the same time, giving the young general information also gave him ammunition. How loyal was Bernard Nordhoff? Brewster stared into his eyes, looking for any hint of betrayal. He found nothing—yet the man had always maintained a streak of independence that he didn't like.

So, he did what any good negotiator did—he chose the middle ground. He would tell Nordhoff what he needed to know; no more, no less. "I am going to do what the archon has asked me to do. I am going to unleash a war on the nations of the former Free

Worlds League. You will lead the assault into the Marik-Stewart Commonwealth. I will pummel the Duchy of Tamarind-Abbey. We will move faster than the timetable the general staff has laid out, and by the time Trillian Steiner realizes how severely we have crippled our foes, there will be no peace for her to negotiate.

"The worlds that fall will need leadership—new leaders, not one of these Steiner women. Someone strong, someone the Lyran people can respect. Victory will give that role to me."

He stopped speaking. What he wasn't telling Bernard Nordhoff was that once he ruled the worlds he had conquered, he knew the press and the Lyran people would see him for what he was—a true leader, a leader in both war and peace. It was simply a matter of time before he consolidated his holdings on Hesperus II with the realms he smashed in the war. A matter of time before a new archon came to power.

By the time Melissa Steiner knew what was happening, she was going to find herself part of a former regime.

General Nordhoff saluted. "Very good, sir. Now that I know what you intend, I will do all I can to ensure your victory."

As his pocket general left the room, Vedet said firmly, "See that you do."

Bernard shut the door behind him and walked briskly to a sparsely furnished office set aside for his use. As soon as that door closed behind him, he let out a long sigh. Being around Duke Vedet always made him nervous. The man was difficult to read, as befit a successful businessman; it was hard to figure out where his mind was headed at any given moment. Of course, Brewster was tremendously successful. But if you own the largest armaments business in the Inner Sphere during a time of war—well, it was hard to see how anyone could fail to succeed.

Nordhoff looked at the noteputer clutched in his hand, then tossed it to the table. Walking to the window, he stared at the parade grounds below. Three squads were marching, drilling, preparing for war. The sergeant's voice barking out commands was muffled but audible.

"I hope he dies." He startled himself by saying the words out loud, but then grinned at the idea of speaking his true feelings. *He's playing war with the lives of thousands of good men and women simply to advance himself.*

This callousness toward others, this selfishness in achieving his own ends—Nordhoff knew it was typical behavior for the duke. Even though the duke had sponsored Bernard's training at the Nagelring—an act that might be considered charitable—Bernard knew the duke only did it to achieve his own goals. His family had served the Brewsters for generations, and on the surface the duke had rewarded that loyalty. When Bernard's father was diagnosed with poisoning caused by exposure to fumes in the smelting unit he managed for the duke in the early years of his career at Defiance Industries, he was provided excellent medical care by the Brewster family; but in the end he still died from working for them.

Bernard doubted the duke even knew how his father died. From his perspective, he continued to support the Nordhoff family by improving Bernard's position in the military—all in anticipation of the moment when he could leverage him for his own gain. There were other wide-eyed cadets and graduates that he would rally to him when this war erupted. The First Hesperus Guards was a collection to the duke, more than a unit. A collection of people that he owned, controlled, dominated.

He doesn't own me.

Hammerfall would put the duke at risk. It was a military operation, regardless of who he gathered to protect him. He would be shackled to the plan, and if things went well, it would kill him. If he were killed or captured, then it would be possible—even reasonable—for Bernard to rally his own loyalists to seize the worlds the duke conquered. Duke Vedet envisioned a fiefdom for himself, but if circumstances came together correctly, it would be Bernard who took a throne. With the head of the Brewster family out of the way, the rest of the family would be momentarily crippled. If he moved fast, Bernard could even seize control of Hesperus II.

All it would take was shuffling a few resources. *The duke is right about one thing—loyalty is everything. And there are many officers who resent the duke as much as I do. We will see who is in charge. . . .*

Eliminating the duke and seizing his assets would not bring back his father . . . but it might set a few things right.

He smiled at the thought.

5

LCAF Staging Base Boelcke
Cavanaugh II
Bolan Military Province, Lyran Commonwealth
21 May 3137

The BattleMech, a *King Crab*, stomped the ground hard, so hard that everything around it shook. A wave of missiles swished out of the launch tubes mounted on the Pegasus hovercraft and crossed the field, slamming into a row of houses. Orange blooms of flames billowing sickening black smoke burst from the remains of the buildings. Hapless infantry tried to flee the building. Two were on fire and dropped and rolled, but one didn't get up. In a defiant gesture, a handful of the survivors fired back at the 'Mech with assault rifles. Their small arms fire was nothing against the fury of the BattleMech.

The *King Crab* strode over a once-pristine fence, smashing it with its massive footfall. It paused for a moment, leaning forward. It fired again—this time a blast of autocannon fire. Not at the buildings—this was directed at the tiny infantry that dared to fire at it. The autocannon rounds turned the pavement and grass where the infantry stood into a furrow, as if a massive blade had tilled the soil. The ground erupted as each of the high-explosive shells went off. Sod, chunks of concrete and bits of the defending infantry rose into the air and fell. They didn't stand a chance.

The holocamera image swung back to the *King Crab* and focused on the image on its torso. A shimmering hawk in flight, claws extended, painted in silver and outlined in regal purple. The image froze.

"Memories of the Silver Hawk Irregulars remain vivid with the people of the Lyran Commonwealth," the voice of the news commentator said. "The Silver Hawk Irregulars have led numerous incursions in their history, as this footage from the early thirty-first century shows. They have always been the vanguard of attacks on our borders by the Free Worlds League.

"And now this ghost from our past has resurfaced." The image switched from the BattleMech to stock footage of Anson Marik. "Lyran intelligence has confirmed that Anson Marik, leader of the Marik-Stewart Commonwealth, has reformed this infamous unit. In a public statement two weeks ago, Anson confirmed LIC findings but claimed that the Irregulars were being rebuilt for defensive purposes. At the same time, Duke Fontaine Marik of the Duchy of Tamarind-Abbey announced that he was increasing his military presence along our borders to discourage any Lyran intrusions into Free Worlds League affairs.

"This reporter wonders who they would be defending against. The Republic? Hardly. The Republic of the Sphere is no threat to anyone at this point, especially now with the formation of Fortress Republic. Jessica Marik? Are any of the Free Worlds League governments a serious threat to each other? And since when has the Free Worlds League ever had to defend its borders from us? Haven't our people always suffered the brunt of invasions by our neighbors? When was the last time we launched a war against the Free Worlds?"

The holoimage changed to that of the reporter

standing at a military base; vehicles, 'Mechs and infantry all could be seen moving purposefully in the background. "The answer to that is, of course, never. It seems obvious that these movements along our border are a prelude to some sort of military operation. The question we all have is, Are we prepared to deal with it? What will be the response of the archon to this threat?

"This is Frank Folgar, Donegal Broadcasting System. Back to you, Jayne."

Trillian rose and shut off the newscast. It had begun, just as she and Melissa had planned it. Digging up the old footage proved that the Silver Hawk Irregulars still had the power to inspire fear.

And fear was a powerful tool.

Leutnant Roderick Frost was a man of medium height with short blond hair. He frowned at his surroundings until he spotted Trillian. Suddenly, his stern face was transformed by a broad grin. He quickly crossed the room as she rose from behind the holo-viewer and gave her a hearty embrace. "I should have known you were behind these cryptic orders, Trillian," he said, holding up the paperwork that had summoned him.

"I figured it was the best way for us to meet without drawing too much attention."

"Pretty funny joke," he said. He looked at the papers for a moment and then quoted from them: " 'Report for a meeting with the archon's liaison to oversee the formation of a new military unit.' At first I figured it was a mistake, and then I assumed it was a joke."

Trillian shook her head. "Think again, Roderick. The orders are no joke."

He lifted his eyebrows, and his green eyes, uncommon in his family, widened slightly at her words. "I'm working for you?"

"It appears so."

Roderick laughed. "I assume my superiors had no

objections to my transfer." His words dripped with sarcasm.

"Oddly, no," she returned in the same tone, then continued more seriously. "To be honest, I was pleased when I saw you piloting your 'Mech the other day. I was afraid that after Algorab, you'd still be piloting a cubicle."

He eyed her warily. She could almost read his thoughts. He was wondering how long she had been on Cavanaugh, how long she had been monitoring his activities. Knowing Roderick, he was fighting his suspicions—even of her, even though they had been close all their lives. Trillian decided to go on the offensive and not give him a chance to interrogate her about her activities. She pulled out a hard copy report and tossed it on the table between them, giving it a slight twist so that it spun to face him. The title on the cover sent a flush to his cheeks: The Incident on Algorab.

"You know it all, then," he said, casting a distasteful glance at the report, then looking back at her.

"I know it all. More than the public, that's for sure. I know that you were made a scapegoat for the failure of your commanding officer and the men above him. If you had followed the orders of Colonel Quentin, you and many more good people would be dead. This is one of those rare times that the press was right, Roderick. You were innocent."

"The court-martial ruled in my favor."

"They didn't clear your name," she said. "For God's sake, you rolled over." She hoped she sounded as frustrated as she felt. *I expect more from you. What are you holding back?*

He sat up a little straighter. "I'm an officer. You're a diplomat. You wouldn't understand."

"I'm family," she said firmly. She knew it was a cheap shot. Roderick had spent his entire life doing everything he could to avoid her family. His father had been the same way.

"I know," he said in a repentant tone, sounding more like the young boy she had played with so many years ago. "Okay, Trill, for you, the truth.

"I did what any good officer is supposed to do. I took responsibility for the operation because it was expected of me. I defended myself at the court-martial, but to try and clear my name was only going to draw attention to me. It wasn't going to bring those men and women back. If anything, it would continue to drag their families through the pain over and over again. Those families had been through enough."

She watched him. "You were afraid that if you pushed too hard, your secret would get out, weren't you?"

He snapped back quickly, "I am not afraid of my family, Trill."

"Bad choice of words—sorry," she replied. "I was just surprised and a little angry that you took the shot that should have been aimed at Quentin. He comes from a connected family, sure—but that was no reason to spare him and his career at the cost of yours. Screw-ups should be booted out of the military."

Roderick hesitated. "Normally, I would agree, but you weren't there. My orders cost people's lives. I *did* violate the orders of a superior officer, regardless of the results. Quentin made sure I knew he would fight it if I tried to label him as incompetent. I couldn't bear the families being drawn into this."

She studied him silently for a moment. This trial by fire had not just matured him; recent events had taken their toll on his spirit. He needed something to reignite his spark—and Trillian believed her assignment was just the thing.

"Well, I'm not here to revive all that or to interrogate you. Melissa has put me in charge of some aspects of this operation, and I have a need that you can fulfill."

"Whipping boy?" He grinned at his own comment, but they both knew there was a grain of truth there.

She smiled back. "I need an officer with special talents to lead a new unit being formed under my personal command. This unit will take on special missions, some of which are political in nature."

Roderick shook his head. "My grandfather always warned me against getting involved in politics. You know that."

"He warned everyone against politics!" She laughed. "I disregarded his advice, and now you need to as well. Let's face it, regardless of what Adam Steiner said about politics, he was a very successful archon both politically and militarily. He played the political game when he had to, Roderick. Now is the time for you to test those waters."

"Why me, Trill? There are other officers with better records and more experience."

She paced around the table and started at him intently. "Yes, there are those with better records. But you have something to prove—and that's a powerful motivator. More importantly, I trust you. We have known each other our entire lives. I know you won't fail me.

"But most importantly, you have something that none of the other officers have—a family name with the impact I might at some point need. You are Steiner through and through. Whether you admit to it has been your choice up to now."

His face flushed. "You know I don't use that name. Not outside of family gatherings. I don't want the rest of the Inner Sphere to treat me differently because of my heritage."

"I understand your reasoning, but you can't expect to deny who you are forever. I have no intention of revealing your secret without your permission, though I have told my aide who you really are.

"This unit I'm pulling together is going to be special; part of their responsibility will be to protect the archon. That's a mission I can only trust to family, Roderick."

The leutnant looked down, avoiding her gaze. "My grandfather, your great-uncle, told me that this day would come, even though it never did for my father—he was raised in peacetime. You are asking me to risk revealing my identity by openly associating with you on a familiar basis."

"I'm asking you to do your duty," she clarified. Both she and Melissa had known he would be a tough sell for this mission. *But I've worked hard to not lie to him, because I truly believe I will need him to be a Steiner before all this is over.* She knew she had him with his next sentence.

"The Lyran command staff is going to hate this. They hate military units that are not under their control, you know?"

"I am aware of their concerns. Frankly, they seemed happy that I was taking you off their hands."

He chuckled. "I bet. And giving them a little frustration to deal with might just make up for some of what I've gone through this last year or so."

"So you're interested."

"Okay," he sighed. "Assuming I do this, I'll want to pick the troops to be used in this unit."

For the first time in several minutes, Trillian allowed herself to smile. "I wouldn't have it any other way."

Roderick was already mulling over the possibilities. His face was more animated than she had seen it in a while. His pacing became a little quicker. "There are a few men who graduated with me two years ago from the academy . . . I can trust them and they know me. Spending those few months in jail might also turn out to be helpful. I'm not the only officer who's taken the fall recently. And those officers talked about good MechWarriors who could use a second chance. Many of these people are looking for a way to redeem themselves. Redemption can be a powerful incentive, cousin—I ought to know."

She nodded and reached for a small box sitting on the table. She flipped it open and showed him the rank insignia inside: hauptmann. "You will report directly to me."

He looked at the pips and then at her. "I guess if you're going to piss off general staff, you might as well do it right."

Trillian's grin was his only answer.

"I won't let you down, Trill."

"I know," she replied. *I only hope I don't fail you. . . .*

BOOK II

Hammerfall

"In strategy the longest way round is often the shortest way there; a direct approach to the object exhausts the attacker and hardens the resistance by compression, whereas an indirect approach loosens the defender's hold by upsetting his balance."

—B. H. Liddell Hart

Algorab
Former Republic of the Sphere
Months Earlier

"**C**olonel, the Republic commander indicates that they have formed up on the ridgeline at two-zero-three to the northeast. We should break off from the Jade Falcons and move to cover their flank."

"What?" shouted Colonel Drew Quentin. "Say again, Ice Wind." The colonel had seemed confused since scouts had located him at the perimeter of the battle zone. General opinion agreed that Quentin had never been the brightest bulb in the pack, and a few rounds with the Jade Falcons had left him dazed, panicked and even more confused than usual.

Roderick closed his eyes in frustration. "Sir, we need to break off from the Falcons and fall back to the left of the Republic and militia line."

"We can't break off now," Quentin's voice came through a hiss of static. "We've got the Jade Falcons right on our front."

Roderick wheeled about his *Rifleman IIC* and sent a barrage downrange into a Falcon *Goshawk*. His autocannon rounds caught the side of the emerald-painted BattleMech as it bore down on a hapless

Lyran JESII missile carrier. The explosions ripped into the hide of the *Goshawk*, mangling its shoulder plate and weapons pod. A stream of smoke came from the damaged laser, but the 'Mech continued to close with the carrier.

"Sir," he said through gritted teeth. "This isn't our fight. For God's sake, we came here to go on maneuvers against The Republic, not tangle with the Falcons. If we fight them here, we might invite reprisal attacks along our border." There was more at stake here than just fighting the Jade Falcons. The lives of many people who lived near the Clan Occupation Zone depended on what the Lyran commander decided.

"I want—" The colonel's voice was cut off in a wave of static. "Oh God. I've lost my 'Mech's arm. They're pushing us too hard."

"Sir, request permission to fall back by lances. We need to get out of here and let The Republic and the locals fight this battle."

"Damn it, Hauptmann!" Colonel Quentin fired back. "You need to do what I tell you to do."

Then give me an order, you old fart. He watched as the *Goshawk* ran to point-blank range with the JESII missile carrier. It pointed its functioning laser at the vehicle at a range of less than a few meters and fired. Thick, ugly black smoke billowed out of the hole it carved. Swinging his right autocannon into play, he locked on to the *Goshawk* and fired another deadly salvo of armor-piercing rounds into his foe.

It was too late for the carrier. It tried to make a break for it, but the *Goshawk* fired again, hitting its steering fans on the rear. The hovertank weaved wildly, spinning out of control in a wide circle. Roderick's shells tore into the side and back of the Jade Falcon 'Mech, sending armor plating flying. Slowly the Falcon MechWarrior turned to face him. He knew that 'Mechs couldn't smile, but he felt as if the face of the green 'Mech were grinning at him—looking forward to the fight.

"All units, this is Ice Wind. We are going to fall back to the left of the Republic line. Break off your attacks."

"You insubordinate bas—" His commanding officer's words were cut off by a swell of hiss.

"You heard me, damn it. All units, break off and fall back by lances!"

"—ou'll pay for this, Frost!"

6

Loire River Valley
Shasta
Free Worlds League
25 July 3137

The rolling grass-covered hills were divided by a grid of trees and hedgerows. These thick lines of vegetation marked the edges of individual farms and larger properties. The embankments represented centuries of growth, the only openings allowing access for farm vehicles. Seen from above, they created a mosaic pattern. From the ground, they were just barriers that had to be breached.

"This is Guard One," Vedet said over his command channel. "Moving north toward their base at Jonville, west of the river." The drop had been flawless. Now his blood was pumping.

It had been a long time since his MechWarrior training. His family owning Defiance Industries had given him access to the best instructors money could buy. Vedet had skipped the rigors of basic training and instead had relied on private instructors to learn the basics of 'Mech piloting. Naturally, he had scored well in his simulations. He was acutely aware, however, that this was not a sim. This was the real thing.

General Nordhoff was overseeing the assault on the

Marik-Stewart Commonwealth; his strike was tagged Anvil. Vedet's army, tagged Gauntlet, was hitting the Duchy of Tamarind-Abbey and consisted of several attack forces striking different worlds. The duke had chosen to lead this arm of the assault personally; the Duchy was anticipated to offer the least resistance, and Duke Vedet wanted his set of targets to allow the media to show him as victorious. He suspected that in this war, his expertise in manipulating the media was going to be important.

The generals that nominally reported to him chafed at what they considered his interference in the battle plan. They were the professionals, and he was willing to grant them that. At the same time, he felt that they were ignoring what he brought to the table in terms of a fresh perspective. Lyran generals understood politics, but were not trained to recognize and consider the political implications of military operations. Politics, Vedet Brewster felt, was an arena he understood.

As much as he disliked accepting her help, he had to allow that Trillian Steiner had supported him in making several important points with the general staff. She had been in most of his meetings, and had provided a voice that understood both the military mindset and the point of view Vedet was trying to convey to them. They listened to her; it probably helped that she was stunningly attractive, though of course Vedet was not taken in by her appearance. Not once did he forget who she worked for and where her true loyalty lay.

Shasta was a soft target. Not aligned to either the Duchy of Tamarind-Abbey or the Marik-Stewart Commonwealth, it was wedged along the border between the two nations. There would be no reinforcements for Shasta, no cavalry riding to the rescue. The people tasked with defending this planet stood alone. They had days to prepare, to concentrate their forces as the invasion force burned in, but the duke knew that it would not be enough.

His comm unit snapped to life. "Guard One, this is

Tiger One. We are on the flank along the riverbed. Our advance lance is picking up signals due north of our position along the river. They appear to be attempting to punch through right where we are. Recommend Command and Dagger companies wheel to an angle. When they hit us we can hold them on the banks of the river. You can sweep in and envelop them." Hauptmann Klein's voice was calm and deliberate. He was a professional soldier, as were all the troops Vedet had incorporated into his First Hesperus Guards.

He glanced down at the tactical display. Yes . . . the suggestion made perfect sense. The Shasta Home Guard had deployed quicker than he had expected, and were showing some good insights when it came to moving out. They had not counted on his force anchoring itself solidly on the Loire riverbank with Tiger Company.

They didn't yet realize just how outgunned they were.

"Very well," he replied. "Dagger Company, fan out to the north and west. I will hold alongside Tiger Company with Command. We will let them try and punch through. Then I want Dagger to swing in behind them. Drive them into the river."

There was a chorus of "yes sirs!" as he finished speaking. He grinned. Now all that remained was for the Shasta forces to play along. They flickered to life on his long-range sensors a moment later. Tiger Company drifted back, luring them deeper into the gulf. With the rolling hills and hedgerows, it was impossible to see the approaching troops. Even the Loire River was nothing more than an occasional glimmer of blue that appeared between the hills. They were down there, though . . . his sensors told him that.

"Tiger One to Command. We are engaged. Enemy is two companies in strength." Hauptmann Klein's voice remained calm, even in battle. *I chose my people well.*

He paused for a moment, then switched back to his command frequency. "This is Guard One to Dagger One. Execute your sweep. We are on your flank and will act as the hinge for this maneuver. Get your fastest units on the far end to cut off their retreat."

He charged his modified 'Mech across the open field. It was a spring planting of oats or wheat that had just been laid, and he cut a swath as the brown and green *Atlas* moved. Brewster kept waiting for an attack from the hedgerow that he was heading toward, but it never came. When he reached it he leaned his BattleMech forward at a trot, and slammed right into it. The trees and brush were no match for tons of moving machinery, but he almost tripped as he stumbled through the line.

The battle was down below, in the next hedgerow. He saw smoke, and an errant laser blast shooting up into the sky. There was a moan, a low rumble like summer thunder. The sound was all around him. Artillery—autocannon fire, explosions. It was as if Shasta itself were groaning under the weight of the war he was unleashing.

Vedet charged his *Atlas* forward across the open field. He knew that when he burst through this time he would see the battle. He slowed his gait slightly, found a thin spot on the row, and clumsily punched through, again almost tripping as he made it to the other side.

An artillery round from Tiger Company's Long Tom hit an enemy Hauberk assault team. The ground under the armored infantry seemed to open up and vomit them into the air. They fell in every direction. He watched two of the men, parts of them anyway, land only a few meters from him. The few survivors tried to flee.

Duke Vedet fired on them.

His company's emergence from the hedgerow had gone unnoticed until he fired. His large laser shots slammed into the crater that the artillery created, and that was now being used as cover by the survivors. They didn't stand a chance. His lasers seared swaths, hitting two or three troopers at a time. The others broke and tried to run toward the river. Now everyone in his company opened fire. He watched as a Fox hovercraft, marked with Shasta V, attempted to juke away. On his right Command Six fired a wave of short-range missiles into it. The Fox was enveloped in flames and smoke and what emerged on the far side of the cloud of death was charred and mangled, the vehicle listing so badly that its hoverskirt gouged the tilled soil.

A maroon *Spider* BattleMech of the Shasta Home Guard leapt through the smoke and fired wildly. The 'Mech on Vedet's left took a hit. Pieces of armor flew off, peppering his own 'Mech. Duke Vedet was amazed by the pilot's audacity at attempting such a move. The *Spider* turned as it ran, clearly hoping to reach the river, but four 'Mechs fired at him simultaneously. Duke Vedet joined in, unleashing a salvo from his short-range missile rack that pushed up his heat. The coolant system kicked up a notch to battle the warmth.

His missiles scattered, most missing by a meter. The few that found their mark joined the withering barrage of missiles, laser and particle projection cannon fire that caught the *Spider* on its right flank. Its arm was blasted off at the elbow joint. The entire 'Mech was blackened by the assault. It wobbled when it tried to move, its right leg oddly stiff—probably an actuator failure. How the MechWarrior stayed operational was a mystery. Vedet stared at him in wonderment as another wave of short-range missiles, this time from Tiger Company, slammed into what was left of the *Spider*. Like a toppled tree it dropped, lifeless, furrowing the ground as it fell.

The Shasta Home Guard seemed to break everywhere at once. They were heading to the river, thinking they could reach safety. Calls on the command

channel told Vedet that Dagger Company had closed
the back door. There was no escape. Command Company
pany pushed forward along the riverbanks as Tiger
Company did the same.

The duke felt as if he were drunk, moving slowly
and awkwardly. He fired wildly at the fleeing defenders.
ers. He watched as a Po tank took a hit at the turret
ring, flinging the turret itself into the air. Flames
roared like a blast furnace from the resulting hole,
churning black smoke skyward. The crew never stood
a chance.

A pair of short-range missiles hit him, shaking him
back to reality. They were a parting shot as the Shasta
forces tried to ford the river. Both hit him squarely in
the center torso and pockmarked the armor plating,
but did not penetrate. He felt a rush of anger that
these militiamen would dare fire on a commander of
the Lyran Commonwealth Armed Forces. He continued
ued forward behind his Command Company as they
rushed toward the riverbed . . . and victory.

Two hours later he stood next to Hauptmann Klein
surveying the remains of the Shasta Home Guard.
Some had reached the river but had not made it
across. Most of the heavy equipment had been destroyed
stroyed in the pincer attack near the banks. Smoke
rose from a dozen ruined machines. Prisoners were
being rounded up. The duke looked at them with disdain.
dain. Surrender seemed dirty to him, worse than
death. *How could you look at yourself in the mirror
after you surrender?* These men and women seemed
less than warriors to him. For the first time ever, he
felt he could understand the Clan warrior mentality.

"Message coming in, sir," Klein said. "The
governor-protector of Shasta would like to discuss
terms of surrender."

Vedet Brewster took a moment to bask in the
words. He had won. It had been easy. Very easy. All
these years military men had been telling him how
difficult war was. Now he had led an invasion of an

ages-old enemy of the Commonwealth. They had landed a few hours ago and now the world was theirs. *It took us longer to burn into this system than to take it.* He was stunned by the carnage but felt intoxicated with power.

"Tell the governor-protector that I will meet with him. There are no terms. Surrender is unconditional. Send him some footage of his Home Guards—let him see what happens when you cross Duke Vedet. He'll agree. He has no choice."

7

The Maas
Gallatin
Marik-Stewart Commonwealth
30 July 3137

General Nordhoff stepped away from the Aurora-class DropShip *Zerkleinerungsmaschine* and saw a glare on his secondary display. It seemed like the enemy forces were everywhere. *Damn it!* This landing zone was supposed to have been secured. The first wave to land had detected nothing and were already a dozen kilometers away.

He heard a thunking sound as his *Xanthos* rocked back under an assault. *No explosion—must have been a gauss round.* His damage readout showed that his left rear leg had been savaged by the attack. *How in the hell did the first wave miss these guys?*

The Maas was a flat plateau dotted by low-lying clumps of dry brush, with a single road cutting across it. There was no place for the enemy to hide. It was big, flat and only thirty kilometers outside the capital city of Valken. It was a perfect landing zone—that is, until they had come under attack.

"This is Hammer Actual. The LZ is hot. What do we have?" He jerked his *Xanthos* to the right, moving farther away from the DropShip and trying to get a target lock. For a moment, his battlecomputer picked up a towed gauss rifle battery, but lost the lock tone a moment later. What the hell did that mean?

"General, we have no idea what's happening. We picked up nothing on sensors when we landed. My advance company is already off the Maas and on our way to the city unopposed. The moment you landed I started getting sniped at. We have taken a defensive posture and are awaiting your orders." The report came from Colonel Dane of the Third Lyran Regulars Regiment, to which Nordhoff had attached himself for the first wave of the assault. Dane was a good soldier, with more battle experience than most Lyran officers of his rank and age. For him to be caught off guard was definitely bad news.

At the edge of his field of vision, Nordhoff saw something stir from the ground, lifting like a flap of soil. A towed LRM launcher emerged, fired in his direction, then dropped out of sight under the billows of white smoke from the missile contrails. The long-range missiles twisted in flight and slammed into a Maxim Mk. II transport. Most of the missiles hit the target, but two went wide. One flew off out of his field of vision, another plowed into the side of the DropShip he had just climbed out of. It did little more than blacken the paint on a closed deployment door, and Nordhoff felt angry all out of proportion to the result of the attack. The missiles that hit violently shook the Maxim.

"Target is hidden underground at"—he stabbed furiously at the controls on his battlecomputer, inputting the coordinates of the firing missile platform based on a ghostlike reading from his sensors—"two-Five-Seven-Alpha. Artillery, drop your spotting round and fire for effect!"

"Sir, we have no FO linked to us," replied the artillery chief nervously. Bright blue smoke rose from the LRM launcher. Without a forward observer, there was a chance of their rounds missing or, worse, hitting friendly targets.

"I know that. Consider me the FO. Let's flush out this bastard."

"Outbound!" the chief replied. There was a roar from the Thumper on the other side of the DropShip as it disgorged its massive barrage. The shells instantly obliterated the spotting round's smoke. The long-range missile battery rose again, knowing it was in trouble, and opened up with two salvos. General Nordhoff's sensors also picked up a towed gauss rifle off to his left firing at one of his 'Mechs—an older model *Panther*. It too appeared for a moment on sensors, then flickered off.

Every BattleMech and vehicle in range spotted the LRM battery and fired at it. The crew attempted to get away, but Nordhoff calculated only one man made it clear. The battery exploded, sending a twist of orange flame into the air.

"We've got a fix on the problem, sir. The soil here is heavily laced with radioactive waste. It generates a null sensor reading on everything at short range. Long-range seems to pick it up." This voice was that of Hauptmann Lanz of the Regulars.

"Is it natural?"

"No, sir." Firing broke out on the flank—this time aimed at the towed gauss rifle. This crew put up a gallant fight, firing three rounds as artillery and every available vehicle locked in on them. Nordhoff watched as the weapon was tossed into the air by a high-explosive missile and landed with its now-twisted barrel pointing up.

Not natural. That meant that they planned this. They identified the Maas as an ideal place for a landing and fight, so they contaminated the ground soil and put a few units up there to shake them up. It had worked, at least for a few minutes. Letting the first wave disembark without firing—that showed a high degree of skill, patience and training. "Who are we up against? This can't be the militia." Anyone patient enough to let the enemy pass right by them and then open fire at point-blank range was better than your typical Free Worlds militia unit.

There was a long pause. "The LRM battery's gun shield says . . . sir, it's the Silver Hawk Irregulars."

Bernard felt cold sweat form on his brow inside his neurohelmet. The Silver Hawk Irregulars always had been the best troops of the Marik-Stewart Commonwealth, easily equal to the best troops of any other House. Their re-formation was one of the chief reasons the Lyran people had gone to war. "Are we facing an entire regiment?"

"Unknown, sir." Lanz was cut off by another voice. "Bogies on the outer marker! Here they come!" barked Colonel Dane.

"Numbers?"

Through the hiss of static, Nordhoff heard the strain in Dane's voice. "My God, they're everywhere. We walked into a trap, General. I have hidden units popping up everywhere. Silver Hawk BattleMechs and vehicles numbering—" His voice was cut off as an explosion dominated the channel. "Son of a bitch, where did that little bastard come from? Sorry, sir, I have about a battalion down here. I am falling back toward the Maas. Suggest you advance and link up with us."

"On our way," Nordhoff assured him. He didn't like the fact that the Silver Hawk Irregulars had already turned the tables on him. They had stolen his initiative and were forcing him to dance to their tune. *They're as good as Lyran intel said they would be.*

He turned his four-legged *Xanthos* in the direction of the fighting. "Third Regulars, form up on this road. We need to get down there and help Colonel Dane. Advance at flank speed."

Dropping off the plateau, he could see the battle a few kilometers away and was surprised at the scale of the fight and the savagery. Little fires burned everywhere, marking damaged vehicles. He watched missiles envelop a BattleMech of the Third Lyran Regulars. A staccato of explosions rocked the *Shockwave* from two sides, peeling open its armor plating into a raw wound. Smoke from the interior damage slithered out in tendrils that followed the *Shockwave* as it moved. He watched a Silver Hawk infantry squad armed with short-range missiles pop out of a concealed hole and blast a wheeled Demon tank, then run to another hole and apparently disappear.

The Silver Hawks had sprung their trap with deadly precision. Now it was up to Nordhoff to turn the tide. "All units, full assault. Extend the flanks. Stealth Company, break off from the main road, juke to the right flank and make a run for their rear. Let's see if we can capture these Hawks."

Artillery suddenly rained down on his force from somewhere. The spotter for the artillery was pretty good to be able to put the rounds right there on the road, but the damage was minimal. "Get our choppers unloaded and in the air. I want that arty found and pounded!" As if to emphasize his point, a hovertransport next to him was clipped by an incoming round, mauling its side armor.

Nordhoff advanced along with the rest of the Lyran forces, and what happened next was the biggest surprise so far. The Silver Hawk Irregulars, seeing the relief force, broke off mauling Colonel Dane's people and began to pull back, slowly, carefully. A hovertransport charged into the middle of the battle and began to load a towed gauss rifle, which fired even as it was being loaded onto the ramp for evac. He admired the crew for its discipline in the middle of battle, but was glad to see them pull out. *That's right, we're here in force now. Run while you still can.*

"We have them on the run. All units advance. Stealth Company, step it up a notch. You can still cut them off."

A sudden ball of red and yellow fire from the flank told him something had changed. "Stealth Two here. Hauptmann Thompson is down. We've hit a minefield in a farm here, both vibramines and antipersonnel. They didn't activate these mines until we got into the middle of the field. Now anything that moves might set one off. I've gotten the transports clear, but it won't be enough. We are pinned and pinned good." An artillery round went off in the vicinity of Stealth Company, which were suddenly sitting ducks.

Nordhoff broke into a run, hoping to reach Colonel Dane's unit before the Silver Hawks made good their getaway. He passed a smoldering wreck, which he tentatively identified as a Tamerlane scout hovercraft churning black smoke into the air. He could barely make out what kind of vehicle it had been, but he recognized the camouflage pattern as one of his own.

Dane's *Uller* stepped out from behind a copse, showing the signs of battle. The armor on his left arm was gone—exposed myomer muscles, blackened, some broken and hanging like torn muscle tissue, were all that remained. His cockpit glass had been hit several times by fire and was both burned and badly cracked. The left leg of his *Uller* hesitated slightly as he moved into view.

"Sit rep," Nordhoff demanded.

Dane's voice was strong but strained. "Recommend we not pursue, sir. We've hit them hard and one of my advance units reports they are heading toward DropShips off to the northwest."

DropShips? This was planned. Why? Why hit us, hurt us and run? "Stealth Company is tied down in a minefield. The rest of our battalion is coming up the road. We can still catch them."

"Sir, they baited us into this trap. I believe if we pursue we will be popped all along the way. My advance units indicate that the Gallatin Guards, the planetary militia, is beginning to advance on the east."

"I don't want to just let the Silver Hawks get away," Nordhoff said hotly.

"Sir, they are *counting* on us chasing them. I've already lost most of my company and you said Stealth is bogged down. And, sir, if they reach those Drop-Ships we will have to contend with that firepower too. You should turn us east, toward the capital city. We can catch the Gallatin Guards and take them out." Colonel Dane spoke with the experience of a seasoned combat veteran, and Nordhoff knew he was right. But he had to admit, he hated what he was hearing.

Damn!

"Colonel, we'll hold here. You and your men did a good job of pasting those Silver Hawks—you chased them right off the planet. You're right, we need to turn our attention to the militia and taking care of our injured." In his mind, Nordhoff was already spinning their actions for the press. It was clear that this was just a few units of the Irregulars. The rest were still out there somewhere.

He saw one of their 'Mechs destroyed on the ground, an *Ocelot*. Even lying there dead it seemed to reach for him with one arm, as if reaching for his heart. *We did drive them out of here.*

"Yessir." Dane's voice sounded almost relieved.

LCAF Staging Base Boelcke
Cavanaugh II
Bolan Military Province, Lyran Commonwealth

The barracks he had commandeered were poor quarters. This was reserve troop housing—dirty, poorly maintained, just kept from falling apart for appearances' sake. Getting even these quarters hadn't been easy, even with Trillian's help. *If I hear "In case you hadn't noticed, there's a war on" one more time, I swear I'll deck someone.* Everyone assumed that the troops he was pulling wouldn't see combat, so they resisted every request. *It's the albatross of Algorab. Regardless of the truth, most officers prefer to see me as a failure—rather than consider that the same thing could happen to them.* Trillian trusted him. She'd even sent Colonel Wehner, her aide, down to observe Roderick introducing himself to his troops.

Hauptmann Roderick Frost paced across in front of the officers and troops he had managed to cobble together. The men and women assembled in front of the billet were a mixed bag. Many he had learned of through the prison grapevine while incarcerated for the incident on Algorab. They were legends in the prison community, skilled fighters who had crossed too many lines to remain in the LCAF. He had come to appreciate such people. *Hell, I am such people.*

Some, like Decker, were old friends. He and Decker had attended the War College of Buena together and kept in touch ever since. Trace Decker was a good officer, but had made mistakes that cost him a chance at command: namely, running an illegal gambling operation. They stood at attention as he paced in front of them, but he did catch Decker winking at him. Frost didn't bother to acknowledge that he saw it.

"I'm glad to meet all of you. A few more personnel will be joining us in the next week or two as we work out our transportation." He surveyed their eyes, looking for the few soldiers he would recognize by sight. Leutnant Jamie Kroff was one. He'd had to work hard to get her into the unit, but she appeared to be bored by his speech. *I'm sure that will change once I get her back into a BattleMech. . . .*

"I chose most of you for this assignment for a few reasons. First, you have demonstrated remarkable aptitude for combat. Your simulation scores and combat records are some of the best in the Lyran Commonwealth." Frost paused for a moment to turn and pace back down the line.

"The second reason is that your careers are in the dump. You either pissed off some officer, stepped on the wrong toes or, in some cases, took matters into your own hands—literally." He stared at Jamie Kroff, who cracked a faint smile. "Because of your political and legal screwups, you ended up in noncombat duties or assigned to units garrisoning some rock that was never going to be a target in our lifetime. The rest of you were rotting in jail."

Roderick saw them sneaking looks at each other. A few nodded. These were bad boys and girls, Roderick told himself, but he hoped they wanted the same thing he did.

"If you don't like what I offer, I'll send you back where you came from. Quite frankly, I don't want you here if you aren't up to the job."

"Sir," Leutnant Kroff cut in. "What exactly are we here for?"

Roderick paused, then gave them a neutral smile. "Combat, Leutnant. Ferocious, dangerous, deadly combat. The stuff we all trained to do."

Turning to the rest of the line, he spoke louder. "The archon herself asked her aide-de-camp, Trillian Steiner, to have me form this unit. We report directly to Lady Steiner. Our missions will be on the front and sometimes past it. When we go in, we'll be in the thick of things. Your posting to this unit gives the Lyran taxpayers some hope of a return on the money spent training you."

He paused. "I'm not going to blow sunshine up your kilts. I don't know where we will be posted. I do know that Lyran high command is not in favor of our existence, which makes this unit all the more appealing to me, and I'm sure to some of you. I know that Lady Steiner has plans to use us. She has personally assured me we will see action. The question is, are you interested in getting into the war?"

Roderick studied their faces and eyes as they stood at attention. He'd chosen them carefully, but he still had to find out if they had the right stuff. "Anyone who wants to leave now, step forward."

He waited. No one moved.

"Very well. I want these barracks so clean that I can eat off the floor in two hours. We will muster here for inspection, and then you will report to the 'Mech bay and simulator facility for drilling."

He paused for a moment. "Welcome back to the army," he said with a grin. "Dismissed!"

Trillian lifted her gaze from the noteputer screen and looked at Klaus Wehner in the dim evening light. She was tired, weary and wondering how the first wave of the assault was going. Without a fully functioning HPG network, she had to rely on courier ships to bring her news. "How did it go, Klaus?"

He took off his hat and dropped into a chair. "Good. Getting them here was easier than I expected because of the number of JumpShips shuffling troops to the front lines. I must admit, though, I'm concerned about this unit of his. He's got some top-notch talent in there, good command staff—but some of these troopers are, well, a challenge."

"Roderick is a good leader. If anyone can turn them into a unit, he can. When we were kids he organized even our water-balloon fights as if they were full-scale invasions. Check his military record and you'll see that he's something of a tactical genius. He knows what he's doing."

Klaus nodded. "I know he's a Steiner at heart," he said, and Trillian felt a minor stab of conscience. She had shared that information with Klaus—the only person she had ever told. "But some of the personnel he's chosen . . . I mean, well, three of them had to be released from military prisons. One nearly killed her commanding officer with her bare hands."

Trillian smiled. "Like you said, Klaus, he's a Steiner. He doesn't like it, he hides it, but he is a Steiner. And, at the right time, that is bound to shine through."

8

Outside the City of Lancaster
Millungera
Duchy of Tamarind-Abbey
30 August 3137

Vedet Brewster looked at his secondary display with a certain amount of disbelief. The Millungera Militia, which Lyran intelligence had painted as being recently reinforced, was on the run. There were four roads that snaked across the countryside, and the militia was using three of them in an attempt to reach the city. He could make out their motion at the extreme range of his vision through the cockpit of his *Atlas*. Occasional dust kicked up from their flight marked their route. Duke Vedet noticed the bare branches of the trees; already autumn was settling in on the northern continent of Millungera. With winter would come a new government as well . . . if this worked as planned.

They have good reason to run—we outnumber them more than two to one. Duke Vedet smiled to himself in the comfort of his cockpit. In a few minutes, the militia would encounter the troops he had pushed ahead. Then he would crush the Millungera force once and for all. He had to—if they reached the confines of Lancaster, they could close the odds dramatically.

City fighting, from everything he had read and studied, was the worst. *They would force me to level the city block by block to get rid of them.* Fortunately, he was prepared to do just that.

The three Cardinal VTOLs loaded with field artillery and armored support infantry dropped down in advance of the militia. The massive turbofans churned up higher plumes of dirt than even the fleeing infantry. Trees were stripped of their bright orange and yellow leaves, leaving only naked branches poking skyward. The VTOLs had positioned themselves on the last two bridges before Lancaster.

The battle erupted quickly. The VTOLs, while mostly used for transport, were also armed. They banked off from the bridges and moved to the flanks to provide cover to the infantry. Their fans stripped more trees naked of their leaves.

"Guard One to Command and Dagger companies. They are boxed in at the bridges. Charge them. Destroy them." He felt an almost physical pleasure in those words. He throttled up the fusion reactor, which throbbed under his cockpit as the 100-ton BattleMech moved as quick as it could jog toward the fight. Dagger Company had been hounding the Millungera Militia. Now, cut loose, they rushed forward. Explosions bracketed both roads.

The *Atlas* seemed to strain at the speed he demanded. He could feel the heat sinks kicking in, attempting to keep the heat of "the pride of Defiance Industries" manageable. Vedet now understood why military men enjoyed this life so much. It was invigorating. He made decisions every day as the head of Defiance Industries. Here, though, on the front, his decisions made the difference between life and death.

He locked his PPC on a small *Locust* and fired. The brilliant white-blue beam of charged particles pierced the air and hit the leg of the militia 'Mech. It bent backward against the actuator, ripping and finally giving way. A salvo of missiles, probably from someone in Dagger Company, hit the 'Mech as did a small laser, its emerald beam slicing at the damaged leg. The *Locust* pilot fought hard to stay upright, but gravity cruelly embraced the BattleMech. It dropped, billowing up dust. Its seared-off foot and leg remained standing upright over it, like an odd grave marker.

A militia SM1, a deadly tank buster, banked off the road to put up a fight and blasted one of his Hesperus Guards. Four comrades of the target responded at once. The SM1 was not built to weather such an assault. The front glacial plate of armor disappeared in fire and laser bursts. Globs of melted armor splattered. The vehicle dropped to the ground and began to shake and rattle as secondary explosions began to go off inside. The sides of the SM1 blew out, followed by churning black smoke. One hatch flopped open, but there was no sign of fleeing crew.

A militia Balac VTOL attempted to provide cover against the waves of advancing BattleMechs, but it had more targets than it could handle and was banking wildly, both firing and attempting to evade missiles in the air. Duke Vedet saw the militia ground units attempt to fan out, to get off the road, but his forces overwhelmed them. He fired at the Balac, hitting it with a burst of short-range missiles. The VTOL swung wide and dropped behind a small hill. The duke saw a ball of orange fire rising into the air, and a moment later the concussion from the blast rattled his *Atlas*.

I killed him.

Vedet slowed his *Atlas* and watched as his vehicles and BattleMechs charged the line. Artillery rained in on the congested roadway, blasting the ferrocrete like black clods of shrapnel. Millungera Militia infantry, in Gnome power armor, attempted to flee to the countryside. He numbly watched as one of his own Rangers rushed right through their formation. One dead man was splayed out on the front armor of the Ranger. A dull wet smear of his blood marked where the body slid away as the Ranger spun for another blast through the squad.

He trembled as he thought about the Balac he had

shot. There had been no hope of survival for the pilot. He thought again, *I took his life.* Vedet Brewster had done many things in his life, but killing had not been one of them. Certainly, his decisions had cost the lives of a few workers here and there, but attacking another vehicle with the intent to permanently disable—he had done this thing. He felt warm; his skin tingled, as if ants crawled on him. He licked his lips and tasted the salt of his own sweat.

A voice called to him, jerking him into a moment of clarity. "Tiger One to Guard One," said Hauptmann Klein. "Sir, we are slaughtering them. I suggest we stand down. They'll surrender."

He heard the words but said nothing. *No.* These men and women were the enemy. History recorded just how many times the Free Worlds League had initiated war against the Lyran people. Per the reports of Lyran intelligence, the Duchy of Tamarind-Abbey had armed these militia units and prepared them to fight—and their most likely target was the Lyran Commonwealth. While the troops he had faced seemed unlikely to succeed in a pitched battle against the superior soldiers the Commonwealth brought to bear, he believed the intelligence reports. Everyone knew that intelligence reports and reality often differed greatly.

If he let these troops live, he would be inviting them to fight again. What if they used a cease-fire as an opportunity to escape—or worse yet, to take the life of one of his own men? No. They had to be *defeated*.

"Guard One," Klein pressed. A distant explosion added to the chaos and carnage erupting on the roads and at the bridges. "Do you copy? I suggest we give them a chance to surrender."

"No," Duke Vedet said softly, then shook his head. Beads of sweat dappled the visor of his neurohelmet. "Negative, Tiger One."

"Sir!" Another explosion, this concussion so strong that it shook his *Atlas*. Something small had been knocked loose and was bouncing around in the cockpit. Probably a BattleMech being blown up. "Sir, this isn't war, this is murder."

Duke Vedet looked at the knoll where the Balac had dropped from sight. A stream of gray smoke still rose from where the militia VTOL had died. "Wipe them out. It is the only way they will know we are serious."

The duke waited a day before visiting the site of the final stand of the Millungera Militia, and he was shocked by what he saw. Even he could not call it a battlefield. Everywhere he turned he saw a debris field of burned and blackened hardware. Chunks of twisted and torn BattleMech armor lay scattered across the field. Vehicle carcasses lined the two roads that led into Lancaster. Some were still smoking, thin gray wisps marking their destruction.

But it was the bodies that sickened him; his stomach pitched as he realized what he was seeing and smelling. Bloated from the heat of the morning sun, the upper portions were sickly pale while other parts, where blood had settled, were deep purple. Most of the victims were torn apart. Pools of blood were now simply dull brown smears and puddles on the grass and ground. The smell of decay mixed with burning 'Mech and vehicle parts was thick enough to taste.

Duke Vedet fought the urge to throw up. *I can't vomit in front of my men . . . what would they think of me?* His skin simultaneously burned with fever and rippled with chills as he breathed shallowly through his mouth. His salvage crews were crawling over a fallen *Raptor II*, apparently attempting to remove hardware from the fallen BattleMech. The *Raptor II* was a relatively new 'Mech; its presence here was one of the few pieces of evidence that Lyran intelligence might have been right about the Millungera Militia refitting for offensive operations. Looking at the mangled remains of the *Raptor*, Vedet found it hard to think of it as a threat.

He took long careful steps. He wanted to make sure

he didn't trip on debris or, worse, step on a dead body. The destruction of the militia had not been a battle, he thought again. Hauptmann Klein had been right— it was murder. With the bridges blocked by his infantry, the river had channeled the militia to its death. Some had turned to fight, some had tried to get away—but it was all futile.

The duke strode to the top of a grassy hill and looked back along where he had walked. Guilt came over him in a wave. *I could have stopped this.* He focused on the *Raptor II* salvage efforts. *No.* He couldn't think about it like that. Fighting and killing were part of war. His family had created the machines of war for generations; some members of the Brewster family had even fought. Questioning what he had done was paramount to questioning the work his dynasty was built on.

I did what was necessary. If we hadn't killed them, they would have continued to threaten us. He would cling to that thought. It was a thin veneer for the reality of what he was looking at, but he would take the scant comfort it offered. They were the enemy, after all. They deserved what had happened to them.

Something made him think of Trillian Steiner, and he thought, *She would never be able to face what I have—battle and death. She must know that. That is why she stayed behind the front lines.* The isolation of the Steiners from real life was their ultimate weakness.

Turning slowly away from the field of destruction, the duke looked over at the isolated wreckage of the Baltac VTOL he had shot down. If he had not known what it was before the crash, he would not have been able to identify it. The autumn grass near it was charred and the tree it had crashed next to was blackened from the flames. His jaw set as he looked at it. *They were the enemy, they deserved this.*

One of his seemingly endless army of aides approached; he thought his name was Leutnant Schnell. Duke Vedet spun to face the young officer, relieved at the diversion. "Sir, the media is here."

"Our media?" He realized it was a redundant question as soon as he asked it. *It's all our media now.*

"Yes, sir."

Brewster nodded. "Let's not let them get too much footage of the battlefield. We don't want to sour people back home on the war because of what we are being forced to do." He strode down the knoll in a direction to put the grassy hill between him and the destruction, and met the interviewer and her holo-video crew at the bottom of the knoll. The duke felt vaguely uneasy as each step brought him closer to the VTOL he had shot down. He could feel its presence, like a ghost, behind him.

"Duke Brewster," the reporter began.

"Duke Vedet," he corrected quickly, with a hint of his best boardroom smile. "I have not forgotten my Skye roots."

The reporter smiled at the correction. "Judy Steffer, Lyran Broadcasting. I have a few questions for you, Duke. It is obvious that your Hesperus Guards have delivered a stunning blow to the troops of the Duchy of Tamarind-Abbey here on Millungera. What is your perspective on the fight?"

He waited for a moment before speaking, aware that the holocamera frame would pair him with the rolling smoke from the downed VTOL behind him. For a fleeting moment he wished he had chosen a different location for the interview, then set his features in a determined expression for the reporter and her viewers. "Ms. Steffer, the Lyran Commonwealth was forced to bring this fight to the Duchy and to the Marik-Stewart Commonwealth, to protect our people and our borders. I am honored to be here on the front lines, helping lend a hand to our brave men and women in the service. What we did here on Millungera was something that had to be done." He was acting—anyone who had ever seen one of his press conferences would know that. The vast majority of the Lyran people, however, would not. The duke intended to play to their sense of patriotism, and to highlight his sensitivity and strength.

"I understand that operations on Alorton and Saltillo were highly successful as well," the reporter followed up. "The Second Lyran Regulars allegedly took Saltillo in only three days of fighting. Would you say that resistance to our actions has been weaker than expected?"

He replied immediately, but wondered how she had heard news of those attacks. Vedet himself had received word only the day before, along with reports from the Marik-Stewart Commonwealth, which were far less positive. If she knew about Alorton and Saltillo, she would know about the Commonwealth as well. Vedet chose to seize the initiative. "I would never characterize war as easy or resistance as weak. Take what has been happening in the Marik-Stewart Commonwealth as an example. While we were able to drive the Silver Hawk Irregulars off Gallatin, they gave us a good fight. Now I understand that they have appeared on Uhura as well. We are sending some of our best forces to deal with these elite troops."

He was telling a partial truth: the Silver Hawk Irregulars' attack had caught Bernard off guard on Gallatin and had surprised everyone, including the LIC's elite Loki branch, by showing up on Uhura. And this information was already out of date, brought by a contracted courier JumpShip. What disturbed Vedet was that the Hawks were setting back the Lyran timetable for seizing these worlds. They hit hard and fast and evaded direct battles that they might lose. General Nordhoff currently was on Uhura with the Third Lyran Regulars and their losses were already way over what had been projected. By addressing this problem proactively, he hoped to disarm more embarrassing questions from the reporter.

"Word is that you personally led the attack here, Duke Vedet," she commented.

He responded with useful but fake humility. Waving his hand in the air as if to brush away her words, he said quite seriously, "Ms. Steffer, it is true that I was in this fight. I believe in leading from the front." *Take that, Trillian Steiner.* "But the real leaders who created this victory were the men and women of the Lyran Commonwealth Armed Forces."

She flashed him a smile, and he wondered if she was flirting with him. "This is Judy Steffer for the LBC." She signaled her camera crew, and they lowered their cameras. "Thank you very much, Duke. I appreciate your comments."

"I thank you." He said it as if he meant it. He folded his arms and watched the camera crew trudge back up over the grassy knoll toward the destroyed Militia forces. He motioned for Leutnant Schnell to approach. The young officer bowed his head slightly and clicked his heels together.

"That news crew that just left, will they be using our JumpShips to transmit their footage?"

Schnell nodded. "I believe so, sir. The media covering us has had to rely on our ships to broadcast their reports."

"I want you to have one of my media people review the footage," he said, glancing up the hill to make sure the news crew was out of earshot.

"Sir?"

"I have a number of my media people on staff. Make sure they see the footage and edit it accordingly. The people back home don't have to see how badly we crushed this militia force. They just need to know that we won the fight and they are safe. You have to trust me, my staff knows what to do."

"Sir," Schnell said nervously. "This is an unusual request. We usually allow the news people to use their best judgment."

The duke grinned, but not unkindly. "Trust me, Leutnant. And another thing—get our crews out here to clean up this battle site. Nothing will make a local population dig in their heels like a constant reminder of defeat. Get it buried and disposed of."

"Yes, sir." Schnell saluted.

"And, Leutnant?"

"Sir?"

He turned and pointed to the fallen VTOL, the one he had taken down. "Start with that wreck behind the hill."

9

Trillian Steiner sat with Klaus Wehner in her ad hoc office, studying the reports from the Lyran Intelligence Corps. Klaus continued to be a godsend. He had organized the data on the first wave of targets and summarized the reports in a succinct manner. She found battle-damage assessments and action reports boring, especially when they were intermixed with intelligence and military data and the countless statistics compiled from battlerooms and sensor feeds. Digesting just a single battle could be a daunting task. Klaus made it easier for her by pulling out the details that were of interest to her or worthy of note.

The office she had adopted as her own was just down the hall from the communications center in Boelcke Base. As JumpShips arrived in-system and transmitted their reports, Klaus compiled the data for her review. Lacking a fully functioning HPG network, this method was the best way to stay on top of what was happening. Duke Vedet had managed to seize the newly operational HPG on Millungera and had already transmitted reports of his success as well as uploaded a wealth of communications traffic detailing the status of Operation Hammerfall. He would be poring over the data with his staff, sorting through the enormous amount of information for slivers of truth and useful intel. *Will we arrive at the same conclusions?*

Doubtful.

Trillian knew the Lyran high command would be performing the same task. She intended to let them do their job with as little interference as possible at this point, other than making sure she was kept up to date on all information. She had a few angles of her own to pursue: there were the classified plans for joint operations with Clan Wolf; there was the expected friction between Duke Vedet and the command staff to manipulate; and there was the Steiner name to use to its best advantage.

She knew that the high command was deliberately withholding some information from the duke. She heard them whispering "figurehead" when his name was mentioned, and she could practically feel the resentment over his assignment as nominal head of the invasion. Some of this was sour grapes: Vedet was expertly manipulating the media from the field, effectively diminishing the operational role of other commanders who had expected to gain prestige from the long-planned incursion into former Free Worlds League territory. She appreciated the simplicity of not having to ask them to keep Vedet ignorant of some elements of the operation.

She also appreciated that her name carried weight with high command, especially with the archon's personal endorsement. She understood that, far from resenting her involvement, most of them felt grateful that she was on the front lines of negotiating peace with the Byzantine governments of the former League. "Better her than me," they said.

Her final ace was currently tipping his chair against

the wall at one side of her desk, scanning the note-puter logs compiled by Klaus. Roderick Frost came to her office once a day for this meeting—a review of the status of the war, a chance for her most trusted people to evaluate and discuss the situation. Roderick offered a good balance to Klaus. Both men were loyal, but Roderick was family. He was motivated to help her by bonds of blood that, in her opinion (and experience), always trumped an oath or even personal loyalty. And as a field officer, he sometimes saw things that even Klaus missed. She valued both their perspectives.

She slid the noteputer across the desk to Roderick and rubbed her eyes. "Tell me, Klaus," she said, trying to scrub the weariness from her face with her hands, "you've been looking at the same reports I have. What do you think?"

"About what, Lady Steiner?"

"Let's start with the situation in the Mark-Stewart Commonwealth."

Klaus paused for a moment, and she knew he was organizing his thoughts before he spoke. It was one of the traits she most liked about him. "I would say that they have outperformed their neighbors in the Duchy. So far, they have been surprisingly well prepared for each one of our attacks. While they have lost every encounter, the fighting in that region is costing us many more casualties than we had anticipated."

She nodded, arching her spine and then slumping back in her seat. "The Silver Hawk Irregulars are proving to be quite troublesome."

Her aide nodded. "They are not fighting according to a doctrine I would have expected. Anson Marik seems to be committing them to action, forcing us to spend resources, then breaking them off and abandoning the field."

"Those who fight and run away," she added, "live to fight another day."

"It's more than that," Roderick interjected. He

rarely spoke during these meetings, so his volunteering an opinion now spoke volumes even before he began his analysis. "No offense, Klaus," he said, "but there is more going on here than any of us has taken into account. Anson Marik is using the Silver Hawks as irregular forces in the true sense of the word. He is using them to demonstrate to his people that every citizen can fight back against our invasion forces."

"And?"

"On the one hand, the Silver Hawk Irregulars possess a certain mystique in the Free Worlds League. Anson is playing on their reputation to take advantage of the *idea* they represent, because he knows that you can't fight and defeat an idea. On the other hand, the Irregulars have never been friendly to the captain-general, and given Marik's ambition to become the next captain-general, it seems odd that he would choose to reform that particular unit."

"What are the military implications?"

"As long as he doesn't commit them in force, but rather orders them to hit us, *bleed* us and run away, he creates hope with the people of his realm."

"Sooner or later he will have to commit them in force," Wehner pointed out.

Roderick's face showed that he disagreed with that statement. "Not necessarily. He can spread them out, a lance or two each on a number of worlds. As their reputation grows, people will have more confidence in them and what they represent. Reports already indicate that Marik is using the Silver Hawk Irregulars to mount a resistance movement." He pulled a noteputer out of the stack and slid it across the desk to Trillian. She picked it up. The small screen showed an image spray-painted on the side of a building. There were pockmarks on the wall near the image but it was clear: a silver eagle outlined in purple. The attached report described an attack on a Lyran checkpoint on Gallatin, a world that had already fallen in the Lyran campaign.

Roderick explained his logic. "This account was buried in the reports submitted by the garrison forces. I almost overlooked it. They have been hit a few times—bombings, sniper attacks and so on. This symbol, the logo of the Silver Hawks, always appears in some public area near the attacks. The same thing has occurred on Uhura, and we are not even finished with operations on that world. The same pattern of activities, the same symbol." His casual tone could not detract from how important this information might be.

"Interesting," Colonel Wehner said, leaning over the desk to look at the noteputer. "I would consider it too early to call this a true pattern, but I must admit that I'm a little ashamed at missing these two incidents. By your leave, milady, I will take this tidbit to the intelligence officer of the day. They may have overlooked it as well."

Trillian nodded and he rose, bowing slightly to her, then stepped out of her office. She remained silent until the door closed behind him. "Roderick, that was a brilliant bit of analysis."

Color bloomed in his cheeks. She hadn't realized that flattery embarrassed him. "He's right—it's too early to say there's a real pattern emerging. But I do think my call on how Anson is deploying the Silver Hawk Irregulars is right."

"How did you spot it?" she asked. He was young, and had been publicly painted as incompetent; yet he was able to spot something that men who saw themselves as his superiors had missed. But then, that was Roderick. Even members of the family had underestimated him for years, and still did—but she saw no need to make that mistake. She deliberately had chosen Roderick for her scheme to offset the actions of Vedet Brewster; Roderick would be her shield to parry any political blows that the duke sought to inflict on her.

She could see from his face that he understood where the question was coming from; confidence and trust shone from his eyes. "I spent a lot of time with my grandfather as a child. Did you know that he preferred to be addressed as General?"

She nodded without interrupting. *He needs to talk this out.*

"He had more hands-on experience with the Jade Falcons than almost anyone else in the Commonwealth. They took his home world from him. He was consistently passed up for leadership roles by the command staff. He saw the Steiner name as a weight around his neck, Trill. . . . Those are his words, not mine."

"He was one of the best archons we've had, at a time when we needed a great leader," Trillian said, proud of her great-uncle. And Adam Steiner had proven himself to be much more than a good general. When the time came, he became a great leader of the Commonwealth.

"He told me that he hated being remembered as archon. He wanted to be remembered as a good military leader, not for his ability to negotiate politics. But he taught me an important lesson. Some officers bury their head when it comes to the political implications of their actions. They ignore that aspect, leaving it for the diplomats to deal with. Grandpa warned me that was a mistake. He made sure I understood that every military action had some political impact.

"When I look at reports like these, I remember what he taught me. I look for patterns. In this case, I think I can see what Anson Marik is planning. If I'm right, it is going to be hard for us to engage and take down the Irregulars. He needs them to inspire his people, give them a reason and hope to fight."

She suppressed a smile. *He's got a unique and valuable military mind . . . and his superiors wanted him permanently denied a command position.* "I'm glad to hear that you study the politics of situations, Roderick. I may have a puzzle for you. I heard from Melissa today. She's concerned about the advances that Duke Vedet is making."

The young officer nodded. "The duke is a formidable presence, and has been succeeding pretty dramatically. This war is far from over, but the Duchy of Tamarind-Abbey is not strong enough to hold him or us back. Melissa is right to be worried about him."

"What would *you* do to keep him in check?"

He paused. "I would overtax him. Take away some resources, force him to slow down. He's not trained on the logistics it takes to wage war. He's used to fighting battles across a table in a boardroom. He's chosen to put himself on the front lines in order to suck up some personal glory, which is good for the press back home but it doesn't help him coordinate an operation on this scale. The high command has taken up some of the slack, but so far this has been manageable. Give him a few more things to worry about and he might just get overwhelmed."

She smiled. "Precisely my thought. We have a contingency or two in place to accomplish just that. The first of these is an operation in Skye."

"You're planning on taking on the Jade Falcons?" He sat straight up as if he were ready to bolt out the door to his BattleMech.

"No, no, opening another front like that would create problems that none of us wants. Our plan is to hit worlds that the Jade Falcons haven't taken yet. It allows us to take on the role of 'liberator' while denying the duke the use of some troops, particularly the Royal regiments in the reserve. What do you think?"

Roderick mulled it over for a second. "Sounds good. Is he aware of the Skye plans?"

"Well, we included them in the operational briefing," Trillian replied. "But whether he paid any attention to them is a big question. Even if he looked at that part of the plan, he has no idea that the archon is about to make them active."

Roderick chuckled. "That should piss him off."

"That's the plan. And we've actually got a few other surprises planned that only a handful of officers are aware of—plans that could change the entire face of this war." She slid the small desktop holoviewer from the corner of the desk to the center. Roderick's eyes were fixed on it. "Obviously, what I'm going to show you is for your eyes and ears only. I trust you implicitly, and I believe it will be to our advantage for you to know what else is in play."

She snapped the data cube into place and turned on the unit. A small image of Archon Melissa Steiner flickered to life. She was wearing a smart dark blue business suit and was obviously recording from her office. She didn't move or speak until Trillian pressed her thumb to the security pad and leaned forward so her retina could be scanned. A small red line passed over her face, grabbing the scan, validating the data cube.

The archon moved about her office, pacing slowly. "Trillian, from the initial reports I have seen, it appears that the first wave has been quite successful, especially in the Duchy of Tamarind-Abbey. I extend to you my congratulations and thanks."

She paused in front of her massive desk. "I am sending you this message because of disturbing evidence that has been sent to me earlier today. Our operatives on Arc-Royal and agents in the Clan Occupation Zone have indicated that Clan Wolf has apparently disappeared. Their garrison units are simply melting away on the front line. This may be an indication that they are fulfilling our bargain, but we still have not received any word from them of their planned military operations. I am letting you know this, per our discussions, so you can plan and act accordingly.

"Neither of us planned on this turn of events. There is no point in speculating about the implications of this, but we may wish to operate as if the Wolves will not be striking at the Marik-Stewart Commonwealth according to the timetable we discussed." Her voice was grave. "While our plans did not rely on the Wolf attacks, we had hoped that they would fulfill their end of the bargain."

"Take care, Trillian. Please pass on my best wishes to Roderick as well. I have complete confidence in both of you." With those words the holographic image faded away. Trillian turned off the unit and looked at her cousin. Roderick's face was more serious than before, and he was frowning.

"You two made a deal with Clan Wolf?" he said in a tone that just missed being accusatory.

"Yes." She wanted to explain more, to tell him what Melissa had been thinking. It took a lot of restraint to hold back. Roderick was smart. He had put the interests of the Lyran Commonwealth ahead of his personal interests before; would he do it again?

"The Clans are not to be toyed with."

"We're not toying with them," she said. "This is serious. Enlisting Clan Wolf's aid ensures the success our people expect."

"Generations of House Steiner have faced down the Clans. I'm not telling you anything you don't know, Trill. You and Melissa are playing a dangerous game. The Clans don't just disappear. Something has happened—or something has changed. Either way, the rules of the game are now different." He was not judging her, he was just stating facts. *If he ever wants to give up a career in the military, he could be a powerful asset in the Diplomatic Corps.*

"Their disappearing right now is unexpected, I'll grant you, but negotiating with them was a gamble worth taking."

He cocked his head slowly to the right. "Was it? For all you know, the Wolves have lied to you from the start. Right now they could be working with our enemies against us. The Clans are treacherous. They have honor, but they are willing to redefine honor to fit their needs."

When she had first seen the message from Melissa, she had to admit that the thought of betrayal had crossed her mind. At the time of their meeting, she had believed that Patrik Fetladral was being honest with her, but now she wondered. Roderick had simply given voice to what she had already contemplated in the back of her mind. "It doesn't matter now," she said flatly.

"You're kidding, right?"

Trillian smiled. "There's nothing we can do one way or another at this point. All we can do is issue the orders to commit some of our reserves to the strikes in Skye. Whatever the Wolves are doing, we can't control it. We simply have to take them at their word."

Roderick opened his mouth like he wanted to say something, but was unable to form the words. Slowly he closed his jaw, then flashed her the grin she had known her entire life. "You know, you're right. There *is* nothing we can do about the Wolves. What we *can* do, however, is give Duke Vedet a few new ulcers."

"You surprise me. I thought you didn't like politics."

Roderick grinned broadly, with a confidence she hadn't seen until this meeting. "This isn't politics—this is family. What you and Melissa have cooked up, that's up to you. But Duke Vedet obviously has his eye on the throne. That seat belongs to the Steiners . . . not the Brewsters. That makes him fair game as far as I'm concerned."

Occupation Headquarters, Governor's Palace
Lancaster, Millungera
Occupied Territory, Lyran Commonwealth
Six Days Later

"That bitch," he said, staring at the image of Trillian Steiner on his holoviewer. Duke Vedet had watched the recording three times, and three times he swore. He wasn't as mad at Trillian Steiner as he was at himself. He had underestimated her—no, he had underestimated the archon. *Melissa is more crafty than I gave her credit for. It's a mistake I won't make again.*

He shut off the unit and paced around the former

governor's posh office. Pulling the Lyran Royals Regiments, units he was counting on as a reserve, and sending them to Skye was going to stall General Nordhoff. He had been slugging his way into the Marik-Stewart Commonwealth for a while now. The Silver Hawk Irregulars had been toying with his forces. Bernard had been aggressive in pursuit, but it was as if the Irregulars knew his plans. They always seemed to be one step ahead of him.

Damn!

Duke Vedet crossed his arms in defiance as he stared out the window at the fall afternoon. The time had come to leave Millungera. If Melissa wanted to try to keep him off guard, that was her prerogative. He could do the same by simply winning the war and completely crushing the Free Worlds League. A few more successful strikes and her little efforts would be all but forgotten. This war was not about Skye . . .

. . . it was about him proving to the Lyran people that he was worthy of their support.

10

Roderick leaned into the turn as his *Rifleman IIC*
banked hard in a running arc. Physics reached out to
the BattleMech, fighting what he was trying to do.
The machine's balance system, merged with feedback
provided by his neurohelmet, fought the imperative to
let the 'Mech topple. The Clan-manufactured technology of his *Rifleman IIC* held true even as he pushed
it beyond the design specifications.

Midstride, he swung his right-arm autocannon into
play. The gun purred just outside his cockpit as it
disgorged its rounds. Even in simulation, these rounds
laid a hard impact of kinetic energy on their target.
He fired right into Dewery's *Firestarter*'s tender right-
flank armor. The rounds erupted with white puffs of
marking powder. His own battle computer registered
the hits, as did Drewery's. Indeed, the *Firestarter* suddenly slowed under the simulated damage.

Frost swung around, satisfied that he had injured
Drewery enough to keep him away for a while. He

ran around the base of a massive hill and fired a cutting swath of laser fire at a fast-moving Zibler strike
tank. The lasers were powered down, but it was hard
to tell just by looking at them. The bursts of emerald
energy seemed just as menacing as if they were at full
power. One shot missed the offset turret, but the other
beam found its mark, registering as a solid hit. The
Zibler fired back. Its dummy autocannon rounds hit
Roderick's *Rifleman* in the right leg, leaving a stream
of white marks from the foot actuator up to the thigh.

His battle computer registered real damage, and
even shook the *Rifleman IIC* as the shells landed, to
mimic real hits. His secondary display flickered for a
moment, indicating the simulated damage. It wasn't
too bad. He angled down the hill and spotted a Po
tank, one of his team in the sim, firing a blast at the
Firestarter he had winged earlier. The damaged 'Mech
weathered the attack and returned fire, sending the
Po scampering for some distance between them.

We are at least holding our position. The circle of
hills was the objective. His force, roughly a company
in strength, was supposed to hold it. Trace Decker
and Jamie Kroff, with a somewhat heavier assault
team, were trying to take the position.

Roderick had been running simulated battles for
weeks now, honing the skills of his new unit and learning their strengths and weaknesses. Because he had
known Trace for so long, he could anticipate his tactics. Trace had patience—a trait Roderick admired
and admitted that sometimes he lacked. Leutnant
Kroff, however, did not hold back. Even her BattleMech, a modified *Violator*, was geared for close-in
fighting. The massive claw hand and mounted anti-
'Mech drilling bore were made for ripping apart
enemy 'Mechs and vehicles. It typified her personal
style—in your face. There was a bet in the company
that the name she had given her 'Mech was obscene,
and the odds were two to one favoring it.

So far his officers were proving themselves true to

form. Decker was holding back, providing long-distance covering fire to allow Kroff to move up and do her dirty work. She had pounced on Leutnant Lasalle's *Shadowhawk* and taken it out of the fight. Even in a simulated combat, close combat assaults were dangerous for the MechWarriors. Lasalle was fine, but she complained that Kroff had been too aggressive.

Nothing new there. He grinned to himself. At the moment, Roderick was counting on her aggressive nature.

"Sir, we have incoming bogies crossing the inner marker. Savage One is in the lead," came the voice of one of the infantry squads on his command channel. Savage One—that was Kroff. He checked his chronometer; she was a little later than expected, but other than that she had matched his predictions.

"All units," he said in a clear voice as he started up the hill. A burst from the Zibler chased him but fell short. "I'm taking the high ground. Slow down Leutnant Kroff as she approaches, then scatter." He kept his 'Mech trotting up the slope but twisted at the waist. The 'Mech's center of gravity shifted, but he leaned uphill to compensate. Not even waiting for the tone, he fired down a burst at the Zibler. This time, the autocannon rounds finished off the hovertank. It powered down immediately as the battle computers logged the damage.

When he reached the crest of the hill, he spotted Kroff's force coming up the opposite side, straight at him. Locking his lasers on target, he unleashed a stream of green laser light down at her. Both weapons found their mark, and he could feel the cockpit heat rise as the systems attempted to simulate the heat of running and battle. Roderick shrugged it off. Hitting Kroff was the plan. It would piss her off.

One of her vehicles on her flank, a Ranger, went down. A *Dasher II* on the other flank turned to engage his infantry at the base of the hill. This was boiling down to her and him. *Good.*

The *Rifleman IIC*'s load-lights flickered green, indicating another autocannon barrage was ready. He leaned out over the crest of the grassy hill and fired as Kroff let loose with her short-range missiles. She was prepared too, apparently. The impact of the missiles caused him to miss with the left arm shot, but the right arm found its mark, hitting her leg with white smoke-powder bursts. Her *Violator* didn't slow. It came straight at him.

"You're going down, sir," she said as he backed up. "I lost the last three exercises to you. Not this time." To emphasize her point she throttled power to her *Violator*'s drill. It whirred menacingly at him as she took a step forward.

Roderick signaled his own unit. "Fire for effect on target Alpha One."

She closed the gap at the top of the flattened hill to almost within striking distance when suddenly puffs of white went off everywhere around the two of them. Artillery. *His* artillery. His battle computer recorded damage as he backed the *Rifleman* away from her. Kroff lunged her *Violator* forward as she realized that the barrage was coming down on both of them. Their battle computers logged the damage as the top of the hill was enveloped in white.

He heard her 'Mech but couldn't see it. His sensors told him the story. Things had gone just as planned. "Cease fire," he ordered. It took two minutes for the marking powder to clear enough for him to see the *Violator* lying flat on its front torso in front of him. It had shut down as she leapt at him.

"Are you okay, Leutnant?"

"You stinking bastard," she replied. "You dropped artillery on both of us."

Roderick felt pretty proud, made even happier by the fact that he was making her mad by winning the simulation. "I knew I was piloting a heavier 'Mech and that you were coming in fast, taking damage all along the way. I assumed Trace would hold back a little and give you cover. When the artillery came down, I knew you'd drop and I'd still be functioning." He glanced at his secondary display and saw that his *Rifleman IIC* was in pretty bad shape after the assault, but still able to engage in limited battle.

"Damn it," she spat. "No one would bring down an artillery barrage on themselves."

"Apparently they would. And watch the language," he replied in a matter-of-fact tone. "That's your lesson. Don't underestimate the enemy. Also, you and Trace have become predictable in your fighting styles. It allowed me to adapt and lay a trap designed to beat the both of you."

She struggled, rocking the *Violator* until she could turn over and stand upright. White powder covered the BattleMech. "Let me guess, we go to the debriefing room. . . ."

Roderick grinned. "I didn't beat you, Leutnant. You beat yourself. Learn the lesson and walk away." Kroff was an angry woman, angry and bitter. He didn't know why and didn't want to know. Her record showed that her gunnery skills were among the best in the Lyran Commonwealth Armed Forces. But if she didn't learn to think things through more clearly, she ran the risk of being just another casualty of war.

He looked out of his cockpit and caught a glimmer on a nearby hilltop. Trill. She was watching . . . again. Frost was tempted to wave the arm of his old *Rifleman IIC* at her, just to let her know that he knew she was there. *I've got work to do. Time to see if anyone learned anything out here today.* "Sword One to all units," he said on the open channel. "We will meet in the debriefing room in one hour."

Trillian lowered her binoculars and looked at Klaus Wehner, who stood next to her. "That was an impressive ending," she commented. She could see from Klaus' squinted eyes that he was not just studying the battle, but wishing he was in it. *It has to be hard for him. He's trained for war, but he's on the sidelines with me.*

"Roderick has done an impressive job of turning this band of misfits into a fighting force. Individually, they're good. He's actually getting them to work together, which is what might keep them alive . . . if they ever see action." Wehner did not lift his gaze from Frost's unit.

"I know that some of the upper command staff think this unit will only be used for garrison duty," she replied. "They're wrong. Roderick reports directly to me and you will have to trust me that when the time is right, they will be deployed on the front lines. It's a matter of waiting for the right opportunity."

"Perhaps we should consider sending them in to assist in the Marik-Stewart Commonwealth," Klaus said. "It feels like things are bogging down there. General Nordhoff is competent, but he continues to face more resistance than we expected."

"The Silver Hawk Irregulars?"

A nod. "Hauptmann Frost was right in his analysis. I took his observations to the intelligence staff, and they had already arrived at the same conclusion. Anson Marik is using the Irregulars as a morale-building force. They are helping him hold together his kingdom. Even on occupied worlds where we have moved in garrison troops, there are rumors and stories of the Silver Hawks on-world, hiding, striking. Most of the resistance movements that have surfaced have adopted the Silver Hawks as their unit, allowing people to believe that the Marik-Stewart government hasn't abandoned them."

"Roderick nailed it, then. We're fighting an idea, here."

"And an idea is a hard thing to kill."

Trillian paused for a moment. "The thing that bothers me is that Anson seems to have elements of the Irregulars poised on every world we strike, even if they only fight and flee. They seem to know what worlds we are going to hit and seem very prepared to meet us."

Klaus crossed his arms in thought. "Lyran Intelligence Corps believes that the amount of preparedness the Marik-Stewart Commonwealth has demonstrated, especially in comparison to the Duchy, indicates an inside source."

"SAFE?"

"The latest thinking is that they are somehow getting advance knowledge of our plans."

Trillian said nothing for a moment, instead letting her eyes follow Roderick's force as it departed. SAFE, within the Lyran Commonwealth Armed Forces? To get a full copy of the invasion plans, a spy would have to be highly placed. SAFE had always been a threat, but a comparatively minor one. If Anson had managed to place or subvert someone on the inside, the security compromise would have far-reaching implications.

For years SAFE had been fragmented, with each of the Free Worlds kingdoms maintaining its own unit. The Free Worlds had lacked a cohesive intelligence-gathering network since the Jihad, when the League had been ripped apart from within and without. There had been talk that SAFE was once again sharing intelligence, but that appeared to not be the case. *Anson has hung the Duchy of Tamarind-Abbey out to dry. Typical Free Worlder thinking. If they ever stop trying to screw over each other, we will be in deep trouble.*

"What do our counterintelligence people say?"

Klaus' eyebrows rose, indicating to Trillian that he did not agree with what he was going to say. "They have shared their plans with me. They want to root out this spy and remove him immediately. As part of that effort, they recommend a series of minor changes in target worlds and LZs. They will filter these changes through different channels. Then—if they are acted on—they will be better able to determine who saw them and passed on the word."

"Does Duke Vedet know about this?"

"No, milady, I don't believe so."

She could see that he was puzzled by the question. Good. She liked catching him off guard. Klaus was a brilliant officer and it pleased her to be able to surprise him occasionally. "Don't let him know. Send on the orders for him to make changes to target worlds, but don't pass on our suspicions."

"May I ask why?"

She grinned. "What if the traitor, this mysterious spy, is someone on his staff? Even better, what if it is him, playing some game we haven't figured out yet? I'd rather not tip my hand until I have more facts. If we could pin this spy on him or his people, it would erode any political capital he's gained leading this invasion. Play it right, and people will want him strung up as a traitor."

Klaus smiled slowly but broadly. "Excellent plan. If you would like, I can personally have myself inserted into the counterintelligence team looking for this agent. Doing so could give us that information long before anyone else who might tip off the guilty party—or the duke."

"Good idea," she replied. "War is hard enough when the enemy doesn't know what you are up to. If there is a spy, then SAFE has pulled off something they've been trying to do for centuries. If we can learn who that agent is, we can turn that to our advantage. Our counterintelligence operatives will want to move quickly and contain the damage. We might be able to use a spy like this to our advantage." Properly controlled, an agent could feed the incorrect information at the right time to cause a total disaster.

"Well played, milady," Wehner replied.

"Now all that's left is to win this war, which means winning the peace."

══ 11 ══

Banja Luka Lowlands
Bondurant, Marik-Stewart Commonwealth
27 September 3137

General Bernard Nordhoff's *Xanthos* stalked past the cluster of conifers and he gazed out into the dense forests. A jagged piece of damaged armor on the rear right leg of his four-legged 'Mech caught on a tree and tore loose one of the branches, snapping back the entire tree with incredible force. As it was with every other living thing on Bondurant, Bernard didn't care if the tree was damaged. He hated this world. It was bleeding him and his troops dry.

Things had been going from bad to worse for the last three weeks. A shower would be nice. Hell, he just wished he could rub his eyes, but he couldn't afford to take off his neurohelmet. Letting down his guard already had cost him far too much. He couldn't remember the last time he'd slept, and every muscle ached.

Damn you, Anson Marik. Damn your Silver Hawk Irregulars!

He knew that cursing his enemy didn't help. But he was mad about their success, and mad about his own failures. It had been like fighting ghosts every time he had tried to engage the Irregulars since the start of this war. Twice before landing on Bondurant, they had hit him hard and managed to get away with minimal losses. Twice they had relinquished the planet, and then the local population had taken up the banner and raised hell for the garrison forces.

He had sworn to turn things around on Bondurant, and at first he thought he had. He had landed in the middle of the rainy season, and had changed his landing zone at the last moment to negate any preparations the Irregulars might have planned. His aerospace elements had confirmed that the Irregulars had been indeed dug in around the original LZ. The LIC had been right; someone had inside information and was feeding it to the Marik-Stewart Commonwealth. This time he had foiled their plans. *I can't wait until Loki gets its hands on whoever is giving Anson his information.* Loki, the LIC's elite secret police and espionage branch, had subtle and deadly methods.

Whoever was commanding the Silver Hawk Irregulars was good. They abandoned their positions as soon as they realized they had been exposed and moved more rapidly than anyone had anticipated—anyone except General Nordhoff.

Bernard had gone after the Irregulars with a speed that had to have shocked them. The Irregulars broke off and appeared to be heading into the swamps of the Banja Luka Lowlands, driving toward the distant plains where his aerospace elements had detected their DropShips. His countermove had seemed perfect: he planned to use two highways through the forest to take both flanks, driving into the swamps to cut off the Irregulars before they could execute their standard modus operandi of striking and fleeing.

True to form, the Silver Hawk Irregulars immediately changed their tactics. Rather than fleeing, they turned on his troops. The three companies of the local militia linked up with the Irregulars, giving them a more vicious bite. Naturally, the local troops knew the swamplands of Banja Luka better than his scouts ever could. Hastily laid vibramines shattered the legs of a half dozen of his BattleMechs. Ambushes and lightning-quick night assaults wore at everyone's nerves. The moment that had offered the potential for a rout of the Irregulars had disappeared, and once again the Lyrans were mired in a bitter struggle.

The fight had torn up his Third Lyran Regulars. Two weeks ago Bernard had been forced to call in his reserves for the first time in this campaign—and it ate at him. His Regulars should have been able to finish the job on their own, but the Silver Hawk Irregulars combined with the local Bondurant Bombardiers had turned Banja Luka into a death trap. He even considered extracting his Regulars, but disengaging from the fight was actually a more dangerous proposition.

I always believed that if I ever got into a fight like this, I would handle it with the forces allotted to me. Now I'm watching good men and women die—and they deserve better. Shelving his ego and asking for help had not been easy—only to be informed that the Lyran Royals Regiments designated as his reserves had been shuffled to "liberate and protect a holding in Skye." The duke had signed the orders for this, but Bernard knew someone else was pulling the strings: a Skye strike had been a contingency plan, and getting it moved into action required someone with more authority than the duke, either Trillian Steiner or the archon herself. Now the help Bernard had been promised was coming from a different source, and he was not happy about it.

I gladly would have taken help from anyone else.

"The First Hesperus Guards are on the field," Duke Vedet announced on the general channel for all the Lyran forces to hear. His voice made Bernard flinch.

His resentment of Vedet Brewster ran deep. Even though the duke had funded his education and helped advance his career, Bernard knew he considered Bernard nothing more than a tool. The Brewster family had profited from the lives and deaths of the Nordhoffs for generations, and his situation was especially galling to Bernard. He didn't like owing anything to the duke or his family. *I have never asked for his help . . . and I certainly don't want it now, in this way.*

"Duke Vedet, this is Stalker Actual," he replied in a neutral tone. "I appreciate your coming." He could tolerate the lie only because he knew the duke's arrival might save some of his troops' lives.

"Indeed, General. I look forward to personally finishing off these Silver Hawk Irregulars."

Bernard shook his weary head. *Brave talk from someone who has yet to face Anson's elite unit.* He knew the duke was looking to make headlines; that was why he had taken the attack corridor in the Duchy of Tamarind-Abbey. *The real fight is in the Marik-Stewart Commonwealth. Now he'll see what war is.*

"Sir, I suggest you move along the edge of the swamp to sector twenty-eight. From there you can enter and move along the old maglev line. You can be the anchor on our right flank."

"General, my troops are fresh," Duke Vedet responded. "Why waste them on flanking duties? We are an assault unit . . . let us do our job. I read the tactical reports during burn-in. Your men are exhausted. Why not simply cut north of our position and hit them directly in the center? They won't be expecting fresh troops."

"With all due respect, sir, they most likely got word of your landing two days ago. The local militia—these Bombardiers we keep locking horns with—is guiding them through the swamps."

There was a slight pause, and Bernard prepared for a debate. The comm channel switched to the discreet line between the two commanders. "Bernard," the duke said, deliberately avoiding his rank and speaking as if they were old and personal friends. "I would hate to pull rank on you. My authority as the commander of this theater gives me the authority to direct this operation as I see fit. I wouldn't want to embarrass you in front of your Regulars."

He had said nothing damaging, yet the threat was there. Bernard slumped forward, sick and tired of fighting both the enemy and his nemesis. Vedet did have the authority he claimed, but Bernard knew his lack of experience would play to the strengths of the Irregulars.

He saw one glimmer of hope. The fighting had been vicious so far. Perhaps his ego would put the duke into a situation from which he could not escape. *They may kill him and do us all a favor—the archon included.* It was a seductive thought. If the duke was killed, Bernard had friendly officers already stationed on Hesperus II, poised to seize the other members of the Brewster family and take control of key installations. *With Defiance Industries in my hands, I could cut my own deal with the archon.*

The last eight hours had been quiet—too quiet. According to their pattern, the Irregulars should have been popping up and striking at the Regulars. They had adapted once again, a trait Bernard found both dangerous and irritating. They seemed to have disappeared into the shadowy swamps just as a thunderstorm rolled in and began to dump down sheets of water. This vanishing act worried Bernard: when they were shooting at him, at least he knew where some of them were. For them to simply fade away alerted his instincts and focused his years of training.

About three kilometers away, Duke Vedet was leading the First Hesperus Guards into what should have been the center of the enemy line. From what little he could make out on his long-range sensors, there was no indication of firing in that area. Bernard allowed himself a moment to close his eyes, to flirt with sleep. His head bobbed slightly as he listened to the muffled waves of rain hit the ferroglass of his cockpit.

Each time his head dropped, a ripple of cold sweat forced him to snap it back up. The comm chatter had been sporadic. Most of it he simply ignored in his dreamlike haze. Then the voice of the duke cut through, loud and clear. "Stalker Actual, this is Guard One." In the background he heard the rumble of artillery, a sound he knew all too well. Now it was the duke's turn.

"Go, Guard One."

"I've got contact with the enemy. They have a lot of artillery dug in. We can't seem to locate them, but they sure as hell have a bead on us." Bernard could hear the nervousness in the duke's voice, and didn't bother trying to suppress a grin.

"The Irregulars broke off from us. They must have swung around into your path of advance," he said.

"I need you to get up here with at least a company," the duke demanded as a rumble, either thunder or another artillery barrage, echoed in the background. "You can move up the right flank, and together we can take them."

General Nordhoff knew better. These were the Silver Hawk Irregulars. They were prepared. They knew the ground. "Sir, we're fighting on their terms. The swamp in your sector is almost impassible. My hover units can get in, but that's about it. Infantry support will be hampered. I suggest you get out of there and fall back to sector nineteen. There's high ground there where we can operate."

"I do not intend to fall back," Duke Vedet snapped. "I didn't come all this way to retreat."

"Sir," Bernard said, as calmly as he could. He understood exactly what the duke was saying, and he agreed with him. That bothered him; if he could identify with the duke, it made his superior more human. He didn't want to identify with the man. "Now that you and your Guards are here, we can take back the initiative. We can force them to dance to our tune for a change."

"You have a plan?"

Bernard did, though it was still sketchy. He knew one thing for sure: spending another few weeks in the Banja Luka Lowlands during the rainy season was not the way to seize the initiative. No—they would have to take the fight somewhere else, somewhere they could draw the Silver Hawks and the Bombardiers into fighting the battle he chose.

"Yes, sir, I do."

"Very well," the duke replied. This time there was a rumble of thunder over Bernard's *Xanthos* as the storm intensified for a moment. A wave of rain swept through the trees and pummeled his BattleMech. "I will divert our supply vehicles to your encampment. When I arrive, I want to hear your ideas. Then I will lead our forces out of this swamp." The duke's voice was cut off by the explosion of another long-range artillery round near his 'Mech.

A deep unease gripped Bernard Nordhoff at the duke's assumption that he would lead their combined forces. If the man had a military background, he would know that the most experienced officer should lead, regardless of rank. But he was a businessman, and in business perception ruled. Bernard waited a moment before responding, trying to choose his words carefully enough to avoid insulting the duke.

"Sir, with all due respect, I must point out that I have tangled with the Silver Hawks several times in the past few weeks. I concur that our forces should unite under a single commander for this operation. Given my tactical experience and familiarity with the Irregulars' style, I believe I should lead. You would, of course, oversee strategy."

"Your track record with these Irregulars has not been exactly stellar." There was a pause, which told Bernard the duke was probably issuing orders on another channel, or moving to another position.

"Sir, I have forced the Silver Hawks into retreat in every engagement. I have beaten them off-planet each time we fought."

"We will discuss this when I arrive at your position. For now, you may assume I will be leading these forces. If anyone is going to get the credit for crushing Anson's prize regiment, it is going to be me. Guard One out." The channel went silent.

Bernard stared at the sheets of rain falling in front of his 'Mech. Anger and frustration tore through his chest like a living entity. *If he would give me these combined resources, I would mop up the Irregulars and the Bombardiers, here and now.* He sucked in a deep breath and blew it out, then closed his eyes and rested his head against the side of his command couch. *The duke assumes that I am his man, but I'm not.*

"I'll show you what I'm capable of," he murmured to himself. Outside, the wind whipped the rain against his cockpit and lightning flashed through the soaked trees.

12

LCAF Staging Base Boelcke
Cavanaugh II
Bolan Military Province, Lyran Commonwealth
3 October 3137

Trillian watched the massive Prime Hauler grind its way up the ramp and into the DropShip *Archon's Pride*. It was piled with crates, barrels, massive bundles of supplies—the stuff of war. She knew the loading process had been going on most of the day. Roderick's battalion was preparing to deploy.

Most of the first-wave objectives, except for a few in the Marik-Stewart Commonwealth, had been taken. The lack of HPG resources put some gaps in their information, but the intelligence projections looked promising. While some worlds were stubbornly resisting their occupation, still the Lyran Commonwealth Armed Forces were coiling like a massive snake, ready to strike at new targets. Trillian knew that Duke Vedet had gone to reinforce General Nordhoff's efforts on Bondurant, a situation she had forced by diverting some of the heavy reserves to strike at Skye. He had complained, and Trillian had ignored his complaints, which added to his frustration.

With Bernard Nordhoff and Vedet Brewster both

on Bondurant, Trillian felt she had consolidated her troubles. The duke had earned good press with his successful attacks against the lightly defended Duchy of Tamarind-Abbey. Trillian had tempered his self-promotion by calling in some favors to carefully edit the content of the duke's news bites. Because of his relationship to the duke, Trillian was also closely monitoring General Nordhoff's activities. He did not seem to be seeking the limelight—he apparently just wanted to fight a war, and was getting more than enough action with the Silver Hawk Irregulars seemingly one step ahead of him on each planet he struck. If Nordhoff had an ulterior motive, he was keeping it close to his vest.

Trillian leaned against a ferrocrete retaining wall, apparently ignored in the bustle of the spaceport. She usually liked the feeling of blending in, though it happened so rarely that she also found it somewhat disconcerting. She decided that, at the moment, she was okay with a lack of attention from the military personnel. As she watched the crew of the *Pride* unload the hauler, Trillian considered her knowledge that the war was about to enter a new phase.

She had a message ready to send to Melissa in the next diplomatic pouch, in which she personally recommended that the archon approve the second wave, a decision the Lyran high command had been worrying over for more than a week. There was more in her communiqué to the archon, however—suggestions that would help her cousin in his current mission. If he knew about her very necessary machinations, he'd be furious, so she was happy to keep him in the dark.

Roderick emerged from the crowd about two dozen meters away. Wearing his olive drab jumpsuit, he too seemed to blend in with the background; his family background didn't make him stand out from the MechWarriors and troopers in his command. His dark sunglasses obscured his eyes, and his casual stride made him appear to be one of the cast, rather than one of the key players. He veered off his path toward her, then leaned against the barrier next to his cousin and studied the *Archon's Pride*.

"I don't suppose I can get you to reconsider coming along?"

She shook her head. "You're smart enough to not ask. You saw your orders? I assume they met with your approval."

Roderick cast her a suspicious eye. "If I got the orders because of my family connection, I will request that the high command reconsider. You know that I don't want special favors."

Classic Roderick. Always wanting to make sure that he advances on his own merit. "You got these orders because of me."

"That's almost as bad, Trill."

"Labourgiere is a key world in the Duchy," she countered. "The strikes into Skye have forced us to shuffle units to act as reserves for the efforts in the Marik-Stewart Commonwealth."

"I am aware of the current situation," Roderick said. "I was suspicious of these orders the moment I found out that we were being sent to the front line. New units get garrison or reserve duty—especially a new unit made up of some of the biggest rejects of the LCAF." He didn't bother trying to keep his voice neutral.

She was on thin ice here. She knew Roderick well enough to know that he would balk if he knew the full extent of her involvement in getting his untried unit into combat. "All I did was point out to some of the high command the advantages of sending your unit to Labourgiere. If you succeed in taking it, they don't have to shuffle other units around, and they have a victory to declare. If you fail, they would be rid of you, and any mention ever again of the events on Algorab."

The mention of Algorab seemed to allay his suspicions for a moment. "I'm sure that more than a few of them would be happy to see me disappear."

"Apparently," Trillian returned. She congratulated herself on avoiding a direct lie, which was good because Roderick would spot it immediately. "LIC says that there are two companies of recently reinforced troops on Labourgiere right now. Intelligence projects that they might be planning to hit a few of our worlds in an attempt to capture initiative from us. Your job is simple enough. Crush them, and take Labourgiere for the Commonwealth."

He paused, staring across the tarmac as the Prime Hauler, devoid of its cargo, moved away from the DropShip. "I've never been a fan of the intelligence corps. They never actually go in and have to do the fighting, so they're not always accurate. Also, it's a little disheartening when your commanding officers are sending you on missions with the hope you might die."

"My advice is to ignore what they're hoping, and just be aware that getting killed is a possible outcome, particularly for a soldier in war. My orders are to *not* be one of those casualties."

She got a wry grin in response. "I have no intention of getting killed. And most of the personnel in my unit have something to prove, so they'll also work at staying alive."

"Let me rephrase, cousin," she said slowly. "I need you to remain alive because I need you in order to keep Duke Vedet in check."

Roderick glared at her. "I've never even met the duke, and he's off in the Marik-Stewart Commonwealth right now. How can I help keep him in check?"

She thought about all the plans she had in motion that hinged on him, but that she couldn't reveal. "Suffice it to say that you and your unit factor into plans the archon has entrusted to me. I trust her, and you know you can trust me. All I'm asking is that you honor that trust and avoid getting yourself killed."

He glared at her for a moment longer, then stiffly declared, "I promise not to get my ass killed or captured on Labourgiere, Lady Steiner."

She smiled. "That wasn't so hard, was it?"

"Saying the words was easy. . . ."

"Very well. This assemblage of jailbirds you call a combat battalion—do they have a name?"

His chuckle told her there was a story behind his response that she was not likely to hear. "I can tell you that the subject has come up. At least three of the names proposed are not allowed under the decency guidelines of the Lyran Commonwealth Armed Forces."

"What do *you* call the unit?"

"Their official designation is Auxiliary Battalion B1. We've pretty much decided that until we prove ourselves in battle, we are going to hold off on formally naming ourselves. For the moment, when we need to call ourselves something, we use the Broken Swords."

"Where is that from?"

"It's an old Terran military phrase. In the days when officers carried swords, either as their weapon or as a ceremonial weapon, officers who were busted from ranks had their swords broken as a way of marking them as failures. It's a little-known custom now, but seems to fit my officers."

"The name actually sounds impressive."

"Let's hope the Duchy of Tamarind-Abbey feels the same way. Anyway, it's just until we find out who we really are—after we've been in a fight or two." Warning sirens and flashing lights drew their attention back to the *Archon's Pride*, and they watched as the massive bay doors began the closing procedure.

"It looks like your ride is ready," she said. "Oh— I'm sending a package to the archon. Any words for Melissa before you leave?"

Roderick Frost grinned. "Tell her I said hello, and I'll try to not screw this up. As for you, Trill, all I can say is, it's time for me to make a little history."

13

Bernard Nordhoff maneuvered his *Xanthos* around the building from which the attack had come. It was a five-story structure; the lower floors already showed pitting from previous attacks. The shots that had hit him had come from the upper floors, a wave of short-range missiles that had dug into the top of his 'Mech and ripped open the armor. None of the shots had reached his internal structure, but they had gained his attention.

Each thud of the missiles impacting on his BattleMech made his temples throb. The headache had been his constant companion for days now. Combat stress, hell—just sitting in the command couch for days at a time was enough to wear down even the most physically fit body.

His feet instinctively manipulated the foot pedals as he throttled to reverse. Compensating for his weariness, his years of training kept the 'Mech's movements smooth and efficient. Sweeping his targeting reticle across the building, he watched the first wave of fire from his unit converge on the old brick structure. The façade of the building erupted with explosions and dropped down in a pile of debris, exposing rooms and warehouse floors.

An SRM squad on the fifth floor scampered back like rats. He saw them at the same time as the rest of his unit. Their random shots into the structure now converged on the fifth floor. One of the enemy fell, plunging into the spreading cloud of dust that had been the building's front. *Good. One less.*

A wave of long-range missiles fired by Verheiden's *Catapult* in Nordhoff's six o'clock hit two floors below the infantry. The missiles channeled deep into the old building and exploded. The blasts shook the entire warehouse. Then, slowly at first, the building's support structure gave way. It collapsed, the upper floors plunging straight down into the lower floors. In a few heartbeats the entire building collapsed. A cloud of gray-brown concrete dust rose up like a tombstone. There was no way the infantry squad could have escaped. The dust spread out and obscured his own vision, forcing him to switch to infrared tracking on his cockpit viewscreen.

Chalk up one dead squad. One less to kill later. I hope it was worth it.

"Stalker Actual to Stalker Four—good shooting, Verheiden," he said into his neurohelmet's microphone, his voice completely without emotion.

"Hell of a way to take a city—sir," Verheiden replied.

Bernard wanted to laugh, but generals didn't laugh. Generals led good men and women to their deaths. At least, that was what was happening on Bondurant. They had been tied down in the Banja Luka Lowlands for long, tedious days. Duke Vedet's arrival as reinforcements had given them a momentary edge, but the duke's insistence on rushing straight at the Irregulars and the local militia had turned the battle into one of attrition.

Nordhoff had devised a plan to seize the initiative. The Lyran forces had broken out of Banja Luka and moved to seize three nearby cities that he knew must be supply bases for the Irregulars. Two had fallen relatively easily—Westhaven and Chesterbrook. Goldsburo was a different story. Once again, the Silver Hawk Irregulars and the Bondurant Bombardiers had figured out the Lyrans' strategy. By traveling along a dry riverbed, they had reached the city ahead of Duke Vedet's forces and dug in. Now his forces were taking Goldsburo one block at a time and they were paying for it.

His viewscreen readjusted to a normal view after the dust subsided, and he looked ahead to the next block. Hanging on a banner—really just a sheet—was the silver and purple eagle of the Silver Hawk Irregulars. The citizens were blatantly defying the Lyrans again, as they had on previous worlds, mocking his troops' deaths. On this world, Bernard knew things were different. On Bondurant, he had prevented the Irregulars from escaping, had forced them to dig in, to fight, to die. The local militia had suffered casualties, and the Irregulars were suffering too, even if it was one squad at a time.

"Stalker One, this is Guard One," the duke's voice sounded in his headset. Bernard no longer cringed when the duke spoke to the troops. Much as he hated the man's arrogance, he had to concede that the duke had stayed in the thick of the battle, his Hesperus Guards bleeding alongside Nordhoff's troops. Yet the duke still managed to prove that he wasn't a true military commander by keeping a small cadre around him for protection during battle. Bernard knew the patches on his *Xanthos* testified to his own willingness to stand on his own.

As further proof that Vedet remained more a businessman than a soldier, the duke had found and taken multiple opportunities during their running battle to remind Bernard of their relative positions. A good military leader would not let such pettiness interfere in the struggle to win an engagement. It made him furious every time; every time he heard Vedet's voice, he steeled himself to hear it again.

"Guard One, this is Stalker One, go."

"General, my air recon on the north side of the city reported enemy activity in that area. Further recon in that direction has given me an unconfirmed report of a DropShip to the north. Are you aware of this?"

DropShip? His headache suddenly became more intense. No, he didn't know. But without recon assets of his own, he would know this information unless the duke passed it along. Was this another jab at him, a prodding at his expertise—or were they both just tired? Bernard closed his eyes. "Negative, sir, this is the first I've heard of this. Do you have the coordinates?"

"I'm sending them to you now."

His secondary display autoloaded the map of Goldsburo and the surrounding area. There were a number of athletic fields outside the city, and the DropShip had been sighted on one of them. He backed out the image of the map and saw the roads between the city and those fields. Two good, wide roads—perfect if you wanted fast egress.

The Silver Hawk Irregulars were going to make a run for it. Bernard was sure of it.

So where did that leave them? How could they best cut them off? He found an intersecting avenue that would work; if the First Hesperus Guards could shift there, they could block the Irregulars' withdrawal. Just at the moment when he thought he had it figured out, he stopped himself. *That's exactly what they want us to do.* He reminded himself that in every encounter with the Irregulars so far, they had succeeded in leading him into a trap. Not this time. Bernard backed up the image of the map again and spotted another road on what would be the Irregulars' west flank. It was a longer route and a smaller road, but it would allow them to place troops behind the LZ. The only troops in position to take advantage of this potential cutoff were the Hesperus Guards: he just had to figure out how to make this move seem like the duke's idea, so that he would execute it.

That road would be a tight fit. The duke and his Guards would be constrained and isolated. Anything might happen there . . . anything.

"Duke Vedet, I assume that your sighting of the DropShip means the Irregulars are preparing to make a break off-world. We cannot afford that. Do you concur?"

"I was thinking the same thing, General. I am in the northwestern suburbs. From here, I can break my Guards due north. There're some good roads here, particularly the Verdun Pike. I can be on that DropShip in a matter of minutes."

"Sir. The Silver Hawk Irregulars have achieved an ambush in every engagement—even when we were expecting it, they succeeded. I assume they expect to lure you into a trap on those main roads. My recommendation is that you take your Guards and head west, then north on the Maurveux Highway. It's a longer route and a little more restrictive, but it will put you north of their LZ and let you hit them from a direction they won't expect."

"It would give us the element of surprise—for a change."

"Affirmative. We are on the south side of the city slugging it out street by street with the Bondurant Bombardiers and a few of the Irregulars. I will disengage with my troops here and move up into the eastern suburbs. We will converge on the LZ, but you will get there first. Priority will be to take out that DropShip. Without it, the Silver Hawks are stranded here. We'll catch them in the open and finish them off."

There was a pause as Duke Vedet considered what he was going to do. Bernard began keying in the orders in anticipation of the duke's agreement, keeping the transmission in the queue. "Sir, we need to move."

When it came, the duke's voice was crisp. "I will move my Guards as you suggest and make an end run on their rear. Don't leave me out there alone, Bernard. That DropShip is a tough nut to crack if the Silver Hawk Irregulars are there."

Bernard smiled, and hit the TRANSMIT key. "Don't worry, sir. My forces will be there just as fast as we can. Listen for our artillery, then watch for us to the east."

Duke Vedet's *Atlas* moved down the road near the middle of his column. The *Atlas* was a slugger, built for assaults—not for speed. Maurveux Highway was not much of a highway, really, just a narrow, two-lane ferrocrete strip surrounded by hedgerows and old stumps, indications that it might once have been a prestigious area. He felt claustrophobic, especially in the massive *Atlas*. The heavily armored shoulders ground into the low trees along the roadway, shredding leaves and branches as he moved.

Both he and his lead unit were picking up activity at the edge of their sensor range, no more than faint ghosts. The transponders tentatively marked them as non-Lyran. He was confident it was the Mariks, but what he didn't know was if his flanking move had caught them off guard and was forcing them to respond, or if this was itself a trap.

Bernard's plan had seemed solid when he'd agreed to it, but it was possible that the Irregulars had once again outfoxed him—Nordhoff had been bested by them more than once already.

Paranoia lurked around the edges of his exhaustion; days of fighting had left him groggy. He resented that his unit commanders were holding up better than he was, no matter how hard he pushed himself. Of course, the MechWarriors he had chosen for his Guards had years of physical and mental conditioning to their advantage—he had spent those same years maintaining and managing his family's empire. He was happy to acknowledge that military personnel endured a lot, but he was sure they had no idea of the stress and guile required in the battlefields he had been fighting on for years.

Now the instincts that he had used to build his family's empire were telling him that the Irregulars were playing Bernard once again. Duke Vedet trusted his instincts.

"Guard One, this is Tiger One," Hauptmann Klein signaled. "I have a definite contact on our right flank. A *Warhammer* is shadowing us. I marked her as a Silver Hawk in my battlecomputer a week ago."

I was right! "General Nordhoff was wrong—they are shifting to catch us. All units, this is Guard One. On my command, we are going to turn to the right flank and move through these hedgerows to take out those Silver Hawks. We will bring an end to them once and for all."

"Sir," came back Klein's voice. "What about the general? He's expecting to link up with us."

Duke Vedet blinked, trying to push away his exhaustion. "I'll inform him as soon as we engage. Guards, on my word, wheel right!"

Bernard looked at his long-range display at the tiny icons marking the transponders of his own Regulars and the Hesperus Guards, and slammed his fist on the console as he listened to the duke describe his actions four kilometers away. *Damn that man!* The Silver Hawks were baiting him, and he had fallen for it! Bernard's own scouts, a fast-moving pair of Rangers, had skirted the drop zone and had found the *Overlord* DropShip there, waiting for the Silver Hawks.

"Sir," he pleaded, "you must disengage and return to the highway. We have the LZ pinned. The DropShip is there. But we have to combine our forces to have any hope of keeping the Irregulars on-planet."

"I'm dealing with them now," the duke snapped back. "General, divert your forces to my position. Get them here now, and we don't need to waste manpower on that DropShip. It's the Silver Hawks we want."

"Sir—"

"Follow your orders, General!"

Bernard Nordhoff gritted his teeth. *Damn that man to hell!* Vedet technically outranked him; to defy him was to face court-martial. Even if Bernard could prove he was right, the duke had enough officers planted in the Lyran Commonwealth Armed Forces to ensure that justice would not prevail. "Regulars, we need to reinforce the Hesperus Guards. All units converge to the left flank, top speed. Get those Long Toms out to the front and lay down a rolling barrage across the following coordinates." He jabbed in the firing coordinates, which matched Duke Vedet's last known position. "Don't bother with spotting rounds, just lay down a barrage as soon as you are within range!"

"Sir, there are friendly units in the area. They will be caught in the—"

"I know. Stop arguing and get your cans in gear. If you don't lay down that barrage, we're going to lose a lot of good people!"

The Silver Hawk Irregulars' *Warhammer* had seen better days. A nasty gash tore up its right torso, the armor was pitted and peeled back from the wound where a particle-projection cannon had ripped open her hide. Autocannon hits from previous days marked the BattleMech with blackened burns and cratered armor plating. Regardless of its damage, however, the 'Mech was obviously still in the fight.

It fired down at one of the Hesperus Guards' *Jaguars*, catching it on the right front leg. The four-legged BattleMech was moving so fast it simply hit the ground, furrowing the turf and ripping up ferrocrete fragments of an old industrial-plant foundation.

The duke took careful aim, angling his targeting reticle onto the enemy 'Mech. His *Atlas* rocked slightly from a long-range missile hit sent from an LRM carrier hiding on a side street. The barrage of missiles hit over the course of a full second, pockmarking armor up his left arm and leg. He didn't waver. It simply took a few moments longer to lock on to the *Warhammer*.

He heard the tone in his neurohelmet and triggered his primary target interlock circuit, firing the massive PPC the *Atlas* toted with a whirring, high-pitched crackle of focused energy. The charged beam hit the *Warhammer*'s lower torso like a bolt of lightning, crossing its right thigh. He watched as the BattleMech reeled under the assault, staggering backward slightly, then slowly regaining balance. A blackened scar marked where the particle cannon had torn into the *Irregular*.

The *Warhammer* obviously saw the *Atlas*, but had tried to ignore it thus far. Not anymore. The *Warhammer*'s arms both ended in PPCs. They lowered as the 'Mech twisted at the waist to face his *Atlas*. Suddenly, alarmingly, the duke realized this was a fight to the death. This time he was not facing a weak VTOL: this fight was with an enemy that might win. His skin rippled with fear and sweat broke out on his entire body. His fingers hovered over the trigger to fire his short-range missiles, but instead he discovered himself jogging the *Atlas* several steps to the right, as if to dodge the inevitable incoming attack or to seek cover in the open field.

Panic! It was the first time the duke had felt that emotion since he was a child. It was nauseating, hot, smothering. His ears rang as the *Warhammer* fired its PPCs at him. One went a little wide, crossing right in front of his *Atlas*. The other shot slammed into his center torso. Static filled his ears even over the ringing as the azure bolt discharged its excess static electricity in white-blue arcs in front of his cockpit. Vedet Brewster twisted his *Atlas*, but the movement was slow and cumbersome.

He drowned his panic by summoning up a wave of

rage that this Marik-Stewart scum dare fire at him. He leaned forward to get his bearings. Wisps of gray smoke hung in the air, and through them the duke spotted the *Warhammer* moving slowly across his field of fire. *Oh no you don't.* He locked on with his short-range missiles and waited for the instant that the targeting tone came to his ears. He fired the second target interlock, sending all six missiles into the leg of the *Warhammer*. They found their mark on the already damaged leg, each one exploding within a moment of the others, each one ripping off chunks of armor. Smoke billowed from one of the holes.

The Silver Hawk 'Mech slowed abruptly. The duke hoped it would fall, that his battle with it was over. As it emerged out of the low smoke, he saw the leg of the *Warhammer* hanging limp at the waist. *It's not over.* The 'Mech listed slightly to the side, dragging the mangled limb as it hobbled awkwardly along. Severed myomer muscles sprouted from holes all down the leg.

Duke Vedet moved his joystick to center the targeting reticle on the *Warhammer* as it tried to move away toward the flank. As he tracked the *Warhammer*, the duke saw one of his Hesperus Guards, a *Galahad*, take a wave of autocannon rounds from another defender. The depleted-uranium-tipped rounds punched deep into its arm, ripping off the limb and sending it spinning to the ground, crushing a large metal garbage container. He was distracted for only a moment; when he returned his attention to his primary target, he saw that the *Warhammer* was moving in on him. Far from running from the fight, this Irregular apparently was intent on killing him. Its menacing PPCs swept side to side, looking for a target lock.

Is this how I will die?

Suddenly there was a rumble . . . too loud and too sustained to be a thunderstorm. The ground around the *Warhammer* exploded. The Silver Hawk 'Mech wobbled for a moment, and as it began to fall its warrior punched out. The ejection seat blew clear of the cockpit and rose into the air as the 'Hammer dropped. Another blast hit the 'Mech as it fell, blasting through its rear armor and gutting the fallen war machine.

Then a round hit the Atlas' right foot. The upper part of his BattleMech lunged forward while his legs seemed to push back. The Atlas pitched hard forward, and the gyro worked furiously to translate signals from his neurohelmet to maintain the balance of the 'Mech. Another explosion erupted a mere ten meters from his BattleMech. A spray of shrapnel slapped into the ferroglass of his cockpit and pitted it. The cockpit canopy barely held together as he tried to get the 'Mech's legs under it before gravity pulled it to the ground.

Gravity won. The Atlas slammed forward and Duke Vedet heard the sickening sound of armor plating moan and pop as he dropped face-first onto the ground. His lean body was thrown across the cockpit as he fell, the straps digging deeply into his shoulders and skin. He felt something wet on his chest and realized that his coolant vest had torn. Darkness swept the cockpit for a moment as he adjusted his view to only the lighting from his controls and display. Another rumble a few dozen meters away signaled another artillery round raining in.

He did nothing for a moment—confused, even frightened. Artillery. He remembered the way a round had plowed through the back of the Warhammer as it had dropped. Should he flee, try to punch out, try to stand up? He pushed at the foot pedals and could feel the massive Atlas rocking. Manipulating his auxiliary controls, he used the arms of the 'Mech to roll it over.

"This is Guard One, I am down." Another artillery round went off, throwing dirt against his cockpit. He saw where the earlier hit had nearly penetrated the ferroglass and realized that he was lucky to be alive. "We are under artillery fire. Someone help me get up and get out of here."

His immediate answer was another blast, this time farther away. Hauptmann Klein's voice came back in his earpiece as he got the *Atlas* to a kneeling position. "Guard One, the incoming fire is friendly. Am requesting cease-fire. We are moving to assist."

The Regulars were shooting at him? *Bernard.* He felt like his brain was on fire. *I treated him like a son and this is how he pays me back?* Hard on the heels of that thought was another that chilled him. Was this attack deliberate? Was his protégé trying to kill him? A new fear touched his nerves. Just how loyal was Bernard?

The artillery had stopped. There was another 'Mech alongside his *Atlas*, assisting him to stand. His damage lights flickered with a little green, a great deal of yellow and red. The fall had crumpled the armor plating on his *Atlas*' front. He saw that it was a *Griffin* that had come to his assistance. He couldn't remember the MechWarrior's name, but then it came to him—Kieran.

"What is the situation?"

"The Silver Hawks that were here have broken and faded into the suburbs. The Regulars have managed to pin down one lance of them, but the others seem to be in retreat. What they did here was some sort of diversion," Leutnant Kieran replied.

"Diversion?"

"Most of the Silver Hawks shifted to the flank and made a run for the DropShip. They will be free and clear in just a few minutes."

"Didn't General Nordhoff trap them?"

"Negative, sir. His forces were diverted here per your orders. They slipped through the noose."

"Damn it!" Duke Vedet replied. *They fooled us. No. It's worse than that. They fooled me.* He clenched his fists against the arms of his command couch. Then his business acumen kicked in. The blame would need to be shouldered by someone else, someone expendable—like Bernard. "Send word to General Nordhoff. Tell him to reassemble our forces. Tell him I want to meet with him."

Five Hours Later

The duke towered over Bernard, his neurohelmet dangling from his hand. Both men wore the shorts common to MechWarriors, stained with days' worth of sweat. The air stung with the acrid smell of unwashed bodies, spilled coolant and welding. The mood was subdued; this was the troops' first chance in days to rest and recoup.

Both men looked exhausted. Neither smiled. They were slick with their own sweat, sore from days in the cockpit, and barely controlling their anger. The duke studied the general and again wondered—had Bernard tried to kill him?

Some of his handpicked loyalists reported that Bernard personally had ordered the barrage and set the coordinates for the attack. He knew where the duke was going to be, and had dropped the artillery on top of him. He knew friendly fire happened on battlefields, but it seemed unthinkable that it could happen accidentally to a duke.

If I die, my family's empire would be at risk. Was he planning to seize Hesperus for himself if I fell?

Vedet hoped that his suspicions were due to a lack of sleep, and did not represent reality. "Bernard. The Silver Hawks got away?"

"Most of them. We managed to take down a few. I had a lance of them boxed in, but they chose to fight rather than surrender. The two we captured punched out and are hospitalized."

"It was a victory," the duke said emotionlessly. "We drove them off the world."

Bernard's brow furrowed with the anger he was clearly trying to hold in check. "If we had taken out that DropShip, we could have bottled up the remains of the Silver Hawks. *That* would have been a real victory."

"We won a real victory," the duke snapped back. "The Lyran people demand that we win, and we did.

Once again, we drove the Irregulars into a full retreat. If you are asked, General, that is what your response will be. Do you understand?''

His answer came reluctantly. "Yes, sir. I do."

"Good. Any hint of failure in this war will be laid at the feet of the military leadership, which means me. Don't forget your place, and my role in this operation. We can ill-afford for public support to fade."

"Even at the cost of the truth," he replied half under his breath.

"Truth? The truth is what I say it is. Remember, Bernard, I made you the man you are today. I can take that away from you." Vedet turned and walked away.

Hauptmann Hans Lanz moved to stand next to General Nordhoff as the duke walked toward his *Atlas*, which the repair crews had given priority. The battle was over, but Bernard's headache remained, throbbing as he watched the duke giving orders to the technicians. *Fixing his 'Mech is a priority to him, not to operations.* "He's a very different man, General," Lanz said.

"You're understating the obvious. He's a politician— a businessman," Bernard said, not shifting his gaze from the lanky royal. "He's no MechWarrior."

"That's what the Guards told me," Lanz said. Bernard turned and faced his subordinate. Clearly he wanted more information, and Lanz quickly complied. "When he was slugging it out with that damn diversion, he got scared and ran for cover. In a goddamned *Atlas* that could smash anything on the battlefield, he ran like a first-year cadet."

That Vedet had fallen for the diversion—a diversion that even a rookie officer could have spotted—was infuriating. *I recognized it, but my advice was ignored.* Bernard ground his teeth in frustration. The thought of that man leading good MechWarriors in battle and then running grated on his few remaining nerves. He had no business leading skilled men and women into battle. They deserved better than that—better than to die while a coward fled.

"Thank you, Lanz. Keep this between us for now."

"Sir?"

"It won't do anyone any good to know that their leader is afraid to fight. I don't want them questioning our capabilities. We keep the lid on this for now."

"Yes, sir."

"There are other ways to deal with men like the duke." He flashed a grim grin. *Sometimes accidents happen on a battlefield.*

14

The Royal Palace
Tharkad, Lyran Commonwealth
13 October 3137

Archon Melissa Steiner looked intently at the holographic map as the officer spoke. Standing at her side, checking his noteputer and glancing at the map every few seconds, was the head of Loki. His name was Gunter Duiven, and his interests paralleled those of the high command in this case. He also had some additional duties.

Loki was one of the branches of the LIC, the Lyran Intelligence Corps. They pursued black ops, and were infamously known as the muscle of the Lyran state's fist. The archon knew that formal channels demanded that she meet with the LIC director, but she chose to meet with Duiven instead. This apparently innocuous choice would help keep the intelligence organization in line. *I have no idea how far or deep Duke Vedet may have reached in the LIC. Having some internal tensions there will play right into my hands.*

"In summary, Archon, as you can see," said the briefing officer, Leutnant-General Maurer, pointing to the holographic image in front of her, "the Duchy of Tamarind-Abbey is reeling under our assaults. The

Marik-Stewart Commonwealth is proving a more difficult enemy than we had anticipated, but the operations in Skye have netted us some unexpected gains."

"The enemy was not engaging us on the Skye worlds," Duvien interjected, without making eye contact with Maurer. "I would be worried if we had run into problems. After all, we were striking worlds that the Jade Falcons hadn't tried to take yet."

Maurer was prepared to make every military advance appear to be a stunning success. "Might I remind you that it was a joint military operation with The Republic on Algorab a year and a half ago that led to a near disaster? None of us expected the Jade Falcons to have a raiding party there. We were fortunate to not run into the same fate that the Algorab Defense Force faced."

Melissa made a minute, involuntary movement at the mention of Algorab. She knew the battle all too well. It was the one in which Roderick Frost had been hung out to dry. Leaning forward in her chair, she made a note to herself to follow up on that with Duvien. "Tell me, isn't the officer that led that operation, this Frost fellow, isn't he leading a new unit in this assault?" It was mock ignorance, and she was always pleased that she could still fool the men around her into thinking she was less aware than she was. Melissa wanted to see if the leutnant-general might use this opportunity to question Trillian's proposed operation or insult Roderick.

"Correct, Archon—very observant of you. His new unit should be en route to Labourgiere as we speak. In fact, they should be landing shortly. The defenses on Labourgiere should be light, and we hope we'll seize it quickly and cleanly—which will line us up to strike at Niihau immediately afterward, though that target has been assigned to the Fifth Lyran Regulars."

He had a chance to question Trillian and Frost and didn't take it. That tells me a lot about him. "And the word from Duke Vedet?"

Maurer cleared his throat, using a moment to gather his thoughts and frame his words carefully. She recognized the technique; it generally meant the speaker was preparing to filter the information being conveyed to her as archon.

"Bondurant fell a week and a half ago. The First Hesperus Guards, the duke's personal unit, suffered thirty percent casualties. The Third Lyran Regulars are now at forty percent of their regular strength. Both units are refitting and repairing."

"And the Silver Hawk Irregulars?"

The leutnant-general shifted on his feet slightly. "The forces on Bondurant suffered extensive losses, in excess of fifty percent. Unfortunately, those forces represented only a battalion reinforced by the local militia. The survivors escaped off-world. Their destination or location is currently unknown."

Melissa cast a glance at her intelligence director, then looked back at the leutnant-general. "I appreciate the update, and look forward to our meeting this afternoon, Leutnant-General. In the meantime, please keep me informed if there is a significant change before then."

He bowed formally. "Yes, Your Majesty. Thank you." He toggled off the holographic display of the worlds, gave a courtesy nod to Gunter Duiven, then left the briefing room. Duiven said nothing until he heard the door snap shut behind Maurer. Even then, he waited for Melissa to speak first.

"I read Brewster's own report of his operation. Duke Vedet may claim that Bondurant is a stunning victory, but the military seems unwilling to slap that label on it," she said. She knew her intelligence head understood the unspoken question in her statement. *Tell me what* you *think, Gunter. . . .*

He snugged his noteputer into the holster at his waist and crossed his arms. "I would say that because the military is not calling it a victory, that demonstrates the tension between the high command and Brewster. That might prove useful in the future."

She nodded once. "And of that other matter I asked you to look into?"

Duiven shook his head. "Clan Wolf is keeping to itself. Our operatives have not reported on Wolf activities, which itself is strange. There have been unconfirmed, garbled reports that their civilian castes seem to have disappeared from some planets. I had one report that implied that they may have abandoned one or more of their worlds."

"That doesn't make sense."

"Archon, to be honest, we don't know what the Wolves are up to. Your query into them at a time when something apparently is happening causes me to ask: Is there something else I should know about our relationship with the Wolves?"

You live in the darkness, Gunter. Best on this subject that you stay there. "Nothing I care to share at this time. Simply curiosity on my part, and I'm glad I asked. You may wish to increase your monitoring of the Wolves from the sound of it. If I hadn't asked you to look into them, who knows when this would have surfaced?"

Duiven remained impassive at her words. "I serve at your bidding, Archon. If you think my people are failing you, or that my leadership is not to your standards, you are entitled and required to relieve me." There was no worry in his voice, no hint of concern.

It was one of the things Melissa liked about him. Gunter was devoted to his duty and to the Commonwealth first and foremost. "That isn't necessary, Gunter, and you know it. I am worried when a large military and political faction simply goes silent, as should you be. That is my duty."

He didn't smile or give any indication of gratitude for her confidence. "I understand fully, Archon. The good news is that I think we are one of the few governments aware of these subtle changes with the Wolves. That in itself may be useful at some point."

Yes, it might at that. She would have to mull over the possibilities of leveraging that information. "In the meantime, I think that this afternoon I will green-light a new wave of attacks in the Skye region. Denying Duke Vedet his reserve troops seems to be a good way to keep him in check and at the same time extend the Commonwealth's influence in Skye." Skye had once been a part of the Lyran Commonwealth. The formation of The Republic had altered that map, not to mention the ages-old push for Skye independence. The Jade Falcons had struck at these holdings but hadn't taken them all. She had been right about one thing—her forces landing on those Skye worlds were seen as a blessing by the local governments: more troops to fight at their side should the Jade Falcons show up.

"The duke will distance himself from the situation in the Marik-Stewart Commonwealth. Knowing his personality and penchant for media opportunities, we anticipate that he will shift his troops and attempt to take down the Duchy of Tamarind-Abbey. When the final push for Tamarind comes, he will be there."

She offered a wry grin. "All as expected, given his ego. That means that Trillian will be there too. She will move to negate him." *And that means Roderick will be there also.*

"A logical move, Archon. But this war is not about Duke Vedet. It's about protecting our people from the Free Worlds League."

She smiled again. "Yes and no. This war is about what the people need, and what is best for the Commonwealth. Knocking out the threat of the Free Worlds League is our priority. Negating the future political threat of Duke Vedet is something I have deemed important."

"I understand completely."

"There is another thing I would like your people to do. We have taken Algorab in Skye. The incident there involving this Hauptmann Frost was embarrassing, particularly because the military was willing to sacrifice him in favor of his CO. I think we need to undo that wrong. I would like your agents on Algorab to track down the militia commanders involved with the fighting there. I want to give them a chance to amend their statements, see if we can set things right."

Duiven cocked his right eyebrow as he pulled out his noteputer and jotted down her instructions. "If I may inquire, Archon, you seem to have an interest in this Roderick Frost. May I ask why?"

"You may ask, Gunter, but I won't answer you— not now, anyway. And for the time being, I'm going to order you to not look."

"Then may I add that we can extend the same courtesy to his former commanding officer . . . the man who benefited the most from the false testimony?"

"Do you really think you can get him to change his statement?"

Gunter smiled. "We are Loki. If you don't ask about our methods, I can assure you that his statement this time will reflect the truth."

"I don't want to know what you have to do."

"Agreed."

She smiled. "Very well. I will see you in the briefing this afternoon."

Clicking his heels in a formal salute, the head of Loki pivoted with military precision and left the room.

Melissa spun her chair to look out the window into the dull gray sky. The war was going well, but it was still early in the game. Trillian might not approve of her digging into Roderick's career blemish, but she had to know the truth. If for no other reason, she wanted to be prepared to mitigate the damage the press might do if they found out her true relationship to him. While she loved Roderick, what if he really was the failure the military had painted him? Melissa wanted the truth, no matter how painful that might be.

Trillian would not have approved of her dealing directly with Duiven instead of his boss, the director of the Lyran Intelligence Corps. She was fine with that, as well. *There are a few things that separate Trillian and me. One is that I am willing to push my luck a little more than she does.*

As for Duke Vedet Brewster—that was a problem with which she knew Trillian could deal.

15

Dropship **Der Samthandschuh**
Nadir Jump Point, Pingree
Bolan Military Province, Lyran Commonwealth
31 October 3137

The meeting had been called by—no, *demanded* by Duke Vedet. When word of the archon's order for another wave of targets in the former Skye holdings had become known, the duke had been infuriated. He had channeled his anger into a request to meet with Trillian Steiner. Trillian knew he would rather have complained directly to the archon, but distance and time made that impossible. Upon receiving his curtly worded message, she had suggested that they jump to an equidistant system, which turned out to be Pingree. Her ship carried lithium batteries, so she was assured of a quick return.

Trillian wasn't looking forward to the meeting, nor did she dread it. Dealing with the duke *was* her responsibility, and she could certainly understand his anger. She had deliberately buried the plans for the Skye incursion among a myriad of other plans and contingencies, precisely so that they had been easy for the duke to overlook. Trillian had taken early responsibility for the overall plan of assault, and so she felt no qualms in facing down the duke and his complaints.

Stripping him of reserves limited Lyran operations in the Marik-Stewart Commonwealth, but Clan Wolf was due to strike at Marik-Stewart planets as well. While Duke Vedet saw only the limits being placed on his capability to strike, she knew that redirecting his troops did not affect the overall strategy for the war.

He had left General Nordhoff to clean up the resistance on Bondurant. The militia there, the Bombardiers, had painted their 'Mechs and vehicles to mimic those of the Silver Hawk Irregulars. Ever since the Irregulars had lifted off-planet, the militia had been lashing out, launching raids all over the southern continent. The local population loved them. *Roderick was right about Anson Marik's plan to use them as an idea as well as a military force.* The locals rallied to them, supplied them, hid them. General Nordhoff would have a busy few weeks.

Brewster's shuttlecraft was coming alongside *Der Samthandschuh* to dock. Using boots with magnetic soles, she was able to walk easily through the lack of gravity to the air lock. There were two fully armed ships' guards waiting there. Trillian's jumpsuit was snug but comfortable—most clothing felt good in zero-g. As the air lock light went green over the doorway, it hissed slightly and opened.

Duke Vedet looked tired. His eyes were more sunken than the last time she saw him. His ebony skin seemed to glisten with sweat. His massive brow was wrinkled, as if he were deep in thought. He also wore a simple jumpsuit, but his revealed the muscles he had developed since the last time they had met. *War has changed him already,* Trillian thought. *How much more will it change him before all of this is over?*

"Duke Vedet," she said cordially.

He stepped through the air lock. "Lady Steiner. I assume you have a cabin where we can talk?" Anger bled into his voice.

"Of course. Follow me." She moved down the gangway. The guards remained at the air lock, securing the hatch. She led him through several passages to a small conference room usually used by the ground troops on the DropShip to coordinate their operations. It contained little more than a single table, a few chairs and a ventilation duct that blew cool air down Trillian's neck. She ignored the discomfort. As the duke entered, she closed the hatch and took a seat across the table from him.

"I came as soon as your message reached me," she said calmly.

"Let's cut to the chase. I need those reserve troops that were diverted to this damned foolish errand into Skye—the Royals Regiments. You have no right to pull them away from me."

She shook her head slightly. "Those troops are already committed. There are numerous political benefits to wooing those Skye worlds back into the Commonwealth fold."

"This is supposed to be a war against the Free Worlds League. Hopping into Skye diverts needed regiments to assignments that have nothing to do with our primary objectives."

"These plans were submitted as part of Operation Hammerfall from the start."

"Bah," he snorted. "The plans contained contingencies for dozens of different scenarios. No one— certainly not I—expected the archon to launch any of those operations."

"The time to have objected to these contingencies was months ago. Matters are out of my hands, and out of yours."

"I will not be treated like an inept junior officer! You forget to whom you are speaking," he shouted, pounding his fist on the table. The thin veneer of control over his anger was melting away. His eyes showed his rage.

"Let me make a few things clear to you, Duke. These plans were devised by the archon. I have known

Melissa Steiner my entire life. I feel perfectly comfortable in speaking for the archon on this matter. Regardless of who you are, or what you think you control, those forces are going into Skye. If you are not willing to follow orders, someone who can will be found and put into your position. Do you understand what I am saying?" Trillian was not lying or bluffing; she knew that Melissa was a difficult person to shift once she had made a decision. More than that, she would not be bullied by this man.

"You have no idea what battle is like," he said, his voice once more under control. "You haven't killed another man or woman. I was there, personally leading assaults. I have seen the results of war up close and personal."

She could tell that his words were sincere, almost like a confession, but there was something he was holding back. "I intend to change that. After the Broken Swords have finished on Labourgiere, I intend to go to Tamarind. The Broken Swords Battalion will follow me a few days later."

There was a pause. The duke focused his reddened eyes on her. "The Broken Swords—is that what they're calling themselves? So far they are untested in *real* combat. The only fighting they've done is in bars. Take them to Tamarind, and they will be quickly crushed by the local defenses. Tamarind is the capital world of the Duchy, Lady Steiner. They won't give it up without a fight. A mere battalion of troublemakers and malcontents is not going to be worth a damn against what is digging in right now on Tamarind." He ended his speech with a chuckle, as if he got a joke that she didn't.

Interesting, he's checking into Roderick. "They may not have to fire a shot. Their primary mission will be to demonstrate their strength, scare the locals—scare Fontaine Marik to the bargaining table if he won't come peacefully. He's already lost nearly half his domain. Having Lyran troops on their capital world will shatter what little morale remains in the Duchy troops."

"We shouldn't negotiate with these Marik wannabes," Duke Vedet argued, leaning across the table toward her. "We should finish them off. The Duchy of Tamarind-Abbey is a hollow shell. Give me the troops you and the archon are frittering away on this crazy Skye gambit and I will hand you the Duchy in its entirety."

She studied him. He wanted to press the war full scale. *How much of what he wants is for his own glory versus the good of the Commonwealth?* Even Trillian found the prospect tempting. The Lyran high command had declared that they could devour the Duchy and the Marik-Stewart Commonwealth. The idea was seductive to her and to them, but she was supposed to be above seduction. Melissa didn't want to wipe out the Free Worlds, only cripple them and remove the threat. It was not up to Trillian, or the duke, or any general to question that. *This is the reason Melissa sent me here.*

"Destroying the Duchy isn't our mission, Duke Vedet. We are tasked with hamstringing the Free Worlds League, and I am adhering to those mission criteria." *As will you.* "I will take Frost's unit to Tamarind. You will reinforce me a few days later. If diplomacy doesn't work, we will do it your way. Do you understand?"

His bitterness at being forced to accept her word twisted his face. "Yes, Lady Steiner."

"I will send you a timetable as to when and where to land on Tamarind. I expect you there on time. If you are right, and the Duchy chooses to fight it out with us, we can only hold a few days without reinforcements."

"I understand completely," he said slowly.

Trillian could practically read his thoughts on his sullen face. There was a good chance he wouldn't be there when needed . . . deliberately. She knew the duke saw her only as an obstacle to the advancement of his own career. *I will have to make sure we—I—don't fail.* "Excellent. I will transmit our timetable to you when you are back aboard your ship."

"I ask again, Lady Steiner. Will you release the troops committed to the operations in Skye? If I don't have those reserves, it will slow down our operations even more in the Marik-Stewart Commonwealth."

"The archon's mind is made up, and I support her decision," she replied. As if to drive the point home, she rose to her feet and extended her hand. He took it, though he offered no pressure in return. "Thank you again, Duke Vedet. Your service in this campaign has been exemplary."

He said nothing in reply, but responded with a slow nod. His silence said more than any words could convey.

Hecla Gorge
Labourgiere
Duchy of Tamarind-Abbey

Roderick crouched his *Rifleman IIC* and lined up another shot as his ammo cycled. The display to his left showed a green light, and he artfully brought the targeting reticle onto the *Stinger*. The planetary militia 'Mech was light and fast moving, but that didn't matter to him. He anticipated its movement and his battle computer adjusted the targeting of his autocannon. Smoothly he squeezed his secondary target interlock trigger. A stream of shells spat out of the arms of the *Rifleman*, catching the *Stinger* on the side and riddling the armor there and on the right arm.

The militia BattleMech shook under the armor-piercing rounds as they burrowed deep into the tiny 'Mech, blasting through her internal mechanisms. The *Stinger* slowed slightly and turned, suddenly pitching back violently. Another hit? No. His shots must have damaged the gyro. Without it, keeping the 'Mech upright at any speed was a dangerous and difficult proposition. It fell back hard, bending at the knees as if pushed down by a punch from the heavens. Its final shot went wild, almost straight up, as if the MechWarrior were defying the owner of the gravity that pulled him down. *Shooting at God isn't going to help you.*

"Sit rep. Savage One, come in, have you got the far bank?" The Hecla Gorge was a dirty little stream surrounded by a deeply banked valley. For two days the Labourgiere Militia, the Fangs of Marik as they called themselves, had been running from his unit. Leutnant Kroff had been sent with her company on a long sweeping maneuver. They should be on the ridge that marked the far bank, opposite the stream. If they were in position, there was nowhere for the Fangs of Marik to go.

"Savage One here. I'm down, the rest of the company is in place and moving toward your position, about one-third of the way down into the gorge."

Typical Kroff maneuver. "How can you be down, Leutnant?"

"One of the buggers, their CO, was piloting a *Marauder*. He needed a lesson in what close-quarters combat is all about."

"You deliver that lesson?"

"My 'Mech is lying on top of his. I'm alive. I don't think he is. At least I'd be shocked if he was, with my drill sunk through the middle of his cockpit."

"Sword One, this is Hilt Five," came back Leutnant Lasalle's voice. "I've got a signal from the enemy. Apparently they have realized we are on both sides of the river and they would like to discuss terms of surrender."

"So much for the Fangs of Marik," Roderick said with a chuckle. "Signal all commands, cease-fire. Tell them I will meet with their designated representative in half an hour at my coordinates. Tell him that we are holding fire, but if his troops move so much as a meter, we will open up, and no one from his unit will walk out of this hole alive."

"Those words, sir?"

"Yes, Lasalle. I've got a timetable to meet."

"Yes, sir," she replied. The next sound he heard was her passing on the word to the other commands to hold their fire. Trace Decker signaled him next. "Word is that the Fangs want to talk peace."

"Yes. Their bark was worse than their bite."

"Kroff is down, again."

"I heard." There was more that he could have said but didn't. Kroff piloted a *Violator*, and it was configured for close-quarters combat. It fit her style. Roderick only wished that he could change her style from time to time.

"I don't think there wasn't a simulation we ran where she didn't go down," Decker added.

"Yeah. I need to talk to her about that. She probably took out their heaviest hitter, but in a long-term fight, I need her at the party for more than a few days."

"Thank you, sir," Trace added. Roderick smiled. They had been friends for years; it sounded good to hear him refer to Roderick by rank. He had been worried about whether he would get that sign of respect in front of the troops.

His Broken Swords had held together very well. Three vehicle and 'Mech casualties, more with the poor infantry. The cost to the Duchy had been a reinforced company of 'Mechs and vehicles, some of which would be refitted and used by his men.

Not too bad for the first time out. "All right, Broken Swords, look sharp. If this is some sort of trick, let these bastards have it." It was too early in the war for him to end up dead . . . that much Roderick Frost knew for sure.

16

The bivouac of forward staging base Stealth had been home to the Millungera Militia only a few months ago. The Duchy forces on Millungera had put up a fight, but in the end it had not been enough. Like so many of the worlds along the border with the Duchy of Tamarind-Abbey and the Lyran Commonwealth, it had been hit hard and fast. The flag had changed, but Trillian doubted the typical citizen would notice much difference.

Perhaps that was part of the problem with what they were trying to accomplish. When governments changed in this part of the Inner Sphere, nothing changed for the common man. It wasn't like the Capellan Confederation's push into the former Republic. They would impose a new order; lives would change on a daily basis. The same was true of the Draconis Combine or the Clans. But here, on the border with the small governments of the Free Worlds League, the flag would change, but life would not.

She sighed, inhaling the stink in the air of the base. Military bases all had the same smell, regardless of which side owned them. There was a hint of petroleum products and 'Mech coolant, a hint of sweat, a musty aroma that clung to the air. She doubted that the men and women of the military even noticed it. As she moved through the base, security checked her badge, then her body. Trillian had gotten used to security procedures over the years and the process didn't bother her. Most of the men who admired her lacked the courage to say anything, let alone take action.

Moving into the 'Mech hangar, she could see the *Archon's Pride* out on the tarmac. Roderick stood near the foot of his BattleMech, the massive *Rifleman IIC*. She surveyed it swiftly; there were only a handful of replacement armor plates, indicating he had suffered only light damage. Good—his after-action report from Labourgiere had been accurate. The fighting had been fast, and the flight of the Duchy forces had been even faster.

Her cousin spared her a quick glance as he signed off on some sort of requisition form that a warrant officer was holding in front of him. Trillian sidled up next to him. "Congratulations on your success."

"The militia, these Fangs of Marik, were not a real test. Even a third-string unit could have taken them on and won. We did some very easy flanking, got them on the run, then boxed them in. I'd love to tell you that I pulled off some sort of tactical miracle, but realistically you could have taken them out with two companies of academy cadets and a handful of monkeys for infantry support."

"You always did have a hard time accepting responsibility for your actions, good or bad."

Roderick looked up at his *Rifleman IIC* as he spoke, rather than looking at her. "I saw your plan for the next operation, Trillian. Pretty gutsy. We anticipate that there will be at least a regiment, maybe more, defending Tamarind. It's their damn capital. I know you don't track a lot of military jargon, but that's three times our size."

"They'll be spread out all over the world. And I'm using the press to stimulate stories and rumors via Loki agents on Tamarind about your victory on Labourgiere. That adds a certain fear factor to your presence there. We will show force, but the real hope is that I can negotiate with Fontaine Marik, get him to see the futility of continuing to fight. We do this right, and we may not have to fight at all."

"There will be a fight," he said bluntly. "People like me have to always pick up the pieces after diplomats and politicians fail."

"The plan is simple," she said, ignoring his comment. "I am going to land a few days before you and attempt to convince Fontaine Marik of the folly of attempting to continue this war."

"Fontaine Marik is a tough old coot," Roderick fired back. "I don't think he's going to roll over as quickly and easily as you expect."

"We've taken away part of his realm. It will force him to do some serious thinking."

He smirked. "If I were him, I'd toss your butt in jail."

"Diplomatic immunity. I'm landing to parlay. There are rules to follow in these situations."

"House Kurita might adhere to all that formality, but this is the Free Worlds League. These folks hosted a nest of the Word of Blake during the Jihad. There's a reason they're all broken up into little fiefdoms— everyone still remembers what happened the last time they were united. Fontaine Marik may be old, but you don't live to become an old Marik without learning a trick or two. You'd better not rely on your court rules to keep you safe." As if to emphasize his point, he handed her a sleek chrome laser pistol.

She held the gun and looked at him. "Where did you get this?"

"The symbol of surrender from the Fangs of Marik.

Their CO gave it to me. I'm not big on souvenirs, but it's a very nice laser. Tuck it away. If diplomacy fails, you'll have something to fall back on."

Trillian looked at the gun. She was trained in its use as well as in martial arts. Paraphrasing her cousin, *One doesn't survive as a Steiner without learning a trick or two.* Yes, she was a trained diplomat and negotiator; at the same time, she had spent close to a year of her life being trained in self-defense. She took the gun and slid it into the hip pocket of her jumpsuit. It was a lot easier than trying to argue with Roderick about it. He was like a big brother, just trying to make sure she was taken care of, and she appreciated that.

"I won't need the gun. If Fontaine doesn't want to play along, your troops will land. People will get scared. It's one thing to talk about an abstract war, it's another when it lands on your doorstep. I'll let him know there are additional forces on the way. He will have no choice but to enter into negotiations."

"Additional forces? This Duke Vedet is going to show up and save our butts if the Duchy opts to resist?"

"Yes." There was more bravado than belief in her voice, and even Trillian could hear it. She wanted to believe that Duke Vedet would do what he was ordered to do. But she could see by Roderick's face that he had picked up on her slight hesitation.

"I have to trust that he will do what is right. He has orders."

"If you die, his orders are left to interpretation," Roderick fired back.

"The part of that scenario that I hate is the part where I'm dead," she snapped sarcastically. Trillian understood the risks. This also was why the archon had sent her: she was willing to take the necessary risks. But she was not stupid. She had an ace in the hole . . . and he was standing right in front of her. "You won't let anything happen to me."

"I may have my hands full if the shit hits the fan, Trill."

She flashed him her best smile. "I wanted your unit put together from day one just for this scenario. That's why you are in command. Melissa and I both know that you are one person who will do whatever it takes to protect me and to protect the Commonwealth."

He stared at her for a long moment in silence. "I don't trust politicians," he replied flatly.

"I'm a politician, Roderick."

He sneered. "Not you—Vedet. From what you've told me, he's gunning for Melissa's seat. I don't trust a royal with ambition."

"Oh, I don't trust him either, cousin. At the same time, if I can broker a peace or surrender of the Duchy quick enough, we'll take the wind out of his sails. His victories to date will be overshadowed—negated—by the peace. It is important that House Steiner comes out as the victorious leader in this fight. If that happens, Duke Vedet becomes a footnote."

"You always were the passionate one, the keeper of the family faith," he said fondly. "All right. I'm there. Not as a Steiner—you know that, and so does Melissa. I'm here because you are my family. I'll do what is necessary to ensure your safety. How could I live with myself if I let anything happen to you?" He patted her on the shoulder in a brotherly manner. Trillian reached up and clasped his hand.

He saw a short female MechWarrior sauntering across the tarmac. "I have to go."

"Problem?"

"Just doing my job." He took off after the other officer at a jog.

She watched him disappear and hoped to see him again soon. Then again, she hoped she wouldn't *need* to see him at all.

Roderick caught up with Jamie Kroff and she gave him a casual salute. He didn't place much weight on formality, but Kroff's performance as an officer was proving difficult to reconcile with unit discipline. Many of his troops, especially the officers, came to him with a chip on their shoulder, but most of them had slowly become less rebellious and more appreciative of the opportunity he was offering them. Kroff was just the opposite; while the rest of the Broken Swords were bonding, she was becoming more insubordinate.

"Sir," she said, eyeing him cautiously.

"We need to talk. Walk with me, Leutnant." He took a long stride out across the tarmac.

"Is there a problem, sir?"

"How are your 'Mech's repairs going?"

"Ball-Buster is just about done. They're just re-stringing the myomer in the left leg."

Ball-Buster . . . it fits her to a tee. "You and I need to arrive at an understanding." Roderick stopped and turned to face her, and she stopped as well, crossing her arms. "In every simulation we have run, you have managed to get that *Violator* of yours knocked out of the fight. I knew you were aggressive, and that works for you—but in our first engagement you did the same thing."

Anger flared in her eyes. "I took out that *Marauder*. That was the Fang's commanding officer—sir. I took him out and crippled their command structure."

Roderick frowned. "Don't feed me that line of crap, Leutnant. You weren't taking down that *Marauder* to hurt the militia. That wasn't tactics. You took it out because you have some sort of problem that you need to resolve. For some reason, you rush into fights and damn near get yourself killed each time."

"That's not entirely true, sir," she retorted. "I came out of this without a scratch."

"Your BattleMech required two Prime Haulers to scoop it up from the battlefield," he said angrily. "And while you were trying to get your brains blown out, your unit was forced to rely on NCOs to hold together."

"We won the fight."

She was right. But he needed her to demonstrate some control—some restraint befitting an officer.

Without it, chaos would take down her entire unit. "Kroff, you are very good. One of the best MechWarriors in our unit."

"Yes, I am," she said simply, but with an arrogant grin.

She has no idea how much she's pushing me. "Here's my problem. I have an outstanding MechWarrior who is an officer, in command of troops that need her expertise, but who has a knack for getting herself knocked out of a battle too quick."

"Like you said, I am one of the best MechWarriors you have, Hauptmann Frost." She stumbled over using his formal rank.

"You know, they pay me to make the tough decisions. Leaving you in a prison cell was a waste of all the training the Commonwealth gave you. Putting you in my unit was a good idea—or it will be, if you can get past your personal issues and learn to fight as part of that unit. Here's the problem put another way. In a command of independent thinkers and self-involved egos, you still manage to find a way to stand out."

"I take it that's not a compliment, sir."

"Knock off the crap, Jamie." He used her first name to take off some of the edge of his tone. "You need special handling. The troops respect you. They know how talented you are. And you scare the crap out of them with your reckless attitude."

"I don't *need* handling."

"I disagree."

"You're a rule-breaker yourself, sir. Everyone knows what happened on Algorab when those Falcons dropped during that exercise. *You* didn't let the rules get in your way."

That stung. Algorab. It was with him all the time. Even when it wasn't said out loud, people muttered about him and what happened there. It was just like his grandfather always said—if people knew the truth, they would judge him on that relationship rather than who he really was. Instead, most people thought that the events on Algorab defined Roderick Frost—a mistake, to say the least. *At least Kroff had the guts to say it out loud.* "Don't try to change the subject. This isn't about me." He gritted his teeth as he spoke, so that she understood just how hard it was for him to control his temper at that moment.

"Leutnant, here's the deal. In the next fight, you keep Ball-Buster operational throughout. I need a fighting commander, not a downed hero. If you don't stay up, I will send you back to the jail cell that I liberated you from. You will not muster out of the army and you will not get a chance ever to pilot a BattleMech in combat again. I will make sure that you spend many long years in jail."

Her face flushed. He knew what she was thinking; it was written clearly on her face. "You're thinking that I wouldn't dare do this. I assure you, I can and will. Do we have an understanding, Leutnant Kroff?"

She still stared at him, her mouth opening and closing without a sound. "Understood, sir."

"Good." He smiled. "Now get over to the 'Mech bay and get those techs to expedite your repairs. I need you primed, locked, loaded and charged for what we're going to be facing."

17

Vedet Brewster felt more alive and energetic than he had in weeks, even though sleep had evaded him during transit to Millungera. The sleeping pills he had taken softened the bitter edge he felt after Bondurant, but then his subsequent rendezvous with Trillian Steiner had made him angry practically beyond reason.

Now she was here on Millungera, and he found his last briefing with her equally frustrating. Just when he felt like things were coming back under his control, he would discover Trillian Steiner blocking his every move. It made him angry again, and in that anger he discovered some solace. Trillian was planning on going right into the lion's den to barter for peace. If that failed—and he was confident it would—she was counting on a unit of misfits, these Broken Swords, to save her. And when they failed, she was counting on him to save them all.

As he stared at the holographic map of the Duchy

of Tamarind-Abbey in the isolated briefing room, he thought of all the troops on the base that were mustering for operations. Hitting Tamarind was one of those objectives, but there were others. The military strategy for finishing off the weakened Duchy was complicated.

The duke stared into the map and at the next target world. He summoned up the anger he had felt when the archon had given the green light to send troops into Skye. The plans for Skye were there, right in front of him, buried in the details. Trillian Steiner and her cousin had used the details to trip him up. There had to be a way to pay them back, to do the same thing to them. *I owe those bitches one for slowing my operations in the Marik-Stewart Commonwealth.*

The door opened, and General Nordhoff walked in. The man was much more slender than he had been at the start of the war. Weeks spent fighting in a cockpit had aged him, made him lean, hardened. Vedet said nothing to his aide until the door clicked closed behind him.

The general's face betrayed no emotion—not joy, not frustration—nothing. The final attack on Bondurant had made the duke suspicious of Nordhoff. His *Atlas* had been pummeled by friendly fire, a barrage ordered and targeted by the general. He had waited for Bernard to apologize, to say something to acknowledge his error, but that admission never came. *I have taken care of this boy, guided his career, ensured his success—and now he tries to kill me?* It was too hard for the duke to believe, and he still didn't fully subscribe to the notion. At the same time, he watched the young general carefully, searching for any indication of betrayal.

"You've reviewed the plans that Lady Steiner provided?" Duke Vedet asked.

Nordhoff nodded. "I have. Lady Steiner's plan is aggressive, perhaps overconfident. And attempting to force the surrender of the Duchy may be premature.

We have pummeled them, but they hold their capital world and can still opt to fight it out."

Vedet Brewster nodded. "I tend to agree, Bernard. Our mission is to bail her out should her attempt at negotiations fail."

"The report I was briefed on says she is taking in this new battalion with her."

"The Broken Swords . . ." the duke replied with contempt.

Nordhoff allowed himself a lone chuckle. "That's not how the Lyran command refers to them. They call them the Misfits, and from their personnel records I'd say the description isn't too far off. The man commanding them, Hauptmann Frost, he's the man who was tagged as being responsible for that debacle on Algorab."

"He has whipped the losers in that unit into shape, from what I have gathered."

"True. But the stink of failure follows him. The general staff thinks this is all folly. More than one of the generals I've spoken to would be relieved if these misfits were wiped out."

"Well, from the plans Lady Steiner has laid out, that may just happen." He stabbed at the controls for the small holotable. The map flickered out of existence and was replaced with the city of Zanzibar, one of the two seats of Fontaine Marik's government on Tamarind. Zanzibar City was the site of the winter palace, and Padaron City was the official capital. The two cities were dramatically different, and on the opposite sides of the planet. Fontaine rotated between the two, but Zanzibar was where he was likely to be at the moment; and it was where the Lyran Commonwealth's embassy was located. After the Jihad, Fontaine had taken to using Zanzibar City for less-formal functions and Padaron City as his formal palace. Sitting alone, in barren wastelands, it looked more like a desert oasis out of *The Arabian Nights* than a modern city.

Bernard stood at parade rest, looking at the map.

"Our current orders are to go to Simpson Desert first. The intent was to hit Tamarind from multiple directions." Simpson Desert was a world nestled deep in the belly of the Duchy of Tamarind-Abbey. Seizing it would split off a third of the Duchy worlds from their capital. Initially, Tamarind was to be bypassed, encircled, then pounced upon. That plan had not changed, except that Trillian Steiner was going to Tamarind first. The duke supported the original plan because it was bold, assertive and left the Duchy reeling. But if Trillian was able to secure a peaceful resolution . . . there would be no victory, no public adoration, no parades, no calls for him to ascend to the archonship. . . .

"Simpson Desert seems like a small challenge. What does intelligence say are its defenses?"

"A battalion of second-rate troops. They have mostly vehicles and infantry, a few BattleMechs. On paper, I should be able to mop them up quickly."

For a moment Vedet said nothing. On paper, the Silver Hawk Irregulars were supposed to be easy to defeat, yet with each encounter they had inflicted heavy casualties and withdrawn. More importantly, their fighting style had hatched numerous partisan groups with alleged ties to the Irregulars. All across the Marik-Stewart Commonwealth, there were units committing crimes against Lyran soldiers in the name of the Irregulars. Professional warriors like Bernard always spoke in terms of battles and timetables. The duke had come to learn that in war, there are only best guesses and approximations.

As he paused to mentally critique the military mindset, his mind drifted back to Bernard's words. "You said that you should be able to mop them up quickly. What kind of time frame are you estimating?"

"I plan on dropping with the two battalions of the Third Regulars that have been refit. Given what the LIC has provided us in terms of identification of defenses, ammunition dumps and so on, I would estimate that we can subdue the defenders in four days with mop-up operations lasting another week." Bernard took out his noteputer and apparently was double-checking his estimates.

"What if it took longer?" the duke pressed.

"It won't, sir," Bernard replied. "My battle plan calls for us to drop right on top of them and to seize their airstrip and supply points in the first few hours of fighting. Isolated, cut off from logistics, driven into the region known as the Verdun Wilderlands—it's really just a matter of forcing their surrender."

"What happens if it does take longer?" Vedet prodded again.

"Our garrison forces arrive to augment us, assist in mop-up operations. But again, it's not going to happen. The defenders on Simpson Desert are not a real threat. I'm not underestimating them—I'm just sure they can't hold out against us."

He isn't hearing what I'm asking. Typical military officer. "General Nordhoff, what happens to Trillian Steiner on Tamarind if your operations are extended?"

The younger man paused, at last grasping the intent of the question. "Ah. Simply put, sir, she is relying on us to show up to reinforce these Broken Swords of hers. If negotiations fail, she may be caught or killed and the Broken Swords could be scattered. If we arrive late, we would miss the party."

"An excellent summation. Her efforts at securing peace may fail. We would arrive on Tamarind in time to take care of the remaining defenders, but there is no way her Broken Swords would be able to hold out. We land, seize control of Tamarind and possibly Fontaine Marik himself and come out of this as the heroes."

Bernard's face remained blank of any emotion. "I am not interested in being a hero, sir."

"What you want is not important, Bernard. Remember what I've done for your career." That brought a wave of red to the younger man's face. *Good—he hasn't forgotten who I am and what I can do.*

"Sir, operations on Simpson Desert could be slowed.

Loki has gotten information wrong in the past, which could cause a change in our deployment—at the last minute of course—if you ordered it. In all honesty, you may need . . . a bigger excuse. We *are* talking about the betrayal of a member of the Steiner family."

Duke Vedet flashed his massive smile for the first time in a long time. "I'm glad we understand each other. Look over the intelligence reports. We can ill-afford things to go wrong on Simpson Desert. It is best that we take this slow and careful, and get it right. In fact, I want you to work out three alternate landing zones, in case we need to divert our forces. As you indicated, we need to be vigilant of all the opportunities. We have to find a way to make this operation drag out longer than necessary."

"I assume no one in the upper command needs to see these plans?"

He shook his head. "Lady Steiner taught me an important lesson. You can make changes as long as there is a good trail of documentation. Let's see how she likes having the tables turned on her."

BOOK III

Undesired Thoughts

"A political problem thought of in military terms
eventually becomes a military problem."
—George C. Marshall

The courtroom was small, hot, humid, joyless. The flag of the Lyran Commonwealth, the massive upright mailed fist, hung on the wall behind the bench where the three judges sat. They looked more like an operations planning board than judges—officers with bright clusters of medals adorning their chests. Roderick stood at attention and studied them carefully. Old men, each one of them; each one had already arrived at his decision—it was written on their faces. *This is all just a formality.* That thought didn't cause him to waver. The heavy, stale air tried to suffocate him with each breath, but he simply resisted.

"Hauptmann Frost." The oldest of the officers, the one in the center, spoke with a deep, dusty voice. "We have heard the testimony of how you were cut off from Colonel Quentin's authority and how you successfully disengaged your forces from the Falcon attack force. We've also heard how you directly defied his orders, even to the point of encouraging a mutiny. Only one queston remains. Why did you do this?"

Why? Yes, they had heard the testimony of Colonel Drew Quentin. He had painted a rosy picture of the events and of his sterling leadership. It was all a carefully constructed lie, but they had heard what they had wanted to hear. "Sir, with all due respect, Colonel

Quentin couldn't find his ass with a flashlight and both hands." The small audience began to growl in protest at his words. *I owe it to the soldiers who died there to tell the truth on record. Their families deserve closure.* He continued speaking before they could cut him off. "The Jade Falcons had dropped on Algorab to hone the mettle of their warriors. We were going to be their fodder. Their fight was with The Republic and the Skye Militia, not with us. I ordered disengagement, per my testimony, because I had the guts to do the right thing."

"I move that the defendant's comments be stricken from the record," the prosecutor said.

"The truth hurts," Roderick said under his breath. He cast a cold glance at his former commanding officer, smug and arrogant in his seat in the audience. Nothing bad was going to happen to Colonel Quentin; he had political connections. The full blame for the operation was falling on Roderick. *And I'm going to take it.*

"You are not helping yourself at all, Hauptmann Frost," one of the other judging officers said.

"Why bury this? Quentin froze in combat, I took command and did what was right. You have the wrong man up here and you all know it. If it weren't for the families of the soldiers who died, I would make sure he got what he deserved."

"Your Honors," the prosecutor pleaded. "You must inform the defendant that his comments are only hurting his cause, and that the Lyran high command must determine who will be brought up and on what charges."

Roderick felt a wave of rage wash over him. *They are more worried about how this plays in the press than they are at arriving at the truth.* "You can do what you want to me, but you have to make sure that man"—he stabbed his finger at Colonel Quentin—"never leads men into battle again. His indecisiveness at a critical moment cost men and women their lives."

"Yes," the prosecutor said. "Fifty-two people lost their lives on Algorab. Fifty-two men and women are dead because you assumed command without proper authority, made a series of bad judgment calls and defied the orders of a superior officer." His tone was acidic. The nods in the room told Roderick that he was very much alone.

"I pray for those men and women each night. But I also thank God for the 187 that managed to get off Algorab alive. The dead are worth mourning, but the living are here because of the choices I made."

"That will be all, Hauptmannt Frost," the judge warned.

18

Marik Winter Palace
Zanzibar, Tamarind
Duchy of Tamarind-Abbey
10 November 3137

Trillian sat in the chair in the waiting area while Klaus Wehner paced about the room. They had been waiting in the plush and gaudily decorated room for two hours. Klaus was not pleased. Arms folded, he walked back and forth across the tiny space while she watched. The dull yellow-orange sun of Tamarind sank slowly outside. She watched the image of the light on the floor and used it to track the time rather than her watch. She understood the nuances of the waiting game.

Their arrival on Tamarind had been uneventful, which was something of a surprise. The capital city of Zanzibar was the antithesis of Tharkad in the Lyran Commonwealth. She would have preferred going to Padaron City, but her embassy told her that Fontaine Marik was currently managing affairs from Zanzibar. Sitting atop the muddy Zanzibe River, the city consisted of buildings that grew to a pinnacle near the center—a planetary communications hub. The spaceport was outside the city, a flat, arid slab of ferrocrete in the middle of a sea of dark sand. As she had entered the city, she passed dozens of tiny markets.

Duke Fontaine Marik had not communicated with her directly, but through channels at the consulate. He had agreed to extend diplomatic courtesies to her and Klaus. Yet there were unmistakable signs of military buildup throughout the city; not the mustering of local militias, but the heavy-duty BattleMechs of the Duchy's regular army. The number of armed squads wandering about was intimidating. Fontaine was doing his best to impress upon her that he was not bargaining from weakness.

Fontaine was one of the old men of Inner Sphere politics. After the Jihad, the Free Worlds League had fragmented into numerous little fiefdoms, each with its own more or less legitimate claim to the captain-generalcy. Fontaine's claim was strong, as he was a direct descendant of Therese Brett-Marik, daughter of former Captain-General Janos Marik. Unlike many of the pretenders, Fontaine had blood on his side, if not age. He was an old man now, but his declining health did not mean that his negotiation skills had diminished at all. This waiting game was a perfect example.

"You should sit down," she said, motioning to the brocade chair next to her own.

"I dislike these stalling tactics," Klaus said.

"That's why they do it," Trillian replied. Suddenly a door opened in the room and a balding man wearing long purple robes, both garish and regal, stepped in. "Lady Steiner, the duke will see you now."

She rose to her feet with Klaus following a good two paces behind. As they entered the main audience chamber, her eyes were drawn to the deep purple curtains draped over the three-story windows. The brilliant colors of the city were muted by the draping, diminished in the massive room.

The throne was audacious, decorated almost to the point of appearing tacky. Like so much of what made up the Free Worlds League, it was a remnant of a much brighter era that was now fallen to decay. Trillian surveyed the room before giving the man on the throne her attention.

Duke Fontaine Marik was old, yet he wore an air of defiance. His face and long nose bore remarkable resemblance to former Captain-General Janos Marik, a look he probably deliberately cultivated. His pristinely groomed eyebrows were oddly dark, hinting at his former striking looks. His forehead held deep furrows of age. He sat oddly askew on the throne, as if he was trying more for comfort than worried about appearance. His grip on the massive arms of the throne seemed to hold him in place on the seat. A goblet in an ornate stand was within reach of his left hand.

Standing at his right side was his grand vizier, Sha Renkin. He said nothing, but she saw complete confidence in his gray eyes. Despite all that had happened to the Duchy, all their losses, he stood behind Duke Marik.

It was the duke's eyes that commanded her attention. They were brilliant, almost on fire, a bluish gray that somehow seemed regal. Despite his age, there was still power in those eyes. Trillian focused on them as she stepped forward to stand before his throne. She bowed her head with respect.

"A member of House Steiner here?" Marik's voice boomed. "I would ask what I have done to deserve this dubious honor, but I assume you have come to finish the blood work of savaging my realm."

He's certainly pulling no punches. She knew that the best way to deal with such raw emotion was to respect it. "Duke Marik, I have come here at the behest of the archon of the Lyran Commonwealth. It is my hope that you and I will be able to bring an end to these hostilities." Slowly she lifted her head and fixed her gaze on his radiant eyes.

Duke Marik paused, instilling even more tension into the air. "You people create false pretenses to start a war. You invade my nation, a peaceful people, and ensnare them. You dare come here and talk of ending these hostilities? Very well, Lady Steiner, tell your cousin to remove her troops. She started this war, she can stop it right now by withdrawing." His words rang with anger.

"You were increasing your military presence along our shared border, Duke Marik," she countered. "And let us acknowledge that the Free Worlds League has a reputation for crossing that same border and invading Lyran worlds. Our actions were aimed at ensuring the sovereignty of our nation and the protection of our people."

He waved his hand as if to dismiss her words from the still air in front of him. "Trumped-up intelligence. Outright lies! You have not found vast armies waiting for you, have you? No. In my realm you have found garrisons and militias that added only a few units here and there to protect *my* realm."

"Duke Marik, I am not here to debate the reasoning behind recent actions. I hope that further loss of life on both sides can be avoided."

"Of course you don't want to discuss the reasons for your illegal and immoral invasion . . . because you are wrong and you know it."

Trillian felt her face flush. "By your own admission, you were increasing your military presence along the border. You cannot deny that both your Duchy and the Marik-Stewart Commonwealth have long pressed claims on worlds that are in the Lyran Commonwealth. We were fully justified in launching this war, if only to ensure that you did not attempt to fulfill those claims."

The mention of the Marik-Stewart Commonwealth seemed to add wrinkles to Fontaine Marik's brow. "Do not presume to associate my nation with that of my upstart relative Anson. Each Free Worlds League nation stands alone, for now at least . . . until the true captain-general emerges to unite the whole. You cannot easily paint me with the same brush as him, Lady Steiner."

There was a note of confidence in his voice that caught Trillian off guard, especially when he spoke of the true captain-general. *What does he know that I do not?* She caught her mind wandering and returned her focus to his argument. *He wants to argue about the cause of the war, not ending it. I need to alter tactics.* "Of course, you are correct, Duke Marik. But surely you see where our nation had reason to be concerned. And surely you must see the value of this diplomatic mission to determine if there is a way we can bring these hostilities to an end."

"You can withdraw your troops," he repeated, in a calmer tone.

She held his eyes. "There are many ways for us to arrive at peace. Yes, we could withdraw, but given the politics involved with this war, I cannot see the people of the Lyran Commonwealth agreeing to such a resolution. There must be some middle ground, a compromise that we can mutually seek, that can achieve an end to this fighting."

Fontaine said nothing for long moments. The room was quiet enough for her to hear her own heart beating as she stood before the elevated throne that held the Marik heir. He cleared his throat, and the moment he did, an aide stepped forward with a glass of water. Fontaine drank it slowly, carefully, released his lock on her eyes for only a moment.

"If we were to engage in talks, will your forces stand down for the duration? Or will you continue to press forward into my realm?"

He was shrewd, much sharper than she had anticipated. Even with armies all around his capital world, he was still attempting to bargain from a position of power. Fontaine was not desperate; he was brave and cunning—a dangerous combination. "A negotiator always seeks to find the means to maintain an upper hand, Duke Marik. With the lack of HPG communications, it would be difficult for me to stop any military operations currently under way, even if I felt inclined to do so. As it happens, I do not feel that doing so would be in the best interests of the Commonwealth at this time. If I feel such a move would assist us in reaching an accord, I will do what I can to slow operations."

"You are brave, Lady Steiner, that much I can say about you. Your nation invades mine, and you come asking me to agree to peace. You brought about this war, not me. The Duchy of Tamarind-Abbey has suffered a great deal under your onslaught only because we were unprepared to wage war, despite your propaganda efforts to the contrary.

"That does not mean we are weak. I have mustered our reserves and have shuffled our troops accordingly. You will find that the remaining worlds of the Duchy are heavily fortified and will not be caught off guard, as we were when you first struck at us. Tamarind itself is an armed camp. We will not be intimidated."

"I have not come to intimidate you, Duke Marik. I have come to try to find some grounds where further loss of life can be averted."

Fontaine paused for a moment before replying. "I have much to attend to, Lady Steiner. Since you are unwilling to suspend your assaults, I must continue to rally my people and prepare them for a long and bitter war. I will hear the terms the archon is considering. Schedule with my grand vizier Sha Renkin for us to meet again in the next day or so. This will give you time to contemplate what your nation has been doing to our people and to refine your archon's vision of peace."

Trillian bowed. "I appreciate your time, Duke Marik, and look forward to our next meeting."

In the privacy of their quarters in the Lyran Consulate, Trillian stood at the bulletproof window and stared out at the city beyond the walls of the compound. The tiny market she could see sported brilliantly colored tent covers. The people of Zanzibar did not seem to realize that war was so close.

"Duke Marik seemed quite agitated," Klaus said.

"It's been a while since we've been on the losing side of a conflict. I'm not sure I would react much differently." She could not conceive of the Lyran Commonwealth losing this war. She would not allow it—nor would Melissa. Not against a divided Free Worlds League . . . not with The Republic of the Sphere paralyzed by its own problems. Not with the Wolves—ah, the Wolves. What were they up to?

"I did not expect him to be so . . . spry."

"This war seems to have shaken the malaise I have always associated with him."

"What is our next step, Lady Steiner?" Klaus pressed.

"We meet with him and sue for peace. Each day he waits, more of his realm is consumed. Soon we'll have troops landing on Tamarind. If that doesn't shake him, nothing will."

"It may require more than that," Wehner added. "It may require us to beat him into acknowledging defeat. Is Roderick Frost really the man for that?"

She flashed a smile. "Yes—and much more, Klaus. Much more."

19

***Dropship* Defiance IV**
Outbound to Nadir Jump Point, Millungera
Lyran Commonwealth (formerly Duchy of
  Tamarind-Abbey)
20 November 3137

Duke Vedet jerked himself awake at the sound of the buzzer in his quarters. The zero-g of his cabin allowed him to drift as he instinctively tried to sit up, bumping his head on a shelf. The sudden stab of pain and the continued ringing of the warning buzzer left him disoriented and confused. A blinking red light allowed him to focus. He pushed off and drifted the two meters across the cabin, fumbling simultaneously with the buzzer and the light switch.

The intercom came on under his fingers as he rubbed his head with his left hand. "Apologies for the disturbance, Duke Vedet. We have a priority-one message coming in for your attention."

His mind flew as he tried to ignore the pain where he bumped his head. Priority one? In wartime, that could only be bad news. He wondered for a moment if something else had gone wrong in the Marik-Stewart Commonwealth. The Silver Hawk Irregulars were still unaccounted for, but the Lyran garrison forces had been reporting attacks on supply bases and barracks by units claiming ties to the Irregulars. Was it a political crisis? For a moment he was worried that Trillian Steiner had been wildly successful. That wasn't possible . . . was it? "Go ahead, authorization Defiance Alpha."

The tiny vidscreen on the wall panel flickered to life. The mailed fist of the Lyran Commonwealth came up first. Then the image changed to a flat 2-D image of Archon Melissa Steiner. "Duke Vedet, I hope this message catches you before you depart the Millungera system. A transmission has come to the high command from Vindemiatrix," she said.

The duke rubbed the sleep from his eyes. *Vindemiatrix? Where is that?* Then he remembered—Skye. It was one of the worlds that Skye still held in the shattered remains of The Republic. "I have had our intelligence people scrub the image. This was taken from the Second Royals Regiment during their drop onto the world." The image of the archon faded and was replaced with a slide show of ten images, each one showing dangerously close DropShips adorned with the Jade Falcon emblem on their hulls. Two were aerodyne *Broadsword*-class ships. The other three were much larger, much more menacing. Two massive *Overlord* ships and a smaller *Union C*-class. It was not just a probe; this was a large force of Clan warriors. And not just any Clan; these were Jade Falcons. *How did they get images with such detail? They must have been close—very close.*

The archon's voice continued. "During their drop to the Plains of Saxonburg, this Jade Falcon force suddenly appeared on the exact same drop vector. They were heading for the same DZ as the Second Royals. We believe that the Jade Falcons' arrival at the same time and place was purely coincidental, but its results were devastating. The Second Royals have suffered over fifty percent casualties in a contested battle for the drop zone."

Sounds just like what happened to Frost back on Algorab.

Melissa Steiner looked uncomfortable. She wasn't in her throne room. Where was she? Obviously a world with a working HPG, like him. It must have taken a hell of a lot to coordinate getting her the data and having her reach out to him. *Now I wish that ComStar had not gotten the HPG on Millungera working again.* She shifted uncomfortably, pausing for a moment. "I must ask for your assistance as the ranking commander in the field. The Second Royals are holding on and have disengaged from the Falcons. They cannot last forever. Since these Royals were designated as reserves for the operations in the Marik-Stewart Commonwealth, we are finding ourselves strained in terms of resources.

"I am asking that you divert some of your and General Nordhoff's forces from the Marik-Stewart Commonwealth and send some experienced forces on to Vindemiatrix. Those forces need assistance. While the Jade Falcons have suffered losses, our forces have been turned and are fighting for survival. Our commitment to Skye cannot be seen as weak. I am counting on you to ensure that none of our efforts in this war lose their momentum."

The duke grinned broadly. "Got your tit in a wringer don't you, Melissa?" he muttered under his breath. He allowed himself a chuckle. "The best part is you need *my* help to get out." He saw that there was a holovid file attached to the message. *This could be what I was looking for, an excuse to not show up on Tamarind to save your cousin Trillian.*

He paused the recording and stabbed at the comm unit with his long fingers. "Bridge."

"Yes, sir?"

"Awaken General Nordhoff. Tell him to meet me in the tactical operations room immediately."

The Jade Falcon *Broadsword*-class ship arced slightly as it came into view. It was close, so close you could make out the lights and silhouettes in the view ports. The turret spun and fired. The ship that the image was being taken from rocked as the stabbing beams of emerald light flickered on. A jagged piece of armor on the target ship, a *Union*-class vessel, was so badly ripped that it appeared in the field of vision. A cloud of hissing gas, probably oxygen, appeared just below the image—a foreboding sign.

Missiles traced through space at the *Broadsword*. At the last moment, the Jade Falcon vessel pitched hard to the side, exposing its underbelly as it moved away. The missiles hit everywhere along the bottom of the *Broadsword*, each silent explosion violently rocking the ship.

Both ships quaked as they plowed deeper into the ionosphere of the world and the turbulence jarred them. The Falcon ship swung wide and another ship, ovoid in shape, came into view. An *Overlord*. This ship was massive, capable of carrying a Binary or Trinary of Clan troops into battle, and bristling with turrets. Each turret rotated as the *Union* ship fired another salvo of long-range missiles. Unlike the *Broadsword*, the massive *Overlord*-class ship didn't rock under the blasts. It was as if the missile hits were lost on the larger ship, they were so small they seemed almost insignificant.

Bernard reached out and shut off the holovid. "I don't need to watch this," he said hoarsely, rubbing his night's growth of dark black beard. "So it was like that all the way to the LZ?"

The duke nodded. He was surprised that Bernard did not want to watch the rest of the holographic file that had come with the message. In a way, it disappointed him. He would have thought that a military man would want to watch it all, to drink it in. "The Falcons apparently were skimming in the upper atmosphere, which was why sensors didn't pick them up. They went in on the same vector as our Royals troops, landing right next to them at almost point-blank range. It turned into a bloodbath."

Bernard continued to rub his thick beard. "I know you don't want to hear this, but the archon is right—we have to divert troops to help the Royals. The Jade Falcons are the nastiest of the Clans, and it would be wrong to leave those troops trapped there."

"I have no intention of abandoning them," the duke fired back. "But what troops can we send?"

Bernard took out his noteputer and thumb-scrolled down the list. "The Fourth Royals have troops designated to rotate off Bondurant and strike at Danais in the Marik-Stewart Commonwealth. While there have been hits by units on Bondurant that claim to be the Silver Hawks, we could strip half of the occupation force there and divert it to Vindemiatrix. That will get a fast response, but it's going to place the forces hitting Danais at risk, especially because we don't know where Anson Marik has put the real Silver Hawk Irregulars."

"Are there any other troops we can send?"

General Nordhoff raised his head slowly. "We could use your Hesperus Guards to assist with operations on Danais. It will force us to use two of my companies of troops as your reserve, but the plan is workable. Whichever of us needs the reserves can tap them first."

That's the right answer. "This could mean that we are tied up on Simpson Desert for longer than planned." He could not hold back the grin that rose to his face.

"It will take us longer with reduced forces. And where my Guards go, I go, General. We will have to fall back on some of the alternate battle plans and drop zones we discussed."

"You see, Bernard—sometimes opportunities present themselves just when you need them. The advantage of the corporate mind is seeing where those opportunities are and how to leverage them."

The younger general nodded. "Sir, I'm doing this because it's the right thing to do. I've tangled with the Silver Hawks. If the Fourth Royals Regiment lands in a reduced configuration on Danais and the Falcons are there, they'll be in for a hell of a fight."

"Yes," Duke Vedet replied. "Of course, Bernard."

"Do you want those orders to go out?"

"Make it happen, General," he said. Ordering around generals gave him a sense of satisfaction. *How many times did I have to kiss the brass' behind to get a sale or an order for merchandise? Thousands? Now the tables are turned.*

Bernard sat in his quarters and looked at the TO&E for his unit. He had made sure that his men were loyal, some more loyal than others. Likewise, he knew that the duke's private unit, the Hesperus Guards, was full of die-hard loyalists. Bernard had pulled up their backgrounds and found similarities with his own history with the duke. Duke Vedet had been a busy man, putting many officers through military academies, manipulating their careers, as well. The difference was that these other men loved it—and Bernard resented it.

He had identified the true hard cases, the ones who were true believers in the duke. When the orders went out, he was going to make sure they were sent to Danais. At the same time, he made sure that any troops that were questionable in his own regiment were also going to be sent on the relief mission.

Yes, I will "make it happen," Duke. But I will do it my way. If the opportunity presents itself, I will not pass up a chance to make sure your trip to Simpson Desert or Tamarind is a one-way voyage.

20

Major Goolies was a less-than-popular watering hole only a block from the military base the Lyran forces were using on Millungera. It was a place that catered to the military crowd—loved their money, hated the damage they inflicted. As Roderick approached, he saw military police vehicles outside, the officers decked out in riot gear, and a few cars of the local authorities. They had the bar surrounded. He shook his head as he approached, showing his ID to the officers when they challenged him.

Nothing good ever starts with a call in the middle of the night saying, "You need to get down to this bar right away, sir." The call had come from a friend who was an MP, a man whose brother had once served under Roderick. No one liked to get a call like this; he was only surprised it hadn't come up before now, given the composition of his unit.

When he finally got into the bar, he stared in dismay. It looked as if a tornado had torn through the middle of Major Goolies. Chairs and the remains of chairs littered the floor, and the mirror behind the bar—usually almost invisible due to the grime—had been broken into jagged shards, along with dozens of bottles of watered-down alcohol. Only two tables remained upright. The air stank of spilled beer and an eye-watering mix of liquor.

Then there were the bodies.

Leutnant Matt Rust of Savage Company was laid out with a nasty gash across his forehead that was still oozing blood down the side of his face and onto the floor. Roderick reminded himself that head wounds always looked worse than they actually were. At least two unconscious and two wounded soldiers were being tended to by comrades wearing the patch of the Fifth Lyran Regulars. He felt a momentary satisfaction that his troops had gotten the best of the fight so far.

At the other end of the room, spread out as if preparing for another assault, were his troops. In the center of the group, her hair disheveled, her eyes blazing, was Jamie Kroff. Trace Decker stood at her side, holding the leg of a broken chair in his hands like a sword, clearly poised to rejoin the battle. *Well, if Trace was involved, I can't level the blame entirely on Kroff.* He just assumed that Jamie had started the fight . . . it fit her style.

He could see nasty round bruises on Kroff's shoulder and arm. Rubber bullets. They had actually blasted her at least once, and still she was up and ready to take more. Her lip was swelling around a cut and her hands were balled into fists—not at the Fifth Lyran Regulars, but at the military police.

The first leutnant in charge of the MPs was holding his club in front of him and barking commands to Kroff. "Listen here, Leutnant, drop to your knees and put your hands on your head." Jamie was ignoring him. Her blood was up and she was still looking for a fight, even one she couldn't win.

Roderick reached out to the MP and touched his

shoulder. The man jerked around. "Who in the hell are you . . . sir?"

"I'm their CO. What happened here?" Roderick avoided giving his name, since this past year it seemed to earn scorn more often than respect.

"What does it look like?" the officer shot back. He seemed as fired up as the brawlers.

"Let me handle this," Roderick said, in a reassuring tone.

"They're all going to the brig," the MP snapped.

"That's not necessary," Roderick said, then raised his voice to carry throughout the bar. "You have to trust me, whatever you have planned for them is nothing compared to what I'm going to do to them."

The MP became visibly calmer. "Even so, you'll need to address the damages, sir."

Roderick looked around. "Seems to me that in these cases, everybody is equally responsible for compensation," he remarked as he took out a wad of bills and divided it in half. "We could spend time in court figuring this out, or you can give the owner my unit's half, and the boys and girls from the Fifth Lyran can foot the rest."

The MP took the money and slid it into his breast pocket. "Seems fair."

"My unit is shipping out tomorrow anyway," Roderick said loudly. "The last thing I need is my officers in the brig. Trust me, the duty they get as a result of this little incident is going to be more than enough punishment." He saw Jamie lowering her fists as he spoke.

The MP smiled. "Saves me a ton of paperwork. Watch her, though." He jabbed his nightstick at Kroff. "She's got issues."

"Really?" he spat sarcastically. "I hadn't noticed."

An hour later he assembled the troops who had participated in the destruction of Major Goolies in one of the empty 'Mech hangars. An hour's time had not improved their appearance. Most bore the marks of a bar fight, the bruises and gouges of hand-to-hand combat. He had them lined up at attention for a full thirty minutes before stepping out in front of them. Between the humidity created by the light rain that had started to fall outside and the warmth of the hangar bay, they stung not only from their fight, but from their sweat.

"Perfect move, people . . . just frigging perfect," he began. "You're damn lucky I had a friend in the MPs who owed me a favor, or you'd all be in the brig right now." Roderick mustered his deepest, most commanding voice as he spoke.

"Sir—" Trace began.

"Shut up, Leutnant!" he barked. No playing favorites. "Let me guess, they made disparaging comments about our unit. They called you some names. You all had a little to drink, you wanted to defend your unit's honor. So the only way to do that was to bust the snail-snot out of a bar and deck a bunch of your fellow troopers."

He paused. "Well, did I hit the mark?"

"It wasn't just that," Trace said nervously. "They called us losers. And a penal unit—and not the kind of 'penal' that means prison. Then they went after you, bringing up Algorab. They said you were a coward and a disgrace."

"So that's what set you off? They slammed me?"

"No, sir," Kroff jumped in. "They said that we were nothing but a suicide unit that Lady Steiner had thrown together. Then they said some things about her that were, well, not exactly ladylike."

"So you were defending the honor of Trillian Steiner? That's why you started the brawl?" That he could understand.

Kroff shook her head, wincing from the pain. "Not exactly, sir. We held off even at that. We owe a lot to Lady Steiner and you, and knew you'd be pissed off if we started a fight, so I held everyone back."

"You did?" That came as a surprise. Kroff was the

definition of a hothead, and bore a lot of wounds from the battle at Major Goolies. It took a lot to believe that she had held her temper in check.

"Yes, sir." Trace picked up the story. "We held off until—well, they said we were not fit to wear the uniform and fight for the archon. Sir, that went too damn far. We've proven ourselves. We told them that . . . but they laughed at us. They goddamned laughed at us," he said bitterly. Trace looked as if he were ready to throw another punch, and Roderick understood why. These folks had all made mistakes in their careers, or, like him, had been a scapegoat for someone else's failure. But they had put their lives on the line like every other soldier. To be laughed at by their so-called peers was just plain wrong.

Roderick bowed his head and shook it in the negative. "You shouldn't have thrown the punch, and you know it. As your CO, I have to respond appropriately.

"Ten-hut!" He thought for a moment as the battered members of his unit snapped to a precision attention. *They are a good military unit. Time to treat them like one.*

Since Algorab, everyone had tried to treat him as a failure, a coward, a liar and a traitor. Negative treatment had not made him a better MechWarrior or leader. What had made him a better leader was that he had moved past that incident, and risen above other people's opinions of him. It was time to teach them the same lesson. It was time for them to learn that he was truly proud of what they had become.

"All right. Consider yourselves punished. Get to your barracks and stay there. Don't let those bozos from the Fifth Regulars see you or I'll end up with a pile of paperwork. Besides, tomorrow you leave to put your butts on the line for the Commonwealth."

They stared at him, shocked, as he saluted them, turned and walked out of the hangar bay.

There was only one thing left to do to make this really right. . . .

Lyran Diplomatic Compound
Zanzibar, Tamarind

Klaus was leaning over the desk, which was covered
with hard-copy reports and noteputers. Trillian stood
silently behind him, watching him work. He was not
as methodical as she had thought. He fluttered from
one pile of paper to another, shuffling reports, shifting
to noteputers, loading data cubes, flipping through another report. It was like watching his mind work.
Klaus Wehner always had a lot of balls up in the air
and somehow managed to juggle them. There were
times when Trillian didn't appreciate how much pressure she put on her staff. It was good to remind herself
occasionally by observing them in action.

"What are you working on?" she asked. She surprised him, and he jumped slightly and started to rise.
She held out her hand to indicate that the courtesy
was not necessary. One of the things that endeared
Klaus to her was his willingness to observe the formal-
ities, even when he knew they were not required.

"Duke Vedet," he said. Two words that carried a
great deal of weight.

"Anything in particular?"

"I've been going over his profile and that of General Nordhoff. We know that Vedet considers Nordhoff something of a protégé. I've been trying to find
a way for us to leverage that to our advantage."

Interesting angle; typical of the kind of work Klaus
did. "Did you find anything?"

"Maybe," he said, shuffling through the papers to
pull out one particular printout. "Nordhoff recently
reassigned several officers in seemingly unrelated but
subtly connected moves. He's loaded the Third Regulars with some friends from his academy days and
childhood buddies from Hesperus. He has positioned
some with him, and has reassigned some back to
Hesperus."

"Why?"

"He's probably just doing some favors for old friends. It happens all the time when someone breaks into the upper command ranks. Regardless of his real reasons, I think we can use this to our advantage. If we were to leak this information to the duke and position it that Bernard is planning some sort of coup back on Hesperus . . . it might drive a wedge between the two of them."

She thought for a moment. It was possible that Nordhoff was simply doing favors for old friends. At the same time, she had to consider the security of the Hesperus Defiance Industries' 'Mech and armaments works, which was critical to the future of the Lyran Commonwealth. Trillian felt it was entirely possible, even likely, that Bernard Nordhoff could be playing out his own agenda. "I like the idea of driving a wedge between them. There was that friendly-fire incident I saw in the reports from Bondurant. Wasn't the duke caught in an artillery barrage ordered by Nordhoff?"

Wehner nodded. "That incident was what started me thinking about this. The preliminary investigation found that Nordhoff did call the strike to the coordinates occupied by the duke and his unit, but that it was an appropriate risk with the potential to catch the Irregulars."

"How were you thinking of taking advantage of this?"

Klaus shifted excitedly in his seat. "Rumor, Lady Steiner. Using loyalists, we circulate a rumor about Nordhoff deliberately seeking to kill the duke and make sure it reaches Vedet. We have a courier JumpShip at the nadir jump point. I send a message to them, they let the word leak out. From what I've seen and read, the duke has a powerful ego. The idea that one of his handpicked people is turning against him, possibly even trying to kill him—well, the duke's not going to sit for it. Causing tension between the two of them will weaken the duke in the long term, with very little risk to us."

"Excellent work, Klaus. Make it happen. Every little edge we can create to keep Duke Vedet in check is useful."

I only hope it's enough, thought Trillian.

LCAF Forward Staging Base Stealth
McKeesport Proper, Millungera
Lyran Commonwealth (formerly Duchy of
   Tamarind-Abbey)

Security had called General Stephen Harper of the Fifth Lyran Regulars to report to the 'Mech bay where his *Mad Cat II* was berthed. It had been a short night for him already. There had been an incident at a local bar with those hoodlums of the Broken Swords Battalion. Somehow that bastard Frost had managed to get his troops out of there before the shit hit the fan. Frost was lucky they already were slated to depart for Tamarind—he'd heard their DropShips lift off an hour ago. If they weren't on their way to the front, hopefully to be destroyed, he would have chewed out Frost till his nether regions were sore. Everyone knew Frost was only where he was because he was somehow friends with Trillian Steiner. After what he had done on Algorab, he was lucky to be allowed to stay in the service.

The general walked briskly to the 'Mech bay and saw the main door was open. There were five 'Mechs visible as he entered the four-story building. His was in the center of the group. He could see immediately what was wrong.

His *Mad Cat II* had been painted for urban warfare, straight stripes of various shades of gray. It wasn't that camouflage really mattered on a BattleMech; it was hard to hide a three-story humanoid-shaped war machine that moved at sixty kilometers per hour. It's not like they could pretend to be a tree. But someone had drastically altered the paint scheme of his *Mad Cat II*.

Buckets of bright paint had been poured over the front of his BattleMech, completely obscuring the cockpit ferroglass. In other spots, it looked as if someone had deliberately splashed paint onto the 'Mech to deface it. He was so mad that he was shaking. *I'm a goddamned general. Nobody does this to my 'Mech. Nobody!*

He walked around the BattleMech, and could see splatters of paint on the floor. A number of soldiers milled about, some pointing up, others fleeing when they saw him coming. He could see what they had been pointing at. Stark black words had been spray-painted over the insignia of the Fifth Lyran Regulars: BROKEN SWORDS RULE!

Frost! "Get a damn cleanup crew in here right now!" he bellowed. "I don't know who that little shit thinks he is, but if I get my hands on him, he's a dead man!" he muttered, loud enough for the other troops to hear. Techs scrambled for painting gear while General Harper contemplated multiple, punishing schemes for revenge.

21

DropShip Archon's Pride
Orbital Entry Approach to Zanzibar
Tamarind, Duchy of Tamarind-Abbey
29 November 3137

Roderick looked at the massive green and khaki globe of Tamarind below him and felt pleased. He had arrived at a pirate point and slid into the flight corridor without any reaction from the planet below. Even in their heightened state of alert, the Duchy forces apparently had overlooked him—for a few minutes, anyway.

Communications would be impossible during landing, so he was reaching out to Trillian now. He hoped she had been successful, and that peace was in the offing. More realistically, he assumed he would have to fight. *If I were in Fontaine's shoes, I think I'd roll the dice and try to slug it out.*

"Glove, this is Sword." His words would be scrambled and beamed via laser directly to the consulate in Zanzibar. "We are on schedule."

There was no response for a full two minutes. He waited. Patience was important in this kind of operation. Finally, Colonel Klaus Wehner, Trillian's aide, responded. "This is Gauntlet, Sword. Glove is indisposed."

"Is the party on?"

There was a pause. "Unfortunately, yes."

"Can you squirt me updates?"

"On the way, Sword."

"Let Glove know we're in town. Let her know that the party will start on schedule."

"Will do, Sword. Godspeed." Even through the imperfect transmission, Roderick could hear regret in Wehner's voice. Klaus was a military man. He knew, and regretted, that lives would be lost. He knew the cost of war.

He switched the comm unit to intercom, and simultaneously broadcast to the other two DropShips, *Rogue Star* and *Sandpiper*. "This is Guard One to all units," he said. He could hear his voice echoing on the bridge and in the adjoining areas. "Diplomatic efforts on Tamarind have not been successful. It looks as if we are going to have to help convince old man Marik that it's time to toss in the towel.

"As such, this is going to be a hot drop. We are going for our primary LZ. Assume all forces to be hostile unless I tell you different. We are going to hit our primary objectives and do it smartly.

"The time has come for everyone to see that a Broken Sword is a truly dangerous weapon." He toggled off the comm unit and addressed Captain Eddington. "Captain, you may take us down. Set condition one. Prepare for combat ops."

Lyran Consulate
Zanzibar, Tamarind

"The channel is clear," said Consul Gustoffson, diplomatic liaison between the Lyran Commonwealth and the Duchy of Tamarind-Abbey. Trillian Steiner's arrival on-planet moved him to a secondary but still important role. Since the beginning of the war between his government and the Duchy, he had struggled to maintain diplomatic dialogue with Fontaine

Marik and his government. Without his tireless work, Trillian knew that her job would be much more difficult.

Though it could not be more difficult than it would now become. With the arrival of Roderick's force in-system, the Duchy government had leapt into action. The holonews broadcasts consisted of little else than wartime rules for the planet's population. There was no panic, but it was clear that the atmosphere of Zanzibar and probably all of Tamarind had changed. Rather than negotiating for peace, Trillian now was going to have to try to convince Fontaine Marik of the futility of fighting.

Trillian nodded for Klaus and the consul to leave the consulate's tiny communications room. Deep, built-in wood bookshelves lined the walls, containing collections of Commonwealth writings. The room was warm and comfortable, like a library. She settled more comfortably into the cushioned chair and took a deep breath.

People always assumed that Trillian lived her life with the benefits that naturally accrued to her last name. They presumed that her life was easy; and that was true much of the time. Being a Steiner had many benefits beyond mere recognition. Yet her current task, facing a tough negotiation, was one in which she paid the price for her heritage. Very few people would choose to change places with her now—on an enemy-controlled capital world during a war. *This is where I show what a Steiner is made of.*

She pressed the button. The holoimage in front of her flickered to life, and the head and shoulders of Fontaine Marik appeared. The anger he had controlled in their previous talks was no longer held in check. His usually pale skin was red, and he looked years younger. The arrival of Roderick's force seemed to have breathed new life into him. His long white hair and goatee were the only evidence of his true age as he glared at her.

"A few minutes ago our defense installations picked up multiple DropShips inbound to Tamarind. Their transponders are Lyran—but you already know that, don't you, Lady Steiner? Is this how you treat me and my people? You land an invasion force during negotiations?"

"I told you more than once, Duke Marik, that military operations would continue, and that I was not in a position to prevent that. The forces landing on Tamarind are those responsible for conquering Labourgiere, the elite Broken Swords. My recommendation to you is that we conclude our negotiations and prevent further loss of life."

Fontaine laughed mockingly. "So this is the Steiner definition of peace. You invade my Duchy, you come to negotiate peace at the end of a barrel of a gun? Well then, it is my duty, as heir to the true line of Mariks, to show you how we deal with such blatant violations of the rules of diplomacy. There will be no peace, Lady Steiner. The liberation of the Duchy of Tamarind-Abbey begins here and now. I will scramble my forces and send them right into your little invasion force. You have confirmed what I assumed—that negotiations are just a trick for you Steiners." The image disappeared.

"Well, I guess Duke Marik is done talking," she said out loud to herself.

She rose slowly and opened the door. Klaus and Consul Gustoffson were waiting in the next room. "Duke Marik has opted for a military solution. He has broken off our talks."

Consul Gustoffson spoke nervously. "Lady Steiner, I expect the duke will move to seize the consulate and take us all into custody. Fontaine would love to hold the archon's cousin as a bargaining chip."

"We need a way out," Klaus prompted.

"We dug tunnels years ago, for just such a situation. I cannot guarantee that they have remained a secret from the locals, but I recommend we position you and your aide and a few guards to exit the consulate immediately via that route."

Trillian unconsciously touched the Cameron star necklace, as she always did in times of stress. "Send a warning to Roderick that they are going to come right at him."

Klaus nodded. "Immediately, Lady Steiner. But you must allow the consul to take you to the tunnels. I will join you shortly."

She realized he was staring at her neck, and abruptly became aware that she was caressing her necklace. She reached for the clasp and unfastened it. "We need to destroy our records," Trillian continued, proud that her voice remained steady. "Leave them nothing to work with if they take this building." *I swore I would never take this off, but desperate times call for desperate measures.* The necklace was unique, and surely would identify her. She suppressed a grin. Her daddy was a Steiner too—he'd understand.

"I will do my duty, milady," Gustoffson replied.

She followed the guards down the hallway, swearing silently to herself. It bothered her that her negotiations ploy didn't work. It bothered her that Roderick was now going into a difficult battle. It bothered her most that Duke Vedet had been right.

Primary Landing Zone
The Harvison Flats
South of Zanzibar, Tamarind

Roderick found the roar of the pair of *Stuka* fighters overhead reassuring as he deployed his command company from the DropShip. They broke off to the north and angled away, obviously in pursuit of a target. "Come on, people, we need to move. Get to those bridges and blow them quick," he barked. Battle-Mechs, vehicles and infantry poured out of the ship and fanned out across the dusty plain. The Harvison

Flats were not strictly desert terrain, but were close to it. A shallow-growing, yellow-green grass barely held down the soil.

He had chosen the Flats for his landing zone because they offered wide-open terrain where he could land his aerospace assets. His VTOLs were being unloaded and prepped for dust-off. A Yasha, outfitted with an autocannon under the cockpit, kicked on its turbofans and rose, sending up billowing clouds of sand and dust. Roderick watched as it moved off to the distance.

A dozen kilometers away, between the capital city and the Flats, snaked the Zanzibe River, a muddy streak bracketed by lush green banks. Only a handful of bridges crossed the river, and their first objective was to shatter those bridges. Doing so wouldn't prevent an attack by the Duchy forces, but it would limit how many of the enemy came and how fast.

The Duchy of Tamarind-Abbey appeared to be spoiling for a fight. A lance of their aerospace fighters, old but still deadly, had swept in to point-blank range against the DropShips as they landed. It took guts to initiate an attack against a DropShip. The *Sandpiper* took three dozen long-range missile hits and numerous laser and PPC hits in the brutal initial assault, but their courage cost the pilots their lives. The ship turrets chewed up the fighters. Two went up almost immediately; the remaining two tried to break and run, but they both crashed on the edge of the Flats. Roderick could see the rising smoke plume from one, a black grave marker to a brave defender of the Duchy.

"This is Savage One, alpha objective is toast," Jamie Kroff reported.

"Good job. Shift to your secondary and prepare for a counterattack," he replied as he angled his *Rifleman* to the west.

"This is Saber One. We are at beta objective. I have bad guys here," Trace Decker's voice said.

Time to earn my pay. "Roger that, Saber One. This

is Sword One. Command Lance, form up on me. We are going to sector three bravo." He throttled up the massive fusion reactor under his seat and the *Rifleman* throbbed to life. He jogged the BattleMech in the lead of his lance across the Flats, his cockpit slowly warming around him. The coolant in his vest gurgled slightly as it began to circulate at the rise in temperature.

His long-range sensors picked up the activity a moment later. The Duchy had sent a strike team, about a company's worth of hovercraft and lightly armored infantry to the river. They came across the muddy waters and up the shallow grass- and tree-lined embankments. The bridge over the Zanzibe was down; Trace had done his job, but the hovercraft were circling him.

Roderick activated his targeting computer and swung the sight along the display, locking it on to the lead Marik Pegasus. The sleek craft was emblazoned with a purple eagle with five-pointed stars in each wing, being clutched at the tail by a human hand. A spray of uranium-tipped armor-piercing rounds mauled the Pegasus' flank and the hovercraft jerked back, swinging wildly, seemingly surprised by the arrival of his lance.

Another two Pegasuses broke formation and swung straight at him, firing their missiles without waiting for a target lock. He heard a rumble to his left but didn't look. Sword Two was there, Warrant Officer Juan Praxis in a *Sun Cobra*. The *Cobra*'s arm-mounted cannons, slightly modified from the original design, sprayed the middle Pegasus, tearing into her hoverskirt and forcing it to dip low into the grass, the pilot obviously fighting for control.

Roderick held his target lock on the lead hovercraft. His second barrage was even more effective than the first. The autocannons seemed to purr at his right and left hands as he slowly squeezed the target interlock trigger. His *Rifleman IIC* held steady as the shells hit in two areas on the Duchy Pegasus. One barrage ate at the rear of the vehicle, devouring the directional vanes, while the second rounds hit in the same area as the first blast, digging deep into the guts of the hovercraft. There was a flicker of red and yellow in the cockpit, an internal explosion and then the hovercraft fell flat onto the sandy soil.

His command lance poured their fire into the other Pegasus craft, which tried to bank around and make a break for the river. Its maneuver only served to spread the damage across all sides of the hovercraft. One of Decker's DI Morgan assault tanks finished off one of the Pegasuses, hitting with all three of its massive particle-projection cannons. The other one made it to the river.

Another wave of hovercraft, tiny Savannah Masters, raced to the rear of Decker's unit. These hovercraft were mostly annoying. Lightly armored and fast as the wind, they carried only tiny lasers. They did little damage, but excelled at diverting attention from other threats. All four of them formed a line and circled around a *Phoenix Hawk*, each one nipping a small gouge of armor as they passed. The *Hawk* fired but couldn't get a bead on any one of them, its brilliant green laser leaving a smoking trench in the dirt instead.

"Sword One to Saber One. Good work on the bridge." Roderick glanced over and saw the smoke from the ruins near the roadway. "Get your Sniper online. Have them lay down a barrage all around those Savannah Masters."

"Yes, sir!" Decker replied enthusiastically. It was easier than trying to go after them individually. A platoon of Kage troops from Decker's company fired at the fast-moving hovercraft and managed to hit one of them, but despite the white trail of smoke it sprouted after the hit, the tiny vehicle seemed unshaken. *Artillery, that's the answer to these nasty buggers.*

Thunder rolled across the Harvison Flats, but there wasn't a cloud in the sky. The first artillery rounds landed behind the Savannah Masters and got their attention. They broke from their formation and started to fan out, a good call given what they were up against. A platoon of hover infantry from his own lance fired at one of the breaking Masters, hitting it and sending it plowing into the ground.

The roar of explosions from incoming artillery suddenly seemed to come from everywhere at once. One of the tiny hovercraft was tossed like a toy. The smoking shell of the previously injured Savannah Master fell in the distance. Flames roared through the burned-out husk of the frame and it flipped twice as explosions went off inside it. He couldn't see the last of the tiny vehicles through the massive dust cloud kicked up by the artillery, but his sensors told him it was making a wide arc around the far end of Trace's formation. *That's a damn brave and lucky pilot.*

He was about to breathe a sigh of relief when Jamie Kroff reported in again. "I've got some bad guys attempting to ford the river in my sector, Sword One. I can bottle them up, but they seem anxious to get over here and are persistent pains in the ass, sir."

"Roger that," Roderick replied. Taking out the bridges was a good start. There were a lot of Duchy troops, though, and they were determined to defend their planet at all costs. He looked in the direction of the capital, and could barely make out the spires of Zanzibar, though the massive communications tower in the center of the city stood out like a beacon.

A cryptic message from Klaus Wehner delivered just as they landed had informed Roderick that Trillian and Wehner had gone underground to avoid capture by Duke Marik. He was confident they were still alive, and he would find them. It was just going to take a while.

22

Verdun
Simpson Desert
Duchy of Tamarind-Abbey
2 December 3137

The carcass of the fallen *Ryoken II* BattleMech was still belching smoke as General Nordhoff marched his *Xanthos* forward. The insignia of the Korps, the defense force on Simpson Desert, was still visible through the smears of black smoke: a pair of palm trees stenciled over a flying eagle. The 'Mech had been one of the determined planetary defenders, and had made a daring charge right into the middle of his company, pouncing on his Padilla artillery. It had destroyed the artillery piece even as the rest of his unit converged on the *Ryoken*. With a single-mindedness that Bernard had to admire, the *Ryoken II* had managed to plow through two squads of Gnome battlesuits before it was finally brought down.

Simpson Desert was not what he expected. The world was lush with beautiful, thick forests, rolling hills and fields—and jagged rock formations that obscured movement and blocked line of sight. Despite the maps, he had expected more—well—desert. The name was a misnomer, a mistake stemming from the first survey of the world.

Four days into the fight, he now understood that the early loss of his Padilla was part of an intelligent plan effectively prosecuted by the defenders.

The last of the Duchy defenders of Simpson Desert had fallen back from the Wilderlands to a loosely formed set of earthworks and fortifications called Fort Verdun. The fort dated back centuries. It was not in the best condition, but what remained was imposing. Deep trenches big enough to slow a BattleMech and stop most vehicles ringed the area. Concrete emplacements held a few artillery pieces. By whittling down the Lyran artillery, the defenders had taken out the firepower that could hurt them the most. They were trying to force Bernard to fight on their terms.

He understood their strategy too late—at least, that was Duke Vedet's often- and loudly repeated opinion. Bernard was fed up with hearing the duke's inexpert views of military strategy and tactics. *He's spent his whole life piloting a desk.* Now *he thinks he understands how to fight a war.* His anger gnawed at Bernard until he could no longer give anything but lip service to supporting his superior officer. "Now we will waste good men in an assault on a fortified position." Those had been the duke's words.

The Verdun complex had been built centuries ago for the Star League Defense Force. Though its basic layout remained strategically sound, even the Word of Blake had found the place too deteriorated to use during the Jihad. The Korps had concentrated their forces in the part of the old fort that was still in relatively good shape. Bernard was confident that there were gaps in their defense that he could exploit, if they could be identified.

The primary disadvantage to the Korps' strategy was this: in an age of mobile warfare, they had dug in. Rooting them out could be costly, but they had sacrificed their mobility—and he had enough Regulars and the remaining Hesperus Guards to surround them. Now it was a matter of probing, prodding, finding the weakness in their position and exploiting it.

General Nordhoff moved his *Xanthos* to the front line just in time for one of the Korps' artillery pieces to drop a massive shell in front of him. One of his Maxim Mk. II transports backed up as clods of sod rained down from the blast. *Well, at least we've pegged their range.*

"Leutnant Schnell," he signaled on the command frequency.

"Yes, sir," Schnell replied abruptly. There was an echo of autocannon rounds in the background.

"I'm on the line in green sector two."

"We have their back door, sir. The roads to Corbyville are blocked," he said confidently. "Their 'Mechs are popping up from hardened positions and taking long-range potshots at us. Mostly eating turf, not armor."

"Understood," Nordhoff said calmly. "You've got three VTOLs with you, affirmative?"

"Roger that, sir. I've got two Cardinals and a Donar gunship."

There was more than one way to take Verdun. He knew he would have to attack from the front, and find and hit weak spots in the line. But using VTOLs to harass the fort from on top and hit them on the inside—that plan had a lot to recommend it. "I have ordered Hauptmann Reed to shift our VTOLs to a staging area along with the airborne troops. I want you to send yours to us as well. Have them skirt out of line of sight and sensor range from the fort. No point in letting the Korps know what we are up to."

"You're planning an air assault, sir."

"I'm planning on taking out the Korps and securing this planet."

"What is the timetable?"

Nordhoff paused. There was no rush, and Duke Vedet did not want to move quickly. The longer they were on Simpson Desert, the more thoroughly decimated Roderick Frost's unit was going be. And why rush in on Verdun when he could pummel it from a distance, wear it down, strip away at least some of the defenders?

In his opinion, the Broken Swords under Frost were a blight on the Lyran TO&E. Yet recent accounts painted the unit as effective soldiers, even if their loyalty could not be guaranteed. By delaying his attack, he was supporting Duke Vedet's strategy and betraying the leadership of the Commonwealth. On the other hand, he despised the duke both personally and professionally. But Vedet held power over his career, and his elderly parents remained within the duke's reach on Hesperus. For now, he must continue to toe the line.

"Take your time, Schnell. Let them rest up and have them move out in the morning. I'm in no rush." *There's no such thing as a hurried siege.*

Hours later, Bernard stood close to one of their campfires. The air was hot and dry during the day, but at night a penetrating chill came down from the hills. The fires were built within view of the Verdun complex; he'd ordered a few extra fires built in case the locals were trying to guesstimate his troop strength. He crossed his arms, warming the front of his body while his backside remained cold.

Bernard allowed his gaze to be transfixed by the flickering flames and the fire's intense colors. His mind was elsewhere—on Tamarind, Hesperus II—*There are a lot of places I'd rather be than here, but here is where I've spent my whole life training to be.*

He thought about Roderick Frost. He'd heard the rumors about what had happened when Frost ran into the Jade Falcons on Algorab, and he'd read about the trial. Nordhoff had been in the military long enough to know that the official story was never the full story, and the expression "hung out to dry" came to mind whenever he considered Frost. But it was only a gut feeling, nothing that he could support.

Now I'm stalling here, and he's fighting, maybe dying on Tamarind. Bernard hated himself for giving in to Duke Vedet's demands. Guilt ate at him even as he tried to convince himself that he had good reasons, valid reasons for delaying the attack on Simpson Desert and delaying the arrival of reinforcements on Tamarind.

It was no work at all to convince himself that he'd end up in the same boat as Frost if he rebelled. The responsible parties rarely took the blame for their failures, especially in the military, and the duke would need a scapegoat if any part of this plan failed. Good men and women always suffered at the expense of those in power.

Bernard closed his eyes. If the duke was killed, he could be his own man. In fact, he could be much more than that. Nordhoff only hoped that Roderick Frost and his men would be able to forgive his transgression, since he wasn't sure he would be able to forgive himself. In the meantime, he was bound to the fate of the man pulling the strings.

He was hardly aware of someone standing next to him until he heard that person sigh. He forced open his weary eyes and saw Duke Vedet standing next to him, his arms folded the same way, his head bowed.

"You've done well the past two days, Bernard," the duke said, keeping his gaze on the fire. The reflections of the orange and red fire on his dark skin made him look more menacing, more dangerous than usual.

"With the Korps dug into that old fortress, it gives us time to pause, make sure we get this right."

The duke kicked a stick into the fire, shifting the coals. "Even the Word of Blake didn't think that old fort was worth wasting time on."

"I try not to base my actions on those of the Word of Blake," Bernard commented dryly. "I like to think the Commonwealth is better than that."

"When do you plan on attacking them?" the duke asked.

"We could begin tomorrow. I would prefer that we rest, give them some time to waste a little more ammunition, realize just how thoroughly they are trapped.

It would be best to resolve this with a nice, easy surrender."

"Do you think that could happen?"

"It's possible," Bernard said, "but unlikely." He frowned. "Loki led us to believe that we were going to be facing second-line troops here. These guys have shown tactical planning and strategic thinking that tells me they are tougher than second-stringers. I think they'll try to slug it out with us, at least for a while. Once the game starts, it's a matter of days, and then Simpson Desert is ours."

"A Defiance Industries JumpShip just arrived in-system from Tamarind—a routine trade mission."

"A   fortunate   coincidence," Bernard replied. *Interesting—the duke is using Defiance vessels to gather intelligence. I wonder whether the high command is aware of this, and if they support it? Or is this just part of the duke's personal game?*

"As a matter of routine, they sent me some news and data files. It appears that the Broken Swords landed on schedule and were immediately attacked by the First Tamarind Regulars Regiment. The battle was still raging when the ship jumped."

Bernard suppressed a wince. *I should be there too. Hell, so should Vedet.*

Duke Vedet continued. "It also appears that Duke Marik has broken off diplomatic relations with the Lyran Commonwealth and seized the consulate. There was no word on the fate of the consul or Lady Steiner."

"You must be quite happy," Bernard said bitterly, and without intending to speak out loud.

The duke turned slowly to look at him. "I have no idea what you mean, General."

A wave of guilt threatened to swamp him. "I could begin our attack on Verdun tomorrow. We hit them hard and fast, and win quickly. Then we can send troops to Tamarind per our orders."

The duke's eyes narrowed as he looked into the

face of his protégé. "We have ample reason to slow down that timetable, General. As you implied, each day they are dug in they become weaker. I would hate for our assault force to be so badly damaged that we cannot be of use to the Broken Swords on Tamarind. No, I believe the best plan is to wait a few days before pressing the attack. Don't you think so?"

He wanted to say no. "Two days, sir."

The duke smiled. "Two days should be more than enough. After that, I will take the Hesperus Guards to Danais to reinforce operations there. You will mop up here. Then you will take your regiment to Tamarind. By then, the Broken Swords will have been destroyed and will have weakened the First Tamarind Regulars. When you land with your battle-hardened troops, you will seize the capital of the Duchy and I will rejoin you there."

Just in time to claim the victory as your own. "I understand, sir."

"Good," said the duke, turning away from the fire. "Then all that is left is for us to do our duty."

Bernard returned his empty gaze to the fire. *Duty. I'm not sure I know what that is anymore.*

23

Trillian walked beside Klaus Wehner as they attempted to blend in with the crowd at the open market. She looked at the wares on the tables at each tent-covered vendor, as if she were casually shopping. Klaus looked bored each time she stopped, using the opportunity to look around the market to make sure that they were not followed.

Fontaine Marik had violated diplomatic protocol when he had sent troops to seize the Lyran Consulate. Usually a formal notification was sent to the capital of another government before such harsh action, the diplomats were formally expelled and so on. Then again, with an invasion force dropping outside his capital city, he obviously felt justified in taking direct action. If not for the speed with which Consul Gustoffson's staff had led them out through hidden tunnels, Trillian would have been captured.

Captured. That was a chilling thought. She was cousin to the archon, but she knew Melissa well enough to know that she would not bargain for Trillian's life. Melissa never let blood ties interfere with the good of the Commonwealth.

Trillian had seen squads of police in every market through which they had wandered. No doubt she was the target of their search. Consul Gustoffson had given her some of the local currency and a shawl to help hide her face, and had urged her to find a way to hook up with Roderick's forces. Klaus had changed into civilian clothing, but he needed the hat purchased early in their flight to hide his military crew cut. She didn't know what had happened to Gustoffson; she only knew that he had remained at the consulate in order to smuggle out the rest of his staff. If she got out of this mess, she would recommend him to Melissa for a commendation.

Klaus touched her arm and nodded subtly at the street. She followed his gaze, catching a glimpse of several police entering the marketplace from the other side of the vendors' shops. She took Klaus' arm and they began moving, her heart pounding with each footfall. Trillian forced a smile to her face as proof that nothing was out of the ordinary. Life as a fugitive was exciting—and she hated it.

The only weapon she had was the tiny officer's laser pistol that Roderick had given her before the start of the mission. She kept it in her boot, since her clothing offered few places to conceal a weapon. Klaus carried a military knife on a shin strap and his own sidearm— a nasty projectile gun. If it came down to a fight, they were hopelessly overmatched.

Their leisurely path took them from one clump of shoppers to the next, which was good camouflage for their effort to avoid looking like they were moving with a purpose. People were stocking up on goods because of the news that the Lyran invaders had landed. One market was playing a holonews broadcast touting the great victory of the First Regulars in trapping the invasion force. There was stock footage of a burning vehicle, a few explosions and smoke in the distance, but nothing that conveyed what the truth might be. She paused and watched the images and worried, not for the same reason as the people in the market, but for the safety of her cousin out there fighting for his life.

The rest of the Lyran forces should be landing any day now. That would tip the scales. Fontaine Marik would be forced to surrender. Any day now . . .

Suddenly a hand grasped her above the elbow, so firmly that she felt as if her arm were locked in a vise. "Papers please," the officer said, roughly guiding her to the side of the street and into a narrow alley. She had been pulled away from Klaus Wehner, whom she saw speaking with a female officer where she had left him. No one seemed to notice them. Nor did anyone seem concerned that the policeman was taking her into an alley.

"My papers, of course," she repeated, reaching into her pocket to retrieve nonexistent documents.

The policeman stared at her. He seemed huge. At first glance he might have looked pudgy, but she could tell it was mostly muscle. He was bald, but the stubble near his ears told Trillian that he shaved his head, probably to look more intimidating. His eyes were hidden behind dark sunglasses, but she could feel his gaze looking her up and down. He still held her arm, and now he pushed her two steps farther into the alley.

She was close to panic. He toggled the radio wired to his collar. "I have a suspect on Westbury."

"If you'll let go of my arm, I can get my papers," she said, pulling at his grip.

He lifted his sunglasses and gazed at her with a nasty expression in his dark eyes. "Well, well, well. It looks like I might have found our wandering diplomat."

With one fluid motion she twisted her arm out of his grip and leapt away, using a classic combination learned in one of her many self-defense classes. She backed a few steps away from him and cast a quick glance down the dark alley. It was a dead end. He closed with her and she kept moving back, sliding into a shallow entryway.

It was nothing more than a place to provide visitors shelter during a storm. She fumbled at the door but it was locked. The officer grabbed her again, this time at the shoulder. She spun, sweeping her leg out. She hit him solidly just behind the knee, but it was like kicking a tree. He dropped to his other knee, pain written on his face. She could see that Klaus was still with the female officer.

God, please don't let me die . . . not now . . . not like this.

The massive officer reached for his sidearm and Trillian let her training take over for thought. She executed a double kick at his face and caught him in the eye, shattering his sunglasses and cranking his head back. Anger twisted his face. With surprising speed he grabbed her ankle and twisted it hard, sending her sprawling facedown onto the ground and knocking the breath from her lungs.

Trillian pushed up in the beginning of a flip, but she suddenly felt his bulk pinning her, grinding her chest and breasts into the tile walkway. Her lungs ached. One of his hands drove her head sideways onto the rough tiles. "You *bitch*, you're going to pay for that."

She struggled. Her right arm and leg were still free. Her attacker shifted his weight to hold her down more securely. His mouth was only centimeters away from her ear. He was breathing hard, but in a husky whisper he repeated, "You'll pay for that, bitch." She believed him. His knee pressed into her crotch . . . she hoped it was his knee . . . and she knew he had more in mind than just hitting her again.

Desperately, she pressed her hand flat against the tile and tried to buck her hips to shift him, but he knocked her hand out from under her, slapping it back toward her torso. Her hand landed against her thigh, and she felt something hard in her pocket. She scrabbled at her pocket, then stabbed at her attacker's face with the object in her right hand.

The Cameron star necklace.

Blood spurted over her hand and the policeman swore, but he did not release her.

She bent her knee and dropped the necklace, reaching for her boot. There! Her pistol! He grabbed for her hand as he belatedly realized what she was doing, but she fired blindly behind her back. She had to hit something, he was so big. He convulsed against her, cursing and hitting her hand, knocking the gun away. He rolled off her.

Trillian twisted onto her back and saw that he was pressing his hand against his side—she must have hit him. She lunged at him. Grabbing the cord for the walkie-talkie clipped to his collar, she used it as a garrote. His thick neck muscles tensed as he tried to lean away from the cord, but she moved with him, maintaining the pressure on his throat.

She arched her back, focusing every atom of her strength on choking the policeman. His eyes bulged as she pressed harder and harder, crushing his windpipe. Blood from the cut she had given him with the Cameron star shimmered as he tried to turn his head. Trillian threw all of her weight against the cord. It dug into his flesh and he made a deep, throaty gurgling noise. His eyes widened and he opened his mouth as if to yell. She could smell his breath, her face was so close to his. Her jaw ached with tension. A roar of pure rage filled her ears.

His free arm hit her three times, each strike weaker than the last. His face was purpling, but she did not let up. He had been going to beat her, maybe kill her, probably rape her. He was not worthy to live. In a few more heartbeats it was over. His body rocked once, then suddenly went limp, but she didn't let go of the cord.

Finally, Trillian let go. Every muscle ached. She

stared at the dead man. He was a brute, ugly, dead. She staggered the few steps across the walkway, breathing raggedly. Sweat washed her body and soaked her clothes, making her hot, sticky, dusty. She stopped when she noticed Klaus standing in that same doorway. He looked down at the body, then at her.

"Jesus," he muttered, bending over to pick up her pistol and the necklace and handing them both to her. "We have to go!"

She didn't even wonder how he had gotten away from the other officer. Taking the gun, she slid it back into her boot. She examined the necklace, then squatted by the dead body and wiped most of the blood off the star onto his uniform. She found her shawl and carefully arranged it over her head. "Yes, we must go."

Taking Klaus' hand, she followed him back into the bustle of the street. She didn't notice the people around her. Her mind's eye was filled with the crumpled form of the police officer whom she—Trillian Steiner—had killed.

As they made their way out of the market, a new thought filled her head. She realized that when the man had died, she'd felt the same rush she got from sex. The same sweat, the same exhilaration. She didn't want to think about what that might mean.

Eighth Lyran Regulars Staging Area
McAffe
Bolan Military Province, Lyran Commonwealth

Colonel Drew Quentin climbed down from his *Orion* and suddenly found himself flanked by two men. They looked out of place—obvious civilians on a military base—but with their close-cropped haircuts, they could have been MechWarriors. Each took him by one elbow. He instantly resisted, and one of them flashed a badge in a small hard plastic case. Glancing at it, he saw the ID badge was for Loki. That explained a great deal. Numbly, he allowed himself to be led to a small, empty office off the 'Mech bay.

One of the men leaned against the door. The other rolled the dull gray office chair out from under the desk and pointed at it. He sat.

"What's this about?" Quentin demanded. "What's going on here?"

"We are with Loki," said the man who wasn't covering the door. He moved to stand in front of the colonel. He could have passed for a common office drone, but spies were like that—and they made Quentin nervous.

"I saw your ID. What does intelligence want with me?" The mere mention of Loki created an atmosphere of tension.

The man paced across in front of him twice, silently. "We're here about Algorab."

Not Algorab! Quentin chuckled nervously. "There must be some sort of mistake. That matter is closed. There was a court-martial and I was cleared. The man you are looking for is Roderick Frost."

"No mistake, Colonel," the agent assured him. "We have been sent here at the personal behest of the archon—on her specific orders."

"The archon?" It didn't seem like it should be possible, but that added to the tension. He shifted in the old office chair. "What does the archon want with me?"

The agent stopped pacing and leaned on the arms of the chair so that he was face-to-face with Quentin. "The archon wants to offer you a unique opportunity, Colonel. One to which you should pay close attention."

"Opportunity? Well, I . . ."

The agent flashed him a fast grin. "You see, Colonel, the archon is not convinced that your testimony regarding the affair on Algorab was entirely accurate. That certain details may have been left out, particularly in reference to the actions of then–First Hauptmann Frost."

"I already testified to what I di—what happened there."

"We know," the agent at the door spoke up. "The problem is that we think you lied."

"I—"

The first agent cut him off. "You see, Colonel, the archon believes you may have accidentally omitted details about that operation. She is much more polite than we are—we'd just call you a liar. We all wonder if perhaps you, shall I say, exaggerated Frost's role in the events. She wants to know the truth. So you are being given a unique chance to amend your testimony, right here—right now. This is your last chance to tell the full truth."

His heart pounded in his ears. *This was never supposed to happen.* He had connections. They had assured him that this wouldn't happen. Frost was supposed to take the fall, and he had. Why did the archon care about *him*? He had no doubt that the two Loki agents were serious. "I won't change my testimony. It would ruin my career. You've got to understand—"

The agent got a little closer to his face. "But I *do* understand, Colonel. Your career is over, regardless. If you tell us what really happened on Algorab, you walk away with your pension and at least a hope for a normal life."

"And if I don't?"

The agent shook his head. "There is an old saying about the truth setting you free. I suggest you embrace that adage, Colonel. Because if you don't—you will never understand true freedom again. Loki's reach is long, surely you know that."

"Why does the archon care about this?" he stammered.

"They didn't tell us that. We simply serve at her pleasure—as do you, if you remember your induction oath.

"So, Colonel, have you decided? Will the truth set you free?"

He sobbed . . . he actually sobbed out loud. Reaching for the noteputer that the agent held out to him, Colonel Quentin began to relate the true events on Algorab.

24

The Zanzibe Pocket
Harvison Flats
South of Zanzibar, Tamarind
4 December 3137

Roderick came up on the levee and used the earthen ridge to protect his lower torso as he fired. The two arm-mounted autocannons spat out a stream of armor-piercing rounds into the approaching JES missile carrier. The shots tore into the soft armor on the side of the vehicle. It had been positioning itself to fire a shot at one of his infantry squads but was suddenly and very deliberately distracted.

The autocannon rounds ate the armor plating on the side and tore into the missile casings. The JES pivoted to face him, which was what he was counting on. Another attack from a little farther down the levee, from a Mars assault tank, poured long-range missiles into the JES, catching the other side of the Duchy vehicle. A flame, really no more than a flicker, appeared near the rear of the vehicle, then turned into a hot red-orange glow. Suddenly the JES rocked violently as some of its ammunition cooked off.

The JES driver fired off the missiles he had. Three, damaged from the shots Roderick had fired, dove into the ground right in front of the JES, spraying shrapnel everywhere. The remaining missiles flew wildly about, like holiday fireworks. The JES shook again, and then the hatches popped. Three crewmen half crawled, half fell out of the tank. Dark gray smoke rose out of the open hatches, followed a heartbeat later by a burst of flame. His infantry scampered forward and apprehended the new prisoners, rushing them back behind the levee.

A Marik *Phoenix Hawk* rose on jump jets to the top of the levee near the Mars tank. It had no idea what it was facing on the other side of the earthworks. The Mars opened up with its front turret, as did Leutnant Vaughn's *Blade*, catching the *Phoenix Hawk* in a devastating crossfire. A nearby SRM squad unleashed a wave of short range missiles into it as well, ripping into the *Hawk*'s legs. Chunks of armor rained down on the Marik side of the berm. The *Hawk* fired its laser into the Mars tank, searing a deep black scar into the top armor of the vehicle. It then slid back down the levee and tried to make a run for the Zanzibe River.

At long range, a Broken Swords *Catapult* covered with replacement armor plates let loose a splatter of autocannon fire and hit the *Phoenix Hawk*. The shots plowed into the waist of the machine, mangling the armor and sending the 'Mech facedown into the riverbed. The soft mud piled up on either side of the 'Mech as it hissed into the water, sizzling from the heat of running and firing. Its MechWarrior struggled for a moment, got it upright, then ducked under the water out of target acquisition. Roderick doubted it was down for good, but it was damaged badly enough to keep it out of the current fight.

"Good work, Swords," he said, looking out on the narrow strip of land where the battle had taken place. One of his Demon armored cars was flipped on its side, probably beyond repair. A *Wasp* was down as well, mangled but salvageable.

"Savage One, get some teams out there and recover those vehicles. Emphasis on the ammunition and reusable parts. Concentrate on the 'Mechs."

"Yes, sir," Jamie Kroff replied. He was impressed. Days of fighting and her 'Mech was still operational, though its armor was nearly a complete patchwork of replacement plates.

Roderick popped open the visor on his neurohelmet and rubbed his eyes. They had been fighting for days, and he hated the fact that he had been right about Duke Vedet failing to bring the relief force. They were two days overdue and there was no sign of them burning in. The Broken Swords had managed to secure a pocket along the Zanzibe River south of Zanzibar, but their hold was tenuous.

He was outnumbered three to one, and the Duchy's First Regulars Regiment kept coming at him, day and night. Roderick had the terrain on his side because he could leverage the river and the hills beyond to whittle away at the Regulars. The defenders had numbers to their advantage, but so far they had sent in their troops piecemeal—like the attack he had just beaten off. A reinforced company had forded the river and attempted to run the gauntlet to the levee. The attempt failed and cost the Duchy a lot of men and materiel, but they seemed to have plenty to spare.

He signed and closed his visor. This was one of those times he hated being right, but the duke *had* hung him out to dry. His ammunition reserves were as low as his patience. The odds remained strongly in favor of the Duchy forces. At any time, they could send their forces in all at once and easily take out his remaining troops. They could be planning that move right now.

Even worse, he'd heard nothing from Trillian. The news broadcasts from Zanzibar said she was a fugitive, and there was an unconfirmed report that she had slain a police officer. Roderick wasn't sure what to make of that report. He wasn't convinced that Trillian was capable of killing another human being, but he did know she wouldn't go down without a fight. It was within the realm of possibility that she had killed someone in order to remain alive and free. *I pray that she's okay. . . .*

Roderick closed his eyes, nearly succumbing to sleep for just a moment. *We can't survive fighting defensively. We have to take the initiative. But how . . . and where?* He reluctantly opened his eyes, and keyed in a strategic overlay map on his secondary display. With twenty percent of his own forces either down or being refit, he needed a fast solution. While the Regulars had suffered more losses, they had more they could afford to lose. He studied the map.

Did he want to try to take Zanzibar itself? He didn't have enough troops to hold one of the seats of Marik power, not against a potentially hostile population. No, the real target was the First Regulars Regiment. Wipe out their ability to wage war, and he wouldn't have to invade the city—the local government would find itself unprotected. They could retreat to Padaron City, but the loss of Zanzibar would be a staggering blow to their morale. Such a retreat would be so demoralizing that the government would be better off leaving the world entirely.

So, how do you take out a regiment operating on friendly ground? He considered what he knew about the enemy's assets based on data from a signal bouncing off a communication satellite. At this point, both forces had roughly equal aerospace assets. They would have to be taken out. Any operation he conducted would have to be done in secret . . . that was doable as well if he used one of his fighters. He would need to hit their supply depots, steal what he could and burn the rest. Most importantly, his Broken Swords would need to keep moving. He needed to abandon the conventional, stand-up war.

He activated his command circuit. "Attention, all company commanders. Deploy your forces to repel another assault, then meet me at the LZ."

"Trouble, sir?" Trace Decker asked.

"Not for us. But the time has come to put these Regulars in a world of hurt."

" 'Bout damn time . . . sir," Kroff piped up.

They stood under the shade of the *Archon's Pride* near one of the massive landing struts. Repair crews were hovering over his *Rifleman IIC*, quickly attaching replacement armor to the left shoulder, which had been mangled during the last assault. Roderick ignored them. His focus was on the officers gathered around the map.

"It's time we take the initiative. I propose to split our command. The two units will operate essentially as independent companies. We will avoid the Regulars to the north and instead head south. About thirty kilometers from here is a bridge we can cross. One company will hold the attention of the Regulars, keep them on the river. The other will sweep to the south, cross the Zanzibe there and move up to hit them. At the same time, we will use every transport we have, VTOL and otherwise, to take a fast-moving force and sweep to the west. They will strike at these two supply depots. Their mission is to steal what they can and destroy the rest.

"Finally, we will deploy our DropShips to the north along the western flank of the enemy. They will drop directly on the airstrip designated as Randolph Field and take out the Regulars' aerospace assets, then come back."

"Sir, how can we move those VTOLs with them watching us?" Jamie asked. "I guess the same question can be asked about any part of this operation. There are satellites over us all the time—hell, we're bouncing signals off them to get a picture of the Regulars."

"Simple," Roderick said. "We remove those satellites."

"I like the idea of being on the move," Trace said. "But risking the DropShips seems a little radical."

"We need to negate that airfield. They are using it to maintain and arm their aerospace and VTOL assets. Most military commanders coddle their DropShips. We don't need them. This is the fight for the entire Duchy of Tamarind-Abbey, right here. I don't care if the ships are ruined in the fight. Their turrets are damned powerful and we are outnumbered and outgunned right now. They can help level the playing field. If they get destroyed in the process—well, I never had plans on us leaving Tamarind in the first place."

"Where are our reinforcements, sir?" Kroff asked.

Roderick had the same question, but didn't want her to know it. "It doesn't matter, does it? They aren't here yet. Until they get here, we're the only show in town." He eyed his officers carefully. "Look, this is not going to be easy. So far we've been forced to react to a superior enemy. Tomorrow morning, I intend to shake up the Duchy commander—force him to dance to our tune."

"Sounds like fun," Trace put in.

"I prefer attack to defense," Kroff added.

"All right, then," Frost said with a broad grin. "Get your people moving. I will coordinate the larger elements of this operation."

Warrant Officer Zachery Dorn angled his *Stuka* aerospace fighter to high orbit. It felt good to be back in space. He and his wingman, Francine Burns, were on an orbital approach to the commercial satellite band. So far there had been no pursuit.

He toggled his targeting and tracking system. Yup, there they were. Ten satellites either in geosynchronous orbit over Zanzibar or crisscrossing the area. Dorn punched in the coordinates of each target and tagged some as his, some as Burns'.

"Go faster," Burns said, a hint of urgency in her voice. "No sign of the Duchy fighters yet, but they did see us take off."

"I don't want to be caught up here alone either, Francine," he said, finishing the last of the tagging. "Targets are designated. Break to your two o'clock and begin the sweep."

He arced his *Stuka* over and spotted the first of his targets, a small news-service satellite. Barely a meter in diameter, the tiny satellite was hard to spot visually, but his sensors picked it up. Switching his four large lasers to his primary target interlock, he let go a blast of energy. He could hear the whine of the capacitors as they began the recharge cycle. The satellite disintegrated, momentarily becoming visible as a cloud of bright, shiny pieces.

"Tallyho!" he shouted, switching to another target.

"Get moving, Dorn. I just picked up something on long-range sensors. Let's dust the rest of these and get out of here."

Roderick watched as Kroff's rear guard crossed the Auburn Bridge over the Zanzibe River. It had taken hours to get everything in place, especially since the operation had unfolded under the cover of night. Now they were on the same side of the river as the Duchy's Regulars—and they were on the move.

"All right, Savage One. Let's begin our move to the north and east."

"Roger, Sword One," Kroff confirmed. He could see her *Violator* outlined by the first rays of the dawn light. In silhouette, it was hard to see how damaged it was. Frost knew she had taken a lot of hits over the last few days—he'd seen all of the replacement armor plates. He was pleased that she'd kept her word: she hadn't lost her ride since they'd landed.

He marched next to her at the front of the column. He felt grim satisfaction at the knowledge that the Duchy's elite Regulars were going to be reeling in a matter of hours. He didn't smile; the battle wasn't won yet. He spared a moment of worry for Trillian. She was somewhere out there on the run, probably still hiding in Zanzibar. It had to be hellish, with the entire local population looking for you. He knew she was tough: as a child, she had beaten him at most games. But that was years ago, and this was not child's play. The game was now much more dangerous.

Keep your head down, Trill. . . .

"Sir?"

He shook his head. *Jeez, I said that out loud.* "Nothing, Jamie. Just keep your units tight behind us."

The raiding force was small and moved fast over the tops of the rolling hills. Trace was running the show, since his BattleMech was temporarily out of the fight. There were at least three other MechWarriors who could pilot his *Stalker* when it was ready to go, but at the moment, this force needed its CO's leadership. There was no room to sit. Trace simply held on to the back of the driver's seat.

His stomach pitched as the Maxim Mk. II transport pitched down the hill. He could see the Gnome troops in the back reflected in the console, squeezed in so tight that they couldn't fall over despite the speed. Hovering only thirty meters overhead, he could hear the Cardinal and the MHI Crane transport VTOLs. There was a rhythm to the thumping of their rotors that seemed in synch with the butterflies in his stomach.

He leaned forward over the driver. "Range?"

"Two klicks and closing," he said.

Trace Decker activated his microphone. "All troops prepare to debark," he said. The massive armored troops gave no reply, though one gave him a thumbs-up. He nodded in acknowledgment.

"We have company," the driver said. "I am picking up a *Locust* and a *Stinger* on the perimeter."

"You know the plan," Trace said.

The driver stretched his neck side to side. "I do," he said into his throat mic. "That doesn't mean I like it." The Maxim thrummed louder as the driver throttled up the reactor and began a wide turn, aiming for the *Stinger*.

Trace braced himself. He turned on his mic one more time. "We've got Regulars on the border, two light BattleMechs. We're going to do this just as we planned, so grab on to something—it's about to get bumpy."

As they crested the next hill, he saw the *Stinger*. It stood facing away from them, as if it hadn't picked them up yet. If it hadn't, it would in a moment. The driver of the Maxim II did exactly what he was supposed to; he aimed his hovercraft right at the *Stinger* and gave it full throttle. The VTOLs above him broke formation and headed toward the supply dump, but the Goblin transport followed the Maxim's lead and headed for the *Locust*.

The *Stinger* twisted its head and seemed to look right at him. At their speed, though, Trace saw the head for only a second. Then the Maxim II slammed into the treelike legs of the *Stinger*, causing a horrible grinding noise—the sickening sound of ripping metal. Trace lurched forward into the seat back in front of him, his shoulders nearly wrenched out of their sockets.

There was a hiss and a rush of air and light from the rear of the transport as the doors opened. The Gnome troopers jumped out, weapons blazing away at the *Stinger*. The Maxim was badly damaged but still operational. It pulled back a meter, then moved past the *Stinger*'s legs. Trace could see the caved-in plating where the hovercraft had crushed the armor, exposing myomer bundles.

Trace heard the SRM launcher on the top of the transport fire its twin-pack of missiles. This battle was far from over, but it sure as hell got started with a bang.

The Duchy of Tamarind's First Regulars Regiment was attempting to force its way across the Zanzibe River under withering fire from the tree line on the far bank. Roderick could see the troops of Saber Company blazing away from the far side of the river as

Duchy 'Mechs rose out of the water. They were putting up a good fight; it was about to get better.

At the moment, the Regulars had no idea he was on their side of the river. They were about to learn the hard way. "Ready, Jamie? We rush to the river and assist Saber Company by cutting off their second wave."

"Just give me the word, sir."

He knew it was taking all her restraint to not rush in right now. Roderick watched a Duchy *Raven II* crumple as it came out of the water, caught in a broadside salvo. *Now is as good a time as any.* "Leutnant Kroff, go shatter that assault so we can link up with Saber Company."

"Yes, sir!" She switched to a broadband channel. "Savage Company, form up on me. Head for the river and let's cut these bastards in half!"

Roderick cleared the brush and fired at a passing Bellona tank. He caught it by surprise, hitting it in the thin rear armor plating. The autocannon rounds tore up the back of the hovercraft and several shells plowed into the rear-mounted large laser. Sparks flew from torn circuitry as the shocked driver pivoted to face the threat. At the same moment, a barrage from a Long Tom across the river rained down on top of it. The Bellona disappeared as the artillery rounds reshaped the landscape around it.

Kroff's *Violator* had closed to point-blank range with a Regulars *Shadowhawk.* The Duchy BattleMech fired one laser blast, then turned to run. The sudden appearance of the attack force on their flank and rear shattered the unit's resolve. Jamie was able to get in one sweeping attack with her anti-'Mech drill, shredding some of the armor on the arm of the *Shadowhawk* as it turned. The 'Mechs just entering the water turned to face the new threat. Some were caught in the cross fire from both sides of the river. Others followed the lead of the *Shadowhawk* and tried to flee.

Roderick watched an SM1 tank destroyer bank out

over the river and head to the rear. Warrant Officer Dewery's *Firestarter* blazed away with its massive flamethrowers, setting the hovertank on fire as it fled. It left a trail of burning ooze as it rose over the embankment and headed back toward Zanzibar.

Frost gritted his teeth. A platoon of Regular infantry dug in along the marshy land near the riverbank only held out for a few salvos before fleeing. The Duchy attack had been shattered. *Now I need to find out, just how successful were we?*

= 25 =

The pair of enemy *Vulture*s emerged from the tree line, disgorged their wave of long-range missiles and faded back to the dense woods for cover. The hover infantry and the ATV support forces charged out from the road toward the enemy. It was a gallant move, but folly against two BattleMechs.

Marik missiles hit the two J-37 transports. The J-37 carried armor equal to several sheets of reinforced cardboard. They were not front-line combat vehicles, but were designed for transporting munitions and supplies to the front lines. The long-range missiles twisted in flight and slammed into the tracked transports. The explosions instantly ripped into the internal storage cells, and there was a resounding secondary blast from each vehicle.

As Duke Vedet arrived on the scene in his *Atlas*, he could see the treads of the transports still in the mud, but the rest of the vehicles were gone, nothing remaining but a black blasted smear on the thick clay roadbed. He cursed, loud and fluently.

"I want those *Vulture*s," he said through gritted teeth.

"We're on it, sir." A Guards *Hatchetman* and *Arbalest* entered the dense growth from which the *Vulture*s had suddenly appeared. The tree branches snapped back behind them, making them invisible in the thick forest growth. "I am getting new readings, sir. They apparently are moving along some road that is not on our maps. It's going to be hard to get at them," reported Hauptmann Klein.

"How in the hell did they get into our rear area, Hauptmann?" Vedet bellowed furiously.

"Unknown, sir. We did not know about that road. Even our fighters didn't pick it up. The forest was supposed to be impenetrable. Our own probes into it supported that theory. I had a squad lost for over an hour in there. The enemy was able to stage this ambush because they had better information."

One part of the duke's mind noted that Klein had taken responsibility for his failure. But what was the price for that failure? He knew Klein's family; he had funded him at the academy. Now Klein had failed him. He wanted to bust him in rank, verbally castigate the man—but doing so would end up hurting his own interests in the long run. *Down the road, I'll need men like him on my side.* He kept the memory of the artillery attack that had taken down his *Atlas* fresh in his mind as a warning.

"We needed those supplies." The duke left it at that.

"I understand, sir."

The worst part of the whole cluster was the identity of the enemy forces. It was not the planetary militia, the Daredevils of Danais. No, this was a lance of the Silver Hawk Irregulars, possibly more than a lance. They had landed three days ago and had done nothing but snipe at the Hesperus Guards ever since.

Their first day on-planet, his Guards had seized the capital, Breckenridge, with only light resistance. It seemed like the assault on Danais was going to be easy. By nightfall, that impression had changed. The Daredevils and the Silver Hawks had struck, taking out a patrol lance. They came in company strength, three-to-one odds. Only one of his Guards survived, and he was badly injured, his BattleMech a shell. It was obvious he had been allowed to live to bring word of their defeat to Duke Vedet and to spread fear among the other Lyran troops.

It almost worked.

Breckenridge offered nothing they needed. For supplies, he was forced to have his infantry break into retail stores and take what they needed. The Marik-Stewart Commonwealth supporters had sabotaged every facility that could be used for repairs or rearming. It was obvious to Duke Vedet that the city had become flypaper for his Hesperus Guards—they had taken it, and now were stuck with it. It possessed no military value, and capturing it had not demoralized the resistance. In fact, it had become a rallying point for the rest of the population.

We need to retake the initiative here . . . but how? The duke briefly considered gathering his officers and asking their opinions. They were supposed to be the experts in warfare, but what had they accomplished? These so-called experts had let the Silver Hawk Irregulars slip from their grasp time and time again. He ignored his own contribution to events on Bondurant—that was Bernard's failure, not his.

Duke Vedet quickly convinced himself that the military officers knew no more about fighting this war than he did. He could see that he needed to go after them in force, and to keep Breckenridge. If the Marik forces recaptured the city, it would turn the entire population actively against us. *And I want those Silver Hawk Irregulars, once and for all.*

To achieve both objectives he was going to need ample supplies for an offensive operation and some reserve troops. Two companies of Bernard's troops had been placed in reserve for whichever commander needed them. Bernard wasn't likely to need them on Tamarind. Roderick Frost would fight hard and lose, but in the process he was bound to badly injure the Tamarind defenders. Tamarind should be a simple mop-up operation.

The duke, on the other hand, needed those troops and supplies.

Two Days Later

The attack had come from a lone *Spider*. The fast-moving light 'Mech wore the silver and purple eagle of the Silver Hawk Irregulars. It had taken two well-aimed shots at the patrol, one of which hit the duke's *Atlas* just below the cockpit.

They pursued it. The *Spider* broke off and burst into a full-speed run. Hauptmann Klein calmly suggested that they were bound to be heading into a trap. The duke wanted the *Spider*, so he ignored the warning, even though he knew Klein was probably right. His only response was, "Look sharp, everyone."

The road ended on the shore of a small blue-green lake surrounded by pine forest. The moment he saw the lake, he gave the order to halt. The *Spider* continued along the shoreline to the far side. Duke Vedet stopped his column on the narrow forest road, embraced by the shade of the massive pine trees that made even the BattleMechs appear small.

"The lake," he warned.

"I'm not picking up anything on MAD other than the *Spider* on the far side," Leutnant Schnell replied cautiously, almost whispering. "We should be able to pick up 'Mech reactors even if they are hiding underwater."

Hauptmann Klein cut in. "Sir, we should get off this road, move along the flank. For now, let that *Spider* go."

The duke paused. "Fine—damn it! Everyone, move into the forest to the east side of the road."

The line of BattleMechs stepped off to the side of

the road and walked up over the shallow embankment, where they stood on a sea of dead brown pine needles. The forest spread densely in every direction. The low branches were dead; the massive pines opened like umbrellas just at the top height of the BattleMechs.

"Move out quickly. Watch your sensors," the duke commanded. The four BattleMechs fanned out. On long-range sensors he could still pick up the *Spider*. It seemed to be still moving in the same direction, out of visual range, out of weapons reach. It was still out there, though, one light BattleMech against four assault-class 'Mechs. That he would stick around made little sense, and that made the duke nervous. *He must know something we don't.*

Two kilometers into the forest, there was still no sign of vehicles or other BattleMechs—only the *Spider*, which seemed to shadow their movement. Duke Vedet found himself getting more anxious, more frustrated. They were wasting time because of a little paranoia. One quick rush would put them in range of that *Spider*. If they hit it once or twice, it would slow down, enough to fall to the rest of the lance's firepower. He reached out to activate his comm system and tell Hauptmann Klein his idea.

Suddenly, the world around him changed completely.

The deep shade of the dense forest lit up all around him. At first, it looked as if they had reached the edge of the forest and sunlight was pouring in. But the light was too dull, too orange and red. Fire! The entire dry forest was on fire, in front of and behind him. A hot, soot-filled wind battered him from all directions.

We walked right into a trap.

"Hauptmann Klein," he said, an edge of fear in his voice as he watched how fast the flames were spreading.

"I see it, sir. We need to dump our explosive ammo right now and wade into the fire, heading back toward the road. The 'Mechs may overheat, but if we move slow we'll most likely make it out."

Duke Vedet didn't want to run. He wanted to stay and fight, but there was nothing to fight. The Irregulars or the Daredevils, one of them had tricked him. He now knew exactly how Bernard must have felt. He had been so concerned about hidden 'Mechs in the lake that he had failed to recognize the real trap.

"Sir?" Klein pressed.

"All units, dump your ammunition and make for the road. Watch your heat levels, but don't stop, keep moving." He watched a pile of autocannon rounds pile up almost knee-deep to First Leutnant Howe's *Blade*. He released his own short-range missiles, which clanged and rumbled to the forest floor near his *Atlas'* feet. He stared at them for a moment, hating the waste of ammo his troops could ill-afford to lose.

I am going to bring in the reserves and supplies I need. These Silver Hawks and the local garrison are going to pay for this!

He waded his *Atlas* off to the west. Within seconds he was surrounded by roaring flames, drenched in his own sweat. The *Atlas* tried to vent the heat but couldn't. By the time he reached the road, the other 'Mechs of the lance were there, all seared the sickening black color of cooked paint. Some had damaged weapons. All were so hot that they literally had smoke rising off them.

They will all pay for this!

26

Zanzibar, Tamarind
Duchy of Tamarind-Abbey
6 December 3137

She heard the gurgling sound and felt the man quiver
under her, fighting for his last breath. That breath,
its heat, its smell, jarred her. Trillian abruptly sat up,
drenched in sweat, eyes wide. Even the wadded-up
cloth coat she used for a pillow was soaked with her
sweat. The alley where she slept was quiet except for
the stirring of a few other homeless people who lived
there. *The nightmare again.* It ruined her sleep on a
regular basis.

Looking across the alley, she saw the half-raised
head of Klaus Wehner, one eye open to look at her.
The nightmares kept him awake as well, because he
was her guardian. As with Roderick, she could count
on Klaus. He never told her how he got away from
the policewoman who had apprehended him. He knew
how she had escaped.

Trillian lay back down on the cool, wet pile of cloth
and pulled the ragged blanket over her. The chill of
the Zanzibar night seemed to make her joints ache,
but most of that came from sleeping on a piece of
packing cardboard for a mattress. She had camped out

before, but never like this. They survived, one step
ahead of the law, by living with the lowest caste in
the city—the beggars.

They still had some of her money. Klaus had lost
his. Perhaps he had bribed the policewoman? That
seemed doubtful. More likely the officer had simply
taken the money from him. The money Trillian had
accepted from the consul had been enough to buy
food, two blankets; enough to stay alive.

As she lay on the ground she looked across the
street, her gaze unfocused. The nightmare had eliminated any hope of more sleep that night; that was the
way it always went. Her thoughts ran along the same
track they'd been stuck in for the past four days. She
had long ago accepted that, with her being a diplomat,
her actions sometimes led to people dying. But she
had never, personally, killed before. It disturbed her
on a deeply fundamental level.

She sighed, and made a face at the odor she inhaled.
For a day or two she had succeeded in convincing
herself it was simply the smell of the alley where they
slept each night. The truth was, that awful smell was
her. There were no public facilities for bathing or
showering, though a fellow homeless person had advised her that she could have a good wash in the bath-
room in the public library, using the toilet as a source
of water and a cup to rinse her hair. Trillian had assumed it would be a long time before she was that
desperate, but now she wasn't so sure.

What would Melissa think of her actions? Would
she even tell her what happened? Yes, she'd have to.
If—no, when they got out of this, she and Klaus would
have to tell everything that happened. Klaus wouldn't
volunteer the information indiscriminately, but it
would have to be included in a full report. She knew
her aide all too well—he would do his duty. As she
would do hers.

The archon would understand. Knowing Melissa,
she would make sure that the details of the incident—

the murder—were suitably buried. Steiners didn't like to be seen with blood on their hands. But secrets like this were hard to keep. Someone always knew. Eyes would follow her at parties, murmurs just out of ear-shot would brush the edges of her awareness, others would glance at her in judgment. Though no one would have the nerve to say what they thought to her, this murder would plague her forever.

What would Roderick say? He would understand better than anyone else in the family. He understood the judgmental gazes from others. He too had suffered from the murmurs and rumors. Roderick would under-stand the burden she carried.

Thinking of Roderick distracted her mind. By watching the holonews broadcasts, she knew he was still out there fighting. For a few days there had been no news; the networks had cited technical difficulties. But Trillian had heard rumors that most of the plan-et's communication satellites had been shot down by the invaders, and that other broadcast hubs also had been destroyed. She applauded the strategy, which was the best proof she could have that Roderick was out there.

When broadcasts resumed, they were heavily slanted. There was celebration over the First Regulars having destroyed one of the "accursed invaders'" DropShips. The video proved the truth of the claim: it showed a House Steiner *Union*-class ship listing heavily away from a shattered landing strut. But Tril-lian took note of other details. Randolph Field, the spaceport where the ship landed, was a smoking debris field. She thought she could make out the shattered remains of at least two aerospace fighters—a *Stingray* and a *Reiver*—smoldering in the background. Not a single building was left standing. She knew that battle had cost the defense force dearly.

Other reports cheered that the First Tamarind Reg-ulars Regiment was going on extended maneuvers to "once and for all ensnare and destroy the desecrators of our soil." Translation: Roderick was no longer fighting a defensive action, but was on the move. If anyone could confound the Tamarind forces, it was her cousin. As she lay on her cardboard bed, she smiled. Roderick would laugh if he could see her now, and he would be the first one to give her a hug—regardless of the stench.

A few hours later the handful of homeless people who normally huddled in the alley woke up. Trillian had learned their habits and adapted them as her own. They carefully hid the belongings they couldn't carry. Trillian always made sure she had the tiny laser pistol in her boot. It hurt wearing it there day after day, but she wanted the pistol handy at all times. She had killed once and knew that if she had to, she would do it again.

Usually, the whole group moved out to the market, where most of them would purchase a small meal. This morning, an army officer and a squad of troops blocked the entrance to the alley. Trillian stood up straight and quickly draped her dirty shawl over her face. Klaus moved to her side. In her new world, she knew change was rarely good. Klaus touched her arm in support, and together with the other homeless people they stared at the line of troops in silent tension.

"Why are they here?" she whispered to Klaus.

"Wait. Remember, we are just beggars," was his only reply.

The officer cleared his throat, then rapidly rattled off a rehearsed speech. "Duke Fontaine Marik, heir to the throne of the Free Worlds League, Duke of the Duchy of Tamarind-Abbey, has asked that all able-bodied citizens of the streets of Zanzibar take an active role in the defense of this city."

Trillian tipped her head slightly as she cast a glance to Klaus. At least they were not here looking for them.

"You are being ordered to report to barricade construction at the south of the city. You will be assigned work crews. All able-bodied men and women will take part in the construction of barricades to keep the invaders out of our capital. It is the duty of all citizens to assist in the defense of the city." He spoke with a patriotic fervor, as if he believed his words.

Most of the Zanzibar homeless stared at him blankly. Trillian stepped forward. "I'll go. No one will call me a coward."

"Me too," Klaus chimed in. Several other of the homeless people volunteered, but most said nothing.

"Your spirit and backbone are appreciated in the effort to win this war. Get aboard this truck and you will be taken to your work zone." The officer gave her a patriotic grin, until she got close enough for him to smell her.

The work was exhausting and slow. Piles of broken bricks and scrap metal were dumped in the street and the workers were expected to take it and turn it into an antitank trap. There was little supervision other than a pudgy man who barked out useless orders like "Get moving, you bums!" No engineering principles were being applied. It was simply a matter of piling the bricks in a way that looked impressive to the supervisor.

Her fingers, arms and knees ached by the afternoon. She examined her fingers and grinned. Gone were the beautifully manicured nails of which she had been so proud. Her fingers had blisters and were filthy—but not filthy enough for her to clean them before eating the sandwiches they were provided. Trillian behaved exactly like everyone else in the work gang.

On the afternoon break—an hour long because the supervisor was off getting a drink somewhere—Trillian sat down and took a gulp of warm water from the small bottle each worker had been given. Her lips were dusty, and she could taste the metallic flavor of the dirt as she swallowed the water. It didn't matter.

She had already learned there were worse things in the universe than a little dirt.

Klaus sat beside her. She still couldn't get used to his salt-and-pepper beard, which she thought completely changed his appearance. He had a nasty cut on his right forearm, which was wrapped in a white rag of unknown origin. Klaus looked disheveled and his pants were torn in several spots, but his eyes had not lost their fire.

"Not much of a barrier," he said, just loud enough for her to hear.

"How desperate are they, do you think?" she replied in a low tone.

His eyebrows rose at her words. "They are worried enough to start building barricades on the main roads into the city. That says something about Hauptmann Frost's level of success so far."

Wehner was right. If the city wasn't at risk, they wouldn't be putting up barricades. Despite the confidence of their news broadcasts, the city was making an effort at defense and you didn't do that unless you had to.

"No word of General Nordhoff or the duke," Trillian added bitterly.

"Way overdue," Klaus agreed, taking another sip of warm water from his bottle. "Then again, I don't think either of us is surprised."

Her jaw ached as she leaned cautiously against the low wall at her back. The afternoon sun bathed her chest, adding to her existing sunburn. "No. Not surprised, just disappointed. There was always a possibility that even if Vedet chose to hang me out to dry, Nordhoff would follow orders."

Klaus wiped his mouth on his dirty sleeve. "It doesn't matter now. If he was counting on the Broken Swords getting killed or captured, so that he could swoop in and grab the glory . . . well, that just hasn't happened." Klaus still had to consciously prevent himself from ending sentences with "milady."

"Roderick is full of surprises."

"He'd better be," Wehner agreed. "They're going to toss everything they have at him."

"Do you think we should leave the city and try to find him?" Trillian hoped Klaus would say yes. She had asked the question four days earlier, but he had convinced her that leaving made no sense. No one knew where Roderick was, not the military, not the press. Still, she had to ask the question.

"You know my answer," he said. "If you want to find Roderick, I think all we have to do is wait and he'll come to us." He nodded at the low pile of debris growing into a barricade. "And if he does come, there won't be much here to resist him."

She thought for a moment, staring at the barricade. "We don't have much money left. And living the way we are, we could easily be victims if fighting breaks out."

"I don't know if I like where this is going."

She stared at him. "We might be able to help Roderick. We have to find him."

"Help him? How? Have you looked at yourself lately? We can barely help each other."

Trillian shook her head. "I know you better than that. You may not be in uniform, but you want to be out there in the fight too. We have to try."

"I hate it when you're right." His shoulders sagged as he accepted her logic. "As a military man, I have to warn you that this is an almost impossible task. There is a crack regiment out there searching for Roderick and they haven't found him. We have no resources and our chances are very slim . . . but you're right, we need to try. If not for our own sake, then just to irritate Duke Vedet."

"You always know just what to say to make a girl feel good," Trillian replied with a dazzling smile as she got to her feet. She felt a little dizzy and the backs of her knees ached from sitting. Still, she felt a new energy, a sense of determination she had not felt for a while. "Now we wait for the right opportunity. When it presents itself, we move."

"Until then, we work."

"And work a little more," she mimicked. She looked up into the brilliant blue-purple sky. *Roderick, my money is still on you.*

27

Marshes of Malcontent
Southeast of Zanzibar
Tamarind, Duchy of Tamarind-Abbey
8 December 3137

Roderick watched the *Ocelot* rush his battered Kage squad. Their battle armor was pitted, burned, missing and, in at least one case, hanging down like a tattered piece of cloth. They huddled behind the old pumping station, clinging to every loose brick for cover as the 'Mech charged, sensing a quick kill. *Not today, big boy.*

He stepped into the *Ocelot*'s path. The MechWarrior had assumed the *Rifleman* was occupied with the Saxon APC on his flank. He only realized his mistake when Roderick fired an autocannon barrage at him at nearly point-blank range. The AP rounds blasted holes right up the front of the BattleMech and into the cockpit canopy. The 'Mech reeled hard to the right, losing its footing and falling backward into the marshy reed bed. A hiss of steam rose from the fallen BattleMech as it lay in the muck.

His Kage troopers jumped out from behind the pumping station as the MechWarrior tried to roll over and stand up. The infantry fluttered down on their slender carbon fiber wings, like a pack of carrion birds feasting on a carcass. They covered the long form of the *Ocelot* from one end to the other, focusing their lasers and firing into every damaged armor plate and exposed seam. Three of the squad concentrated on the right arm, obviously damaging the actuator. As Frost cycled another salvo of autocannon rounds, he saw that the *Ocelot* had stopped moving. Either the MechWarrior was surrendering or the BattleMech was too damaged to continue the fight. There was always the possibility that the MechWarrior was dead. He found himself hoping it was the latter. He hated dealing with prisoners. They always proved to be more trouble than they were worth.

He saw the MechWarrior hauled out alive by the Kage troops. They stripped off his neurohelmet and waved to him. He waved the arm of his *Rifleman IIC*, acknowledging the victory. *Another POW*. They had captured a number of the Tamarind soldiers and had quickly run out of facilities for holding them. *You don't have to feed dead enemies.*

"Sit rep?" he asked as he checked his own damage display. His right leg had lost most of its armor in the last assault and he was still having an ammunition feed problem in the right torso. *We can't keep this up forever, but we can sure as hell try.*

First Leutnant Duvahl signaled. "That bogie was the last of them, sir. They are bugging out to the north, what's left of them. We have three downed 'Mechs, but it looks like we took out four of theirs—and Warrant Officer Krane managed to capture a Zibler."

Roderick could hear a note of glee in her voice. Krane had piloted a *Thunderbolt* that had fallen three days ago. Roderick had assigned her to help coordinate communication until they secured a new 'Mech. Looking at the fallen *Ocelot*, he believed he had fixed that problem. "Leutnant, get a repair team down here. I have an *Ocelot* I think is salvageable. It might be damaged, but at least you're firing."

"Yes, sir!" she replied. He admired her spirit—the

kind of spirit that had held his ragtag force together so far.

The fighting over the last two weeks had been savage. Trace had staged a stunningly successful raid on the First Regulars' supply base. They had knocked out most of the satellites over Tamarind, enough to blind both sides to each other's actions.

For the most part, his plan had worked out very well. By using the DropShips to destroy the airfield the Regulars were using, he had achieved total surprise. They had been lured into space chasing his *Stukas* while they were destroying the satellites. When they realized that DropShips were landing on their tarmac, they turned and made a beeline home. But there was no place left to land, and Roderick's ships had already wiped out nearly all the First Regulars' VTOLs. The returning fighters put up a good fight, but only the *Sandpiper* failed to get away. The *Sandpiper* was downed on the airfield, having pummeled the tarmac and everything sitting on it for more than an hour. While the local press touted the destruction of their DropShip as a stunning victory, the truth was Roderick had been happy to pay the price to eliminate the First Regulars' air superiority.

Since then, his tiny army had been on the move. After driving back the river assault, he continued south of Zanzibar, moving into the low marshlands, an inhospitable area of reeds and a few ragged trees. The Regulars had retreated to the northwest of the capital, reeling from the confusing array of assaults.

If he had wanted, he could have charged into the capital and taken it, block by painful block. If he knew help was on its way, he would have taken that option. But it was clear that Duke Vedet had betrayed not just Trillian, but him and his Broken Swords.

The unit was holding up, though the stress was starting to show. His troops had become masters of salvage, stealing ammunition and stripping off useful weapons and armor plating like a pack of locusts gutting a dead body. They were keeping most of their BattleMech force operational, but even his *Rifleman IIC* was starting to look like it had been assembled in a mad scientist's laboratory. He had lost his left autocannon to a JES missile carrier two days ago. It had been replaced, but the replacement part was painted for a different camouflage scheme and had some unique coolant hoses and feed assemblies spot-welded into place. It was ugly, but his 'Mech fit in with the rest of his Broken Swords.

He moved to the staging area and powered down as soon as he heard the click of the gantry swing into play. Five techs began to survey the damage from the battle. Already, replacement armor plates, obviously from fallen enemy 'Mechs, were being hoisted in place. Roderick removed his neurohelmet and disconnected his coolant vest hoses. His arms and back ached as he popped the hatch and began the weary climb down to the ground. The cooler air felt good on his hot, sweaty skin. It felt as if he had a visible film of grime, perspiration and dust over his entire body. Any attempt to wash with anything short of a sonic shower only seemed to make him feel worse.

At the feet of his *Rifleman IIC*, he stared upward and at the scars of battle. There was a gouge on his left arm, a laser burst. *Hmm. I don't remember getting hit there.* So much had been happening in the chaos of battle it was hard to keep track of each and every little hit.

The marshlands were only a temporary base. Roderick and Kroff had gone over the maps the night before. There was a tiny village off to the north and east with the unassuming name of Burkettsville. It was nothing more than a wide spot along the highway, but if they seized it intact, it would be a source of petrochemicals and food. This was not just a war against the Duchy of Tamarind-Abbey, it was a war for survival.

He ambled along to his tent. Outside the tent, Warrant Officer Dewery stood at attention, or as close to it as any of his officers got. Dewery was a very good MechWarrior. His biggest problem was that he was a thief. Before coming into the Broken Swords, he had been stealing military supplies and selling them on the black market. It had cost him his career. Dewery saluted and Frost responded. The usually cheerful man seemed drained.

"What can I do for you, Dewery?"

"My ride is down," he said glumly. "Sorry, sir."

"Your *Firestarter*?"

"They got the gyro and the engine housing. I'm sorry, sir. I didn't mean to let you down."

"Let me down? What are you talking about?"

"I want to fight, sir. I just don't have a BattleMech."

Roderick closed his eyes. Lyran command had written off the men and women in his unit as failures and criminals. Here was Dewery, a man who should have been sitting in a prison cell somewhere back in the Commonwealth, and he was upset that he couldn't take part in the battle to win control of the Duchy of Tamarind-Abbey. The irony was not lost on Roderick.

"Have you talked to the techs?" he asked.

"They say they have a *Cougar*, but that you haven't assigned a MechWarrior to it. They say she's a good ride, but her weapons load-out is a hodgepodge of whatever they've been able to duct tape onto her."

"You want to pilot that hunk of junk?" he asked. He had seen the *Cougar* in question, and his description was not far off the mark.

"I don't want to fight this war from the ground, sir. Who knows, we may capture another *Firestarter* and put me back in my normal ride." It was pure optimism.

Frost looked at the young officer and crossed his arms. "Dewery, she's yours. If you're crazy enough to pilot that mess, all I can say is I'm glad you're on our side."

The young officer saluted, smiled broadly and took

off. Roderick entered his tent and peeled off his coolant vest. *This is what it has come to. We're piloting BattleMechs made up of parts from three or four different 'Mechs into battle.* He lowered himself to his cot. He needed sleep—not a lot, but enough to get his mind clear. *Then we will move to this Burkettsville. If nothing else, it will drive those Regulars troops nuts trying to figure out why.*

He closed his eyes and felt nothing.

Burkettsville, Tamarind
The Next Day

The defensive perimeter around the tiny village of Burkettsville was surprisingly sound. This was some of the rockiest terrain that Roderick had seen on Tamarind, and the large rock outcroppings in the area gave his troops good cover. He used his DropShips to shuttle his supplies and most of the troops to the tiny village.

The Broken Swords seized the water pumping station and the oil refinery. The Duchy owned the refinery, but had not taken the steps necessary to sabotage it or shut it down. Roderick was suspicious, but grateful. They didn't need a lot of petrochemicals, but having access to any source was good.

There were a few garages and machine shops in the tiny village, excellent sources for parts that helped with repairs. The village mayor came out to protest as Roderick's people seized the telecommunications systems and cut off Burkettsville from the rest of the world. He ignored the mayor. *This is war.* If their roles had been reversed, he would have complained too—but he would have expected the occupier to respond exactly as he had. They prohibited travel into and out of the village, with no exceptions. The local doctor's office was raided for medical supplies. Foodstuffs were stripped from private families and retail stores. It was an organized looting. Roderick wasn't proud of it, but insisted it was necessary.

The good news was that his troops had seized several tiny motels and bed-and-breakfasts and rapidly converted them into barracks. It was a chance for a night's sleep in a real bed, a shower with real soap, a chance to shave and to recharge. Every protest was ignored or ended by brute force.

As Roderick stepped out of the city hall, one of his troops in Hauberk battlearmor approached him. He was holding a woman by the forearm, but she seemed to be keeping pace with him pretty easily. Through his external microphone the soldier said, "Found this woman. She insisted that she see you. Said it was important, sir."

He looked at the woman, whose bowed head was wrapped with a babushka, really nothing more than a dirty rag. She was filthy; dried splatters of mud on her legs vied for prominence with sunburns and grime. What he could see of her hair was matted and oily. When she lifted her head and straightened up, he could see that she was tall.

The woman looked him full in the face, and without speaking he rushed forward and threw his arms around Trillian Steiner, hugging her tightly. She responded, but slowly. They held each other for a long moment, and then he loosed his arms so he could look at her face. Tears furrowed the dust on her cheeks.

The armored trooper stepped off, passing the woman's companion, who had walked up behind her. Roderick studied the bearded man and was surprised to discover it was Klaus Wehner. He nodded in acknowledgment. "Damn, Trill, it's good to see you!"

Her breath seemed labored. "I wasn't sure we'd make it."

"How did you know we'd be here?"

"We didn't," Klaus answered. "She asked me where I might move if I was on the run. This seemed like one of a dozen good choices. I guess that for the first time since this started, we got lucky."

Roderick held her face in his hands and saw in her eyes that she had been through a lot. "Trillian, I was worried. They said you killed a police officer. I knew they hadn't caught you because they never made an announcement, but I didn't know where you were."

"We had our challenges," she said with a wan smile. "But all along we tracked what you were doing. You've done great."

Roderick shook his head. "We've pounded these Regulars a few times now. They're going to find us and this time they are going to come for the kill—I can feel it in my gut."

"Can we take them?" Klaus asked. *We.* Roderick suddenly remembered that Wehner was a colonel and outranked him.

"What choice do I have? Duke-frigging-Vedet hung us all out to dry. So for now, it looks like it's going to have to be us fighting this war." He couldn't keep the bitterness from his words.

Trillian said nothing, but wiped her eyes with her grubby sleeve. Klaus spoke for them both. "We'll do what we can. I'm rated for a medium BattleMech. It's been a while since I piloted one in battle, but count me in if you have a ride. I may have rank on you, but this is your show. All I ask is for a chance to fight."

Roderick nodded and allowed himself a smile at Colonel Wehner's words. He then turned to his cousin. *Damn! She's alive!* He squeezed her shoulders as if to make sure she was really there. "We need to compare notes. We have to find a way to set these bastards on their ears." *I have to do it before my unit begins to melt away on its own.*

28

Breckenridge Heights
Danais, Marik-Stewart Commonwealth
9 December 3137

Duke Vedet Brewster watched as the gray-green VTOL patrol came across the city to Breckenridge Heights. Despite the misty rain that had fallen all morning, the two VTOLs had been out scrounging the countryside for some sign of the Silver Hawk Irregulars and their Daredevils militia allies. The two tiny Yashas arced over the city at eighty meters and began the approach to the landing pad.

He'd made the Heights his headquarters because the city of Breckenridge proper had been so hostile to him. The locals were passive at first, but then began the insurrection. Minor acts of defiance. Protests, sit-down strikes, all aimed at disruption. The Irregulars' version of the Marik eagle showed up everywhere, painted on banners or on the buildings themselves. The population seemed to be going out of its way to defy him.

There had been a few attacks as well. A sniper or snipers had taken out three of his officers. One shot had nearly hit him, and he made the decision to move his headquarters to Breckenridge Heights, a college campus. Settled on a ridge over the city, it was secure and safe. From here, the locals would have to look up and see him. They would now have a constant reminder of the new administration on this world. The age of the Marik-Stewart Commonwealth was over. This was the new age of the Lyran Commonwealth, a new age in which Duke Vedet saw his role as much larger than ever before.

As the VTOLs angled for the helipad on the far end of the campus, the duke gave an unconscious nod of approval. He had taken over the former dean's office, and Duke Vedet was just returning to a very comfortable chair when a shimmer of something caught his attention. Then came the blast: resounding, ear shattering. The rotor assembly of the first Yasha shattered as the craft dropped to the ground like a rock. The turbofan flew apart, the blades spinning like deadly daggers. One shattered the window of his office and buried itself a full meter into the wall.

Duke Vedet was stunned. Shards of glass covered his uniform, some so fine they appeared only as a glimmer. The wind blew in from the shattered window, caressing his face and reminding him of how warm it was outside. *What happened?* He activated the commlink on his desk and called the helipad. The remaining Yasha banked hard to the right and he saw a smoke trail coming from the city below, and then another one. Missiles!

The missile slammed into the remaining Yasha. It rocked under the blast, a chunk of its lower armor plate tearing off and falling to the campus below. It banked hard and came down on the helipad, out of the field of fire, landing with a grinding noise that he could hear from his office.

"Situation!" he barked.

"We think we've taken fire, sir," came a voice filled with disbelief.

"Of course we're under attack. I want a unit to track down where those missiles came from, damn it!"

The audacity of it stunned him. He stared at the broken blade in the brick wall of his office. It flexed slightly along its length, like a sword. In that moment it dawned on him that he could have been killed.

A chill ran down his spine. The attack on the Yasha reminded him of his first combat kill, earlier in the war, when he had shot down a VTOL. His mind's eye recalled the image of that falling craft. Flinching at the memory, he wondered how many people he had been responsible for killing so far. *I'm in command. I can't have these kinds of thoughts.* He touched the blade and quickly took away his hand. The metal was oddly warm to the touch.

The Fourth Royals Regiment's first and second battalions were the other friendly forces on the planet besides his Hesperus Guards. They had been in the field for two weeks now attempting to pin down the Silver Hawk forces. Now this—a strike right here at the occupation capital. His mind immediately went to blame; who was at fault for this?

The archon? Melissa Steiner had a lot to answer for in this war. Her ill-conceived foray into Skye had stretched resources dangerously thin, but she would never face the blame for it. There were layers of insulation between her and truth. The common man and woman in the Commonwealth would not see her as the person who led to this resistance effort.

Trillian Steiner would be a perfect scapegoat for this, if she were still alive. Nothing had been heard from her since Duke Marik had rejected her attempts to negotiate peace. The chances of her surviving were between slim and none. In fact, chances were good that she would end up in Fontaine Marik's hands and provide a bargaining chip in any peace talks. She had misplaced her faith in a military unit led by a misfit, this Roderick Frost. The defenders of Tamarind certainly would have ripped his unit apart by now.

He grasped the blade between his fingertips, and again felt the impression of warmth. He tested its flexibility, then released it again. No, the real scapegoat was the Lyran Commonwealth Armed Forces. They had been the biggest failure. The Silver Hawk Irregulars always seemed to know where they were going to land and were ready and waiting. Their ability to maintain operational secrecy had been breached time and time again. They demonstrated a fundamental unwillingness to listen to him, to bow to his leadership. That had been their downfall.

Then there was Bernard. Vedet had treated that man like a son. Now his operatives came back to him with rumors that Bernard was planning to kill him to usurp his control over Hesperus II and Defiance Industries. Duke Vedet had caught wind of these plans three days ago and had made plans of his own. The men whom Bernard Nordhoff had slid into positions on Hesperus had been transferred away at his orders.

The duke thought back to Bondurant and the friendly-fire incident that had downed his *Atlas*. Now it was clear that it had been no accident. Bernard had tried to kill him and failed. If he had succeeded, the Brewster family holdings, and the Lyran Commonwealth as a whole, would have been placed at risk. Bernard would have seized Defiance Industries and tried to dictate his own terms to the Commonwealth. As he stared at the fan blade in the wall, he understood that the military and men like Bernard had sold him out—they had betrayed him.

He left his office and walked out toward the helipad and 'Mech bays. He wanted to see the remains of the Yasha himself. The Hesperus Guards counted on his leadership. They were loyal, unlike the rest of the military and political machine that had manipulated him. He saw the smoke first, billowing black plumes. When he saw the Yasha he could not tell one end of it from the other. It was nothing more than a twisted hulk, burning, black, dead.

"Sir," Leutnant Schnell said. "You shouldn't be out here. We need to resecure the perimeter." Fire crews moved in, spraying globs of white foam on the fallen VTOL.

The duke ignored him, moving toward the 'Mech bay, where he could see his *Atlas* standing. *What do I do about Bernard? About Tamarind? About the archon?* His mind whirled with ideas, some legal, most not. He arrived at the foot of his 100-ton 'Mech and looked up. The *Atlas* was magnificent, representing the best of everything of which Defiance Industries was capable. Yet over his shoulder was the smoking symbol of everything that resistance could do.

Bernard would be leaving for Tamarind shortly. If Roderick Frost had done his duty, the Duchy forces would be considerably weakened and Frost's unit would be destroyed. Bernard would land and mop up. Tamarind would fall. Fontaine Marik would be captured. The Duchy of Tamarind-Abbey, this abomination, this shadow of the Free Worlds League, would be crushed. The duke, as the operational commander, would be able to claim victory. He smiled. *Yes, I will always have the victory.*

He had another thought. *What if I held back more than just supplies and reserves from Bernard? I could divert some of his troops directly here. He would be stretched thin rather than me.* He would have to win in an even fight with the defenders on Tamarind. If he won, the duke's victory would be even more impressive. If he failed—well, the duke could come in with his Hesperus Guards and mop up. Bernard would be a casualty, just like he tried to make the duke back on Bondurant.

This is payback. This is how we do it in the business world, Bernard. You screw with me, I screw you over twice as bad. He laughed to himself and patted the leg of his *Atlas*. *I will deny him one-third of his force, divert it here. You should have made sure I was dead, Bernard. Leaving me alive was your biggest mistake.*

Something on the BattleMech near his hand caught his eye. He leaned in closer and sucked in a long breath. It was a stenciled image of a purple eagle outlined in silver, small, about the size of his palm. When he touched it, it was dry. *How long has this been here? They came here, right onto our base, and did this to my BattleMech? Was it a traitor or an infiltrator?* Then, a more disturbing thought . . . *Did it matter?*

My God, if they can accomplish this, no place on this world is safe. He took a nervous step back from the *Atlas* and called for Leutnant Schnell.

29

The Harvison Flats
South of Zanzibar, Tamarind
14 December 3137

The flowing sandy hills and the burn marks, the expended autocannon casings, the blasted little craters of every size and shape, all told a story. As General Nordhoff fanned out his troops, he saw the recent carnage of battle and one thought came to mind: *Is this where Frost and his men died?* As he moved his *Xanthos* through the wreckage on the battlefield, he saw that the fighting here had been spread out all along the banks of the Zanzibe River. The plan Frost had filed called for his troops to blow the bridges over the river to bottle up the defense force and then deal with them piecemeal. Had that happened? The evidence made it seem possible. The only thing wrong was the outcome. Frost couldn't have survived this long. Bernard was weeks overdue. Outnumbered three to one, he had to be a casualty of war.

When Bernard arrived in-system, he hadn't even tried to communicate with Frost's force. The satellite network on Tamarind was gone—probably Frost's doing, to cloak his force from the enemy. Nordhoff had picked up signals from the First Regulars Regiment south and east of Zanzibar. They had to have spotted him as well.

He had landed on Tamarind with far fewer men and materiel than planned—Duke Vedet had seen to that. He had stripped his regiment of one-third of its strength and reassigned those troops to the operations on Danais. He laughed every time he thought of it: the duke had tried to make the Silver Hawk Irregulars seem insignificant when Bernard was fighting them. *Now that he has to deal with them, he needs help— my help.*

But losing his third battalion was no laughing matter. The Duchy of Tamarind-Abbey obviously was not going down without a fight. The debris around his *Xanthos* told him that the fighting had been vicious. He wondered for a moment what had become of Trillian Steiner. Had she been taken prisoner? What would he do with her if she was? Once Zanzibar fell, the Duchy would collapse along with it. He could be her rescuer, or perhaps something more. *She has the archon's ear, and rescuing her could definitely benefit me.*

"This is Stalker Actual to Sky Warden. Do we have any aerospace activity?"

"Negative, Stalker Actual," came back the voice of his regiment's air commander. "We located a Lyran IFF ship transponder about thirty kilometers from your location. We scrambled a flight and have gotten some images. It's the *Sandpiper*, or what was left of it. The burned-out hulk was parked in the middle of a spaceport. It appears they grounded it there to take out the Duchy's fighter defenses."

Bernard listened in amazement. He could imagine the battle. Did Roderick really deploy his DropShips as implied, abandoning any hope of leaving the planet? In Nordhoff's opinion, that was the strongest evidence yet that Frost and his men were gone. No commander would commit such a desperate act unless there was no way to win the battle.

"Acknowledged. Any sign of the other ships?"

"We haven't spotted them yet, sir."

"Keep looking. First battalion, form up on me. Second battalion, you have our right. We are going to find a place to cross this river and make our move on the city from the southwest. Once we take this city, this part of the war comes to an end."

Bernard angled his *Xanthos* toward the Zanzibe River. He hoped the fighting had left at least one bridge, or that he could find a ford shallow enough to cross. Otherwise, this was going to be a long march.

To the Southeast

A blast from the SM1's massive tank-busting cannon tore into Roderick's right side. The shells exploded and rocked back his *Rifleman IIC* like a boxer being hit with a haymaker punch. His head throbbed as he fought to maintain his balance and keep the BattleMech upright, staggering back two steps before regaining his equilibrium. The damage display lit up yellow with a few spots of red. The SM1 hovertank had ripped deeply into his armored hide, adding to missile damage he had received earlier.

"Somebody want to help me with that SM1?" he asked, waiting for his autocannons to cycle.

"On it, Hauptmann," said Jamie Kroff. Looking downrange, he saw her *Violator* burst from the tree line at a full gallop. Without slowing, she broadsided the SM1. Her massive anti-'Mech drill whirred to life. She lifted it upward and plunged it into the SM1. The drill threw shreds and shards of armor in every direction as it burrowed into the tank. It almost pulled her down, but she managed to make her *Violator* hold steady. Soon he could no longer see her BattleMech's fist and Roderick realized that she had burrowed right through the tank.

It dropped hard down on its hoverskirt and smoke

rose from the hole as she pulled out the drill. Her
Violator had pockmarks from numerous hits. It was
still standing, and from where Roderick sat, that was
nothing short of a miracle. "Thanks for the save."

"Sir, these guys are bugging out," Trace Decker cut
in on the comm channel. "They were just hitting us
and suddenly turned tail and ran out of here at flank
speed—thank God."

For a moment Roderick said nothing. Apparently
the fourth battle of Burkettsville was over—which he
considered good news. *I'm running out of flanking
moves and rear areas to strike at.* He could think of
only a few things that would cause the First Regulars
to turn away. At the moment they had his unit on the
ropes. Most of Burkettsville was already trashed from
the attack they had repulsed the night before. He had
used his presence there as bait to lure in the Regulars.
They kept coming, and his troopers kept finding new
ways to batter them.

Fires burned from the refinery. *At least we put some
of the oil to good use.* He gave himself a mental pat
on the back as he thought about the concealed
trenches full of fuel that had been ignited during the
assault. It had caught and eliminated a handful of vehicles and infantry squads, and had redefined the battlefield. Of course, the cost had been the Regulars
destroying Burkettsville with long-range artillery.

And now the First Regulars were moving away—
why? Then it came to him. Was it possible? Switching
to the channel reserved for communication with other
Lyran commanders, he dared to wish for the impossible. "This is Sword One to any Lyran unit on
Tamarind—come in." He paused. "Any Lyran unit,
this is the Broken Swords, please respond."

Static greeted him. He waited, then repeated his
request. Again, only static came back to him.

"What's the word, Hauptmann?" Trace asked.

Were the reinforcements finally there? *If so, why
not respond?* "I'm not sure. Let's get in some quick

repairs and rearm. I want our VTOLs up. Have them follow the Regulars. Let's find out where they went and why."

Bernard stopped his *Xanthos* at the sound of the voice. Roderick Frost was alive. He shouldn't be, but somehow he was. Nordhoff froze for a moment, stunned with disbelief and fear. *Awkward* didn't even begin to describe this situation. If Frost survived this operation, there would be questions about his late arrival. While he didn't care about the implications to Duke Vedet, Bernard did not want to be branded as having left his fellow MechWarriors to die in the Tamarind wastelands. No matter what his victory, everything else would be tainted by that suspicion.

"Sir, we are beginning to pick up ground activity from the forward scouts," Hauptmann Lanz signaled. The sound of his voice drowned out Frost's broadcasts and galvanized Bernard into action.

"What are you getting?"

"Seismic shows BattleMech activity. Someone is definitely skirting the edge of our sensors, sizing us up. Estimates from the scout lances show one to two battalions in strength."

Not only had Roderick survived, but the First Tamarind Regulars Regiment had not been crippled in the field. The outlook on Tamarind was getting worse by the minute. The temperature in his cockpit seemed to be slowly rising; then he realized it was just him. Roderick would want answers or, worse, retribution. Even the reach of Duke Vedet might not be enough to save him.

"Find me a shallow spot and let's get across that river with everything we've got." The priority was to take on the defenders of Tamarind, then deal with Roderick Frost.

His command tent was a hard-shell dome that could be broken down quickly. One of the segments had shattered under a piece of shrapnel and its shards now were held together with repair tape. The air stank of the oily diesel fumes from the fires. The Regulars thought that Burkettsville was important to Roderick. The truth was, he used it as bait to lure them into a series of traps.

"So, we have confirmation?"

"They are on the ground to the north and west of here," Trace said, leaning on his crutch. His BattleMech had been blasted out from under him days ago. He'd nearly been crushed in his cockpit, but had been lucky and managed to punch out. The landing was how he had wrenched his knee. "From what we could detect, Lyran transponders show about two battalions in strength, possibly less."

Doesn't sound like much. They were most likely counting on our destruction sucking up more of the Regulars resources. I hate to disappoint them by being alive. Trillian sat at the collapsible table, apparently concentrating on his words. The shower a few days ago had done much to restore her spirits, though she seemed distant to him, like there was something she was holding back. "We've got what—a company strength, at best?"

"Sounds about right with our losses today," Trace said wearily.

"It's their turn at the dance," Jamie Kroff added. Her forehead bore a brilliant purple bruise from when her neurohelmet had been damaged during an attack two days earlier. "We were left here alone to deal with these guys for weeks. Time the Third Lyran Regulars bled a little."

He understood her feelings; in fact, he felt the same way. Regardless of why they had been delayed, these were comrades in arms. They were all Lyran warriors. Their dying didn't help Melissa or the war effort one bit. "What do the Tamarind Regulars have?"

"About two battalions plus at least two or three companies of local militia that have been pulled into service. They're probably a little low on ammunition, and just about everything they have has been damaged. Their experienced troops are prisoners or casualties. Now they're most likely tapping veterans or putting inexperienced troops into equipment they don't know how to pilot."

Nordhoff is outnumbered and probably doesn't even know it. He rubbed his forehead in thought. "They are ignoring communications from us," he stated, and shot a glance at Trillian. Her face betrayed nothing but she did nod her head, indicating that she understood why.

"They don't want our help," Kroff added. "Let them deal with the Regulars."

"This isn't a democracy, Leutnant," he fired back with a quick show of temper. "I will make the call regarding what this unit does and doesn't do." His eyes fell on Colonel Wehner, who gave him a reassuring nod. He appreciated it. His soldiers and MechWarriors were tired of fighting, running and fighting some more.

Trillian stirred, then rose to her feet. "I recommend a brief recess, Hauptmann Frost," she said deliberately. "I would like to speak with you before you choose your next move."

Roderick checked his chronometer. "Everybody take five. See what else you can have the repair crews fix. When we move, we're going to need every hunk of junk mobile." The officers limped, shuffled and wearily dragged themselves out of the tent. Finally it was just him and Trillian.

"We don't have a lot of time, Trill. What do you know?"

"I'm willing to bet that Duke Vedet held off sending reinforcements here to sabotage your efforts and my negotiations. I also know that if he or his proxy Nordhoff wins the fight here on Tamarind, Vedet will claim it as a victory not just for the Lyran Commonwealth but also for himself. He could use that kind of victory to position himself for a bid to unseat Melissa and become archon—and we've already got evidence that he's heading that direction." Her words were direct and coldly blunt.

"You're usually a little more fun at parties," he replied sarcastically. His joke fell flat. Given his own exhaustion, he understood why.

"I have a confession to make, Roderick. There was a reason I tapped you to create this unit, your Broken Swords. I was counting on *you* securing a victory here. I was counting on this being a victory that House Steiner could claim as its own, with no interference from Duke Vedet."

He began to look repentant as she spoke. "Trillian, I am down to a shadow of a company of troops. Most of my men and women are wounded. We have enough ammunition to prosecute a short fight, and then we are bone-dry, even accounting for our salvage. How can I ask them to go into battle one more time? I'm not sure that even I believe we can do any good. Maybe we should let the Lyran Regulars take up the slack."

She hesitated, and he thought it was one of the few times he'd ever seen her at a loss for words. "*You* can't ask them. You're right. But there is someone who can. Someone you've spent your whole life avoiding. Roderick *Steiner* can ask."

He took a step back. "Trillian, what you're asking me to do . . ."

"Is only what you've always known you would have to do. Your troops are dead on their feet. But if they knew you were Roderick Steiner—if they knew who your grandfather was—it would be enough to send them forward just one more time and win the victory. You have to try. If not for Melissa, or me, then for your grandfather."

He bowed his head. He knew she was right. Damn her, she was *always* right. "You and Melissa are asking a hell of a lot."

"That's what family does." She said nothing more. She didn't have to.

His officers reassembled around the folding table and all eyes focused on Roderick. "We *could* just let the Third Lyran deal with these buggers. I know it's tempting—we're just about spent in every way we can be. But we're not going to step aside. We're going to let the distraction they are providing work to our advantage. We are going to drive toward the capital, turn and hit the enemy in the rear with every ounce of strength and ammunition we have left. We'll leave oneDropShip in reserve for our wounded. The other will shuttle us to a new LZ right smack in their back pocket."

"Sir," Kroff began to protest.

"No debate. This is my command," he said, cutting the air with his hand.

Trace joined in. "Our troops are dead on their feet, sir. I don't know how I can ask them to fight again."

"If they need motivation, I can give you what you need. There's a reason this unit was formed. It wasn't just because we were misfits and I was the biggest misfit of all. No. Archon Melissa chose me for a reason." He looked at Trillian, who nodded once, firmly. "She chose me because she wanted this victory to be for all the Lyran people. She wanted a victory delivered by a member of the family. By a true-blue Steiner."

His audience was enthralled. "I and my family have lived under the name Frost for two generations. My father and I wanted to make our own marks on the universe and not be judged, for good or bad, on our family ties. The name I was born with is Roderick Steiner. My grandfather, Adam Steiner, was one of the Commonwealth's greatest generals and a former archon. So I'm not asking you as Hauptmann Roderick Frost to go into battle one more time. I'm asking you as Roderick Steiner. Fight at my side, and you are fighting alongside the entire Lyran Commonwealth and centuries of history."

"You can't be a Steiner," Trace said wonderingly. "You were hung out to dry a year and a half ago. They wouldn't let that happen to one of their own."

"But I am a Steiner, and living proof that with enough money and the influence of the archon, even a person's name and relationships can be effectively buried. The price I paid for anonymity was that I couldn't curry favors when I got in trouble. What happened on Algorab happened. I could have asked the archon to intervene, but I didn't. Pride apparently is a family trait as well."

There was a stunned silence.

"So you want us to tell our personnel that they should throw themselves into battle one more time because they're being led by a Steiner?" Kroff asked.

"Damned straight. I'm going with or without them. I have to. Obligation is part of the price of the blood I carry. If your troops need motivation, tell them that the archon's cousin is their CO. Tell them he wants them to write their own page in the history book. This might be their one chance to take part in something—well, epic."

Lieutenant Kroff looked at Trillian. "Is this true?"

"Yes," she said proudly. "He's my cousin and my best friend. You already know that you won't find a better man to lead you into a fight. The only thing that's changed is now you know you're following the grandson of Adam Steiner, one of the best generals our family ever produced."

Trace limped forward on his crutch. "I'll be damned! Sir, there's a *Thor* we captured and have already refit. You get me a block of wood for the left pedal and I'll run it using the crutch if I have to."

"You're with me, then?" Roderick's face shone with pride and gratitude.

They rose to their feet, determined grins on every face. Trace Decker summed it up for all of them.

"Who am I to deny myself a page in the history books? Who knows, one day *you* might be archon."

General Nordhoff had made a long sweep to the east toward Zanzibar. He had managed to get about five kilometers north in the middle of the arc when they hit. The First Tamarind Regulars Regiment was not crippled, at least not in numbers. They came at him en masse. Most of their vehicles were cobbled-together messes. Every one of them showed the damage of fighting with Frost's men, but they were all functional.

He lost one company in the first twenty minutes of the fight. He had tossed them forward to buy time to pull back. Now, with the river behind him, there was no place left to go. Attempting to ford the river under fire was suicide. Bernard hated making a stand where he was pinned down, but he had no choice.

An artillery round went off to the right, engulfing an M1 Marksman tank in its blast. The tank backed away from the crater it had been sucked into when the round went off, smoke wisping around it as it retreated. The Marksman tank tried to track a fast-moving Tamarind Tamerlane strike sled that slid in behind it. The medium lasers of the Tamerlane blasted the rear of the Marksman; then it turned and headed farther to the rear of his force, looking for more targets. *Reckless!* His shock troopers fired at it, pitting its armor, sending it scampering. Either the Duchy had elite troops, or these men and women were green and downright dangerous as a result.

A warning tone sounded as incoming missiles slammed into his quad-legged 'Mech. The *Xanthos* rocked hard to one side and Bernard struggled to keep the 'Mech standing.

A moment later there was a crimson burst of light from a pulse laser against his other side that inflicted damage near two of his hip actuators on the right side.

The two massive autocannons on the back-top of his BattleMech locked on to a *Black Hawk* running across his field of vision. He fired the moment he had a lock tone and burrowed a dozen armor-piercing rounds into one massive hip joint. The squat, birdlike 'Mech tipped over, which made him grin until a pair of short-range missiles erupted against the front of his *Xanthos*. Flames roared upward and he cursed as the heat in his cockpit began to rise. Inferno rounds. Nasty, gell-filled rockets intended to toast a 'Mech rather than actually destroying it. Heat was a potent weapon against BattleMechs. He cursed as he backed up a few paces, closer to the river.

The Marksman at his side sent a gauss rifle round downrange, hitting a Duchy *Legionnaire*. The slivery slug hit its left arm and tossed it back with such fierce kinetic force that it must have severed the myomer muscles in the elbow actuator. The arm dropped limp at the large 'Mech's side, yet it pressed forward.

The fighting was a confusing mess. Bernard surveyed the landscape and saw, in the distance, even more Duchy forces pressing forward. *Damn . . . so many of them.* He watched as a Partisan antiaircraft vehicle downed one of his Balac VTOLs. It careened wildly into the ground and exploded on impact. Another one of his tanks, an SM1 tank buster, hit the Partisan with an autocannon burst that ripped the vehicle in half. A tire burst out and bounced away. Bernard watched it until it disappeared in the melee.

The *Black Hawk* regained its feet and his sensors told him that not only was it still operational, but its weapons were charged. It unleashed a salvo of laser energy at the Marksman tank, and this time the tank was not so lucky. The lasers seared black marks all over the vehicle. It threw a tread and ground to a halt in the sandy soil.

An errant short-range missile plowed into Bernard's *Xanthos*, hitting low on the rear right leg. It was a minor hit, but it got his attention. *We have to get out of here. I have to get out of here.*

"All troops, draw back the line. Form a pocket on

the river!" he bellowed into the microphone. Meter by meter, the Third Lyran Regulars gave their ground.

Roderick identified the rear ranks of the First Regulars force on his long-range sensors as he debarked the DropShip. The Lyrans and Duchy alike had written off his force—prematurely, as they were about to find out. "Rush forward, flank speed. Split them down the middle and link up with the Third Lyrans."

His troops moved forward silently for a moment, then broke into a run, howling at the top of their lungs. Roderick was yelling too. He had enough ammunition for nine volleys. After that, he was going to have to go at it the old-fashioned way—brawling. He looked out his right cockpit viewscreen and considered his autocannon. It would make an excellent club.

A pesky Bellona hovertank was pulling back from the battle raging down by the river. Roderick watched as Kroff fired a salvo of long-range missiles at it. It was the first indication to the Duchy forces that they were being hit from the rear. The Bellona, already damaged from the fighting, erupted in flames and ground to a halt. Its crew bailed out and fled.

The rear of the First Regulars' line turned to face the new threat. The momentum of their attack suddenly was spent. A familiar *Mad Cat II* turned at the waist and seemed to stare straight at Roderick. He locked on his autocannons and fired. Some of the shells went wild, cutting through the sandy dunes in the distance. The others hit the *Mad Cat* right in the waist, rocking it backward as it fired.

He switched to the Lyran command channel. "This is Roderick Steiner, commanding officer of the Broken Swords, to all Lyran units. We are hitting the Duchy forces in the rear. Meet us in the center. Let's split these guys up and end this."

Cheers went up on the comm channel. The wavering line in the distance suddenly seemed closer. Roderick throttled his *Rifleman* to a full charge and headed into the center of the line, right at the *Mad Cat II*. At his side, Jamie Kroff in her battered *Violator* joined him, howling louder than anyone.

Bernard felt his entire body go tense at the words on the command channel. Roderick *Steiner*? Suddenly it made sense to him. Melissa had put him on Tamarind to ensure a *Steiner* victory. His stomach clenched at his next thought. *I have hung out a member of the archon's family to die.* There would be no rope large enough for his noose when this was over. As his forces pushed out from the Zanzibe, they roared with cheers. The only person, other than the commanding officer of the Duchy forces, who was not happy about the arrival of Roderick's force was him.

He was tempted to send his forces at Roderick. Perhaps he could convince them it was a ploy, that they should fire on the Broken Swords. No. That would never work. These were professional soldiers; they would never follow such a command. His chest felt heavy at the thought of what he had been a part of. What really ate at him was that Duke Vedet was not here to see his plans fall apart.

A gauss rifle round hit his *Xanthos* in the rear hip, smashing the actuator. The 'Mech fought him, trying to let gravity take its natural course. His arms ached as he tried to keep it upright. It staggered to the side and he finally got his footing. The damaged leg was frozen; it wouldn't move no matter how much he rocked and played with the throttle to change directions. This would slow him down considerably. He would miss out on the battle that now was flowing away from the river's edge where he stood.

In the distance he saw a pair of DI Morgan tanks unleash a hellish barrage of particle cannon fire on an old-model *Apollo*, a leftover from when the Free Worlds League last was unified. The brilliant white-blue beams of charged energy stabbed at the *Apollo* and seemed to coil around the 'Mech like snakes when they hit, tossing arcs of raw energy off in every direction. The *Apollo* staggered, hitting one of the tanks with a salvo of thirty long-range missiles. The explosions left the front portion of one tank gutted down to the chassis. If the *Apollo* pilot survived the assault from the PPCs, the heat would slowly roast him. That was the true beauty of the Morgans.

The plight of the *Apollo* mirrored Bernard's own situation. He surveyed the area, and an idea formed in his mind—rough, dangerous, but possibly the best course of action. *It might just work.* He looked at the river and knew that mere kilometers away on the other side were his DropShips. There were JumpShips in-system right now recharging. He eyed the long, deep, murky brown river. Beyond it lay salvation. *This isn't the course I intended to take.*

"Third Lyrans, advance on the center. Link up with the Swords and finish these bastards off," he commanded. "I have taken damage and will be falling back to the DropShips for repairs." The wounded beast of his BattleMech limped toward the fast-moving waters.

The last of the Tamarind Regulars to fall was taken down by Jamie Kroff. Her *Violator* was missing its clawlike left arm at the elbow and was moving with a limp. Her long-range missile rack was peeled back as if a can opener had been used to rip the armored hide off her 'Mech near the head. Her foe was the *Mad Cat II* that had been slugging it out with several of the Broken Swords and had taken down Roderick's *Rifleman*.

She had run past the *Mad Cat* in search of other targets, turned and hit it from behind. She used her drill to pierce the thinner rear armor of the 'Mech. Her drill shredded the shielding around the *Mad Cat*'s fusion reactor. When she wrenched it free, the momentum sent her toppling to the ground. The *Mad Cat* staggered two steps and fell down beside her. Slick green coolant sprayed from her drill as she shut it off.

A message calling for an immediate cease-fire came from Colonel Chamlin, the Duchy commander. The fighting stopped as the forces of the Third Lyran Regulars linked up with the remnants of the Broken Swords. Roderick managed to get his *Rifleman* back on its feet, uttering a silent prayer of thanks. There was no armor left on his 'Mech. His right autocannon was crumpled, worthless. His unit consisted of a ragtag group of survivors, more than MechWarriors.

Roderick Steiner smiled.

Reaching down to his comm unit, he squibbed a simple numeric code to Trillian to let her know that they had succeeded—and to let her know that he was still alive. "Where is your CO?" he asked on the Lyran command channel.

"General Nordhoff has fallen back with damage, I'm afraid. Several other MechWarriors went back with him. We took pretty heavy damage until you showed up."

The First Tamarind Regulars *were* tough customers—that much he had to give them. They were not mere militia; they fought with zeal. Now that they were gone, Zanzibar—no, Tamarind—actually, the Duchy of Tamarind-Abbey, was wide open for the taking. "Tell General Nordhoff I need to meet with him immediately."

The response came back a minute later. "Sir, I can't reach the general. His DropShip apparently departed a few minutes ago."

Departed? Roderick understood suddenly. They *had* been hung out to dry by Nordhoff and Duke Vedet. The general knew it could be proven, and had run to avoid the charge. He fled like a coward. *On Algorab, I could have done the same, but I faced the music.* Roderick closed his eyes and sighed. Politics was always the downfall of military men such as him. His grandfather had taught him that. Now he had learned the lesson for himself.

"That makes me the ranking unit commander on the field," he said solemnly. "Send the word to your battalion and company commanders. We need to regroup and refit before we move into Zanzibar."

He toggled a channel to Trace Decker. "Trace, I need you to do me a favor."

"Yes, sir!"

"Go get my cousin. It's time to end this damn war."

There was a chuckle. "With pleasure, sir!"

30

The first time Trillian had entered the Marik winter palace, she had thought the room to be gaudy and overdone. Now there was a noticeable element missing in the posh throne room. In the center of the room was a dais, but the throne of the Duchy of Tamarind-Abbey was missing.

Entering Zanzibar had proven easier than expected. The local police put up some resistance at a few barricades, but they were no match for BattleMechs and armored infantry. Roderick had insisted on a quick move into the city, before sabotage or more organized defense could be made, and it was a good call, even though all the troops were weary of the fight. The barricades the government had thrown up had proven more effective for citizen morale than actual defense, and the local population was more interested in random acts of looting than mounting a defense. The Third Lyran Regulars pushed into the city with little resistance and quickly seized the palace. The Broken Swords, what was left of them, marched in with the Regulars.

They had not seized Fontaine Marik and his court.
Grand Vizier Sha Renkin waited in the throne room
alone. The man was roughly the same age as Fontaine
but much skinnier, almost frail-looking. He wore long
flowing robes and a look of pure hate that seemed the
exclusive purview of old men. Trillian regarded him
carefully as the security detachment from the Third
Lyran swept the room for any unwanted devices.

She had dealt with Sha Renkin several times during
her initial talks with Fontaine. He had mostly remained quiet and aloof, looking to Duke Marik for
his lead. Now he stood here alone.

"So, the archon's tool emerges at last," Sha Renkin
said coolly.

"Where is Duke Marik? We have much to discuss."
Her words were a deliberate understatement of the
obvious.

The grand vizier glared at her with pale gray eyes.
"His Highness and the rest of his advisers and staff
departed hours ago for Padaron City and from there
to an undisclosed world. He did not wish to become
a bargaining chip for the safety of his nation. He has
given me instructions in regards to terms for an
armistice."

His anger was understandable, but hers was justified. "I only wish the duke had shown the same con-
sideration for my security when he stormed our
consulate and tried to take me hostage."

Sha Renkin smiled thinly. "He was only attempting
to ensure your own safety, milady. Nothing more,
nothing less. At least he didn't kill a man in cold
blood. Tell me, do you have nightmares about your
crime?" He was enjoying this.

Trillian knew her face was red with anger, but refused to acknowledge the verbal barb. "So now that
Tamarind has fallen, the duke wishes to discuss
peace terms?"

"He does not," the grand vizier replied. "Peace with
the Lyran people is not something he will seek until

the worlds you have illegally taken are once again part of his Grand Duchy. He has empowered me to discuss terms of a cease-fire, an armistice. Though we cannot have peace while you occupy our worlds, we do seek to end further bloodshed at the hands of the Lyran people."

The missing throne was a clear message to her and Melissa. The loss of Tamarind was not going to take the fight out of Fontaine Marik. He was holding on to the throne to let House Steiner know that while they held his capital world, they didn't hold the Duchy. As long as Fontaine Marik lived, the Duchy survived.

Armistice, not peace. She had hoped for much more, but acknowledged that what she had was a victory. While a cease-fire in the Duchy of Tamarind-Abbey did not win the war, it would allow resources to be shifted to the Marik-Stewart Commonwealth as well as the Skye incursion. It was a good first step down the long road to peace.

She had been surprised by how nimble Fontaine Marik had proven to be. He had always seemed like an old man, lost in the wrong era. She, and the archon, had underestimated him. The loss of his capital world was significant, but by staying alive and keeping an operational government, Fontaine did not allow the rest of the Duchy to collapse.

Trillian stared at the grand vizier while she thought. Their intention all along had been only to cripple the Duchy. That goal had been achieved both militarily and politically. It was much better to live with a weak neighbor than a new enemy deeper in the Free Worlds League.

"Sha Renkin," she said calmly, "I believe the archon would welcome an opportunity to extend peace between our people."

The grand vizier chuckled. "Of course she would. I am no fool, nor is Duke Marik. We both know how Anson Marik is handling your forces in his realm. I know that the Lyran Commonwealth has more problems than solutions right now. You need peace almost as much as we do, so stop acting so benevolent, my dear." His words were filled with contempt, but Trillian ignored the provocation. There was no point in arguing with the man—especially when he was right.

She bowed to the tall, elderly man. "Let us adjourn, Sha Renkin, and draft a document that stops this killing."

Breckenridge Heights
Danais, Marik-Stewart Commonwealth

The shock wave of the explosion cracked every bit of mortar in the brick wall near Duke Vedet and tossed him and his aide across the room. His chest and lungs ached as he tried to get his breath. Coughing, he opened his eyes and saw the dust covering the entryway to his headquarters like a dull gray fog.

When he moved, his joints protested. The tall black man got up and two members of his security detachment moved to his side, checking him for signs of injury. Frustrated and angry, he pushed them aside. A fine film of dust rose as he brushed off the sleeves of his uniform.

His ears rang with a high-pitched tone that he noticed only when he couldn't hear the words of his guards. Shaking his head didn't help. He rubbed his ears, but his hearing came back slowly.

"What happened?" He knew he was yelling but couldn't help it. People rushed past him out into the street. The duke was supposed to be getting into his limousine. From the smoke and the people running in the street, he could tell that was not going to be happening any time soon.

One of the guards got right up to his ear and yelled a response. "Car bomb," he bellowed.

The duke moved to the door and looked out. His

hoverlimo was twisted in the middle lengthwise. A crater extended from the opposite side of the street where half of a building had collapsed into a mound of rubble. The crater was not deep, but every window that Duke Vedet could see from where he was standing had been taken out by the concussion of the blast. There were a few people too—or parts of people, a leg and an arm, lying on the sidewalk along with hundreds of thousands of pieces of building.

He moved back into his HQ. The ringing in his ears had diminished to an annoying muffle. Vedet Brewster knew who was responsible for this outrage—the Silver Hawk Irregulars. They had been like ghosts on Danais. Only a handful of them had been killed in actual combat. The rest of the time they were training the locals in a nasty insurrection against the Lyran forces. They refused to fight a stand-up battle against his forces, instead making these kinds of attacks. Bombings, assassinations, sabotage—all bore the mark of the silver and purple eagle.

"I will spit on Anson Marik's grave!" he said.

"Sir?" one of his aides asked.

"Never mind," he spat back, rubbing his ears again. The Silver Hawks' movement was more dangerous than ever. He could not kill this enemy, the belief in resistance to the occupation forces. You could not kill an idea. Anson had provided a rallying point for his people while at the same time managing to tie down a lot of troops.

He motioned for an aide. "We need to get a message out immediately."

The aide took out his noteputer and stylus. "Go, sir."

"We need to pull back a battalion of troops from Gannett." He glanced nervously at the doorway. "We're going to need additional security."

"Yes, sir," the aide said, flashing a salute.

This was not the kind of war he had planned on fighting. At least Bernard was on Tamarind, taking care of matters there. And from Tamarind, he could not make any mischief on Hesperus II. Once Tamarind fell, so would the rest of the Duchy. Duke Vedet would go there personally and declare victory. Then he could leave behind these Silver Hawk Irregulars and their guerrilla tactics. The other professionals in the military could handle the cleanup here. He would bask in the glory of crushing the Duchy of Tamarind-Abbey. Even Melissa Steiner would have to acknowledge his role, which would truly make his victory complete. For a moment, thinking of this future glory made the loss of his limousine almost tolerable.

He would be glad after all of this to return to Defiance Industries. Running a megacorporation was much easier than waging war. In business, politics did not come with blood as a price tag. Bombs did not explode in boardrooms, and when they did, they were public relations problems, not picking up pieces of human beings. He did not understand or appreciate the military mind-set. It seemed inefficient, cumbersome and downright duplicitous. Duke Vedet knew that the other officers resented him because of his title and assignment, but none of them had the courage to say anything.

Then, once the gratitude of the Lyran people was showered on him, he would be a contender against Melissa or any other Steiner for the archonship.

It was only a matter of time. Vedet Brewster forced himself to smile.

══ **31** ══

The Royal Palace
Tharkad, Lyran Commonwealth
28 March 3138

She could feel the flesh in her hands, the thick meat around his neck. She pushed the cord in deeper, deeper. It dug a trench in his throat, cutting through the skin. His eyes bulged. Trillian opened her mouth to scream, but could not inhale. Her stomach roiled.

Trillian sat up. Her body was clammy, covered in a sheen of sweat that made her silk sheets stick to her lithe frame. Air rushed into her mouth, and her eyes stared into the darkness of her bedroom. *Where am I?* The palace. It came back to her. She rubbed her hands against the sheets as if to check to see if the bed was real. The nightmare again. She had endured it every few nights since the incident on Tamarind. Peeling the sheet away from her skin, she slowly lay back and stared up at the dark ceiling.

I killed a man, killed him with my bare hands. It suddenly occurred to her that she didn't even know his name. He was going to attack her, and she took his life. In her mind, it was justified. If it was justified, if she'd only been protecting herself, then why was she still having the nightmares?

She suspected that part of the problem was that she still hadn't told anyone. She had wanted to tell Roderick before they left Tamarind, but couldn't. Trillian knew he would understand; Roderick had taken many lives in his profession. At the same time, she worried that his opinion of her would change—a fear that spawned its own nightmares in the back of her mind. Each day during their voyage to Tharkad, she had contemplated telling him but fought back the urge.

The cool air of the room hitting her sweat-soaked pajamas chilled her as she rose from the bed. There was no point in trying to go back to sleep. She knew her nightmares all too well. Each night was a wrestling match with her conscience and guilt. Some warm milk, that might help. Trillian pushed her feet into her slippers and pulled a robe over her pajamas, mostly for modesty. The royal palace was home, but it was always filled with people and activity, even at this hour of morning.

Her return to Tharkad had not helped her sleep. Her report to the archon had gone well. She had resumed her role of confidante almost immediately. She questioned why her cousin was meeting daily with the director of Loki rather than his boss, the director of the Lyran Intelligence Corps. Melissa had explained her motivation. Trillian did what she did best—she challenged that thinking, pointed out that Melissa sometimes was too cautious, verging on paranoia. Leveraging Loki as she did was like using a machete to open an envelope. Despite their agreement to disagree on this point, it felt good to once again offer her council.

Trillian passed the guards in the hallway and made her way to the elevator. In the first-level basement she silently walked down the corridors into the stainless steel kitchen. The kitchen smelled mildly of disinfectants, the aroma of fresh baked bread that made her mouth water, and something sweet, probably pastries for the coming day. She opened the massive refrigerator unit and poured herself a glass of milk. As she turned to the pulse warmer, she was shocked to see Melissa Steiner standing there in her robe. She jerked slightly in surprise, spilling some of her milk on the steel prep table.

"I don't suppose I could ask you to pour another glass?" the archon said, pulling her robe tight.

"You scared me."

"I've had a hard time sleeping ever since the war started," she confessed as Trillian took out another glass and filled it for her. "My physician wanted to give me a sleeping aid, but I hate taking medication. Plus, I had some late-night messages that kept me up."

The archon paused as Trillian warmed their milk. The archon laid the transcript of the message on the table.

"I didn't think you even knew where the kitchen was," Trillian joked.

"I may be the archon, but this *is* my house. You know I like a late-night snack from time to time. But why are you up at this hour?"

"Nightmare," she replied, handing Melissa her milk. The two of them sipped the warm milk. There was one person whom she could trust with her secret. Melissa would not judge her and could never share the secret. She wanted to tell someone, *needed* to tell someone. Trillian looked at her cousin and finally said, "I need to talk to someone, Melissa."

"The last I checked, I was someone."

"No joking," she said. "This is serious."

Melissa pulled up a stool and sat down. "It has been a long time since we shared personal secrets."

The words came hard, as if her mouth did not want to obey her commands. Trillian felt her face get red, her eyes get wet as she began. "On Tamarind, you know there was a time when Klaus and I were hiding from the police. Duke Marik had everyone looking for us. We posed as locals, wandering the markets, trying to blend in.

"We were confronted by the police. I got separated from Klaus. A policeman dragged me into an alley," she said, watching Melissa's face. The mention of the alley seemed to disturb her, perhaps because she suspected the worst. *She has no idea.* "He tried to force himself on me. I wasn't sure if . . . what he was going to do . . . I think he was going to kill me—or worse."

Melissa said nothing but leaned closer, putting her hand on Trillian's forearm. "I wasn't sure how it happened, it was all so fast. I strangled him with the cord to his radio. I remember thinking he was going to kill or rape me or both. He just kept fighting. I choked him to death. Melissa, I killed another person."

She paused. The archon shook her head. "You protected yourself. If you hadn't, he would have—well—you had to." Her words were reassuring.

"My God," Trillian said, suppressing the urge to cry. "I killed someone."

Melissa got up and hugged her. "Trillian, what you did was survived. You're a Steiner. You did what you had to do. If you hadn't, we might not have had peace with the Duchy . . . at least not as quickly as we did."

Trillian held on to Melissa tightly. "I keep seeing him in my nightmares. I keep remembering what happened."

Melissa leaned back while still holding her. "It will pass with time."

"How do you know?"

Melissa's cool blue eyes locked with Trillian's. "I started a war, Trill. You killed one man. I sent a lot of men and women to their deaths, and caused the deaths of even more. You're not the only one in this house who has nightmares. You are not the only person struggling with her demons. I know your nightmares will eventually fade, but they won't go away. Mine haven't."

"You? You are always so strong."

"I have to be strong. People expect that." She paused. "Does anyone else know about this?"

"Klaus does, he was there. I tried, but I couldn't tell Roderick."

The archon hugged her again. "You've told me. It stays with me. Your aide is a good man and will keep it to himself. I know you are close to Roderick. You may be able to tell him eventually."

Maybe . . . maybe after time. "Thank you."

"We're family," the archon reminded her. She toasted Trillian with her warm milk.

Trillian wiped away the sting of her tears and toasted her cousin back. "I feel like the weight of the world is off my chest."

The archon slid the piece of paper in front of her but kept her hand firmly over it. "We all carry burdens. Sometimes they are negative, sometimes they are positive. Sometimes the things that keep us up at night are the past, sometimes they are the future."

"You're waxing poetic. That's not like you."

"A package was transmitted to us by a courier ship. A set of military plans in exacting detail."

"Plans?" *Are we under attack?*

Melissa handed Trillian the paper. "Then this came in. A message from our friends."

"Clan Wolf!" she said, looking at the message.

"Our friends have emerged from hiding, and not a minute too soon given what the Marik-Stewart Commonwealth is costing us."

With all that had been going on, Trillian had not thought about the Wolves in a long time. The memories of her meeting with them seemed so far away, like a lifetime ago. "Does Duke Vedet know yet?"

"With the jump circuit I have in place—he should shortly." Melissa Steiner grinned broadly.

Breckenridge Heights
Danais, Marik-Stewart Commonwealth
Two Days Later

General Frank Addams stood over the holographic map as Vedet Brewster once again demanded to know his plans. *The man keeps talking in circles—talking about counterinsurgency. I want to know how he's going to end this threat. Damn military mentality!* A sniper attack two days earlier had killed General Leuken, putting Addams in command. The sniper had been caught, but the damage had been done. No place, not even his HQ, felt safe.

The peace with the Duchy of Tamarind-Abbey had been hard to swallow, as had Bernard's dissertion. Food, sleep—nothing seemed to offer respite, lately. When word of the peace, negotiated by Trillian Steiner, had come, that had been bad enough. He had counted on old man Marik to kill or capture her, but she proved every bit a Steiner.

Then there had been the military victory led by Roderick *Steiner.* He had to salute Melissa on that maneuver. She had managed to make sure that the victory on Tamarind was associated directly with the Steiner name. All his work, his leadership, his inspiration—all was forgotten. The archon and her family had robbed him of the glory he deserved.

It's not fair, but I know how the game is played now. I know now that my real hope is to shatter the Marik-Stewart Commonwealth. Once this realm fell, even she would not be able to claim credit for it. The Lyran people would know once and for all what he was able to do.

General Addams opened his mouth to reply, but was cut off by the arrival and quick salute of a courier. Both the general and the duke were handed communications packets. They both paused and flipped through the papers. The duke saw the words on the page but couldn't believe what he was seeing.

From the Desk of Archon Melissa Steiner . . .

. . . Clan Wolf forces will be striking at the following worlds . . .

. . . are to be given a wide berth . . .

. . . considered nonhostile allies in our war against the Marik-Stewart Commonwealth . . .

. . . by order of the archon . . .

He felt dizzy. How was this possible? *That bitch!* All along she had been in league with the Wolves and hadn't told him. With the lack of a full HPG network, the Wolves could have been busy for a month or more without even being noticed. He felt as if the blood were draining from his extremities and his face.

Melissa had bested him.

From the beginning she had outwitted and outfoxed him. The negotiations with the Wolves had to have been in place *before* the war started. All along she knew what they were up to, she had to. She and Trillian both. At each step along the way, they had bested him. *Did they manipulate Bernard's betrayal as well?* The duke slumped where he stood.

He looked at General Addams. "I assume you got the same information?"

"Wolves have swarmed across the border," he said, glancing again at the paperwork. "They hit Gannett, that's been confirmed. Our forces there fired at them, but they sent a coded signal that informed them of the"—he glanced at the paper again—" 'new relationship' with the Lyran Commonwealth. They then ordered us off Gannett."

"Damn her! She never said anything to me," the duke spat back.

"She is the archon," the general replied coolly, not impressed with the duke's theatrics. "I serve at her behest." The words he didn't say were strongly implied. *As do you.*

Vedet Brewster tossed the communication across the room. "Fine, then, let's see how the Wolves deal with these Silver Hawk Irregulars."

"Yes, sir," the general said flatly. It was obvious the meeting was over. He left the room, leaving the duke alone.

The war was different now. His mind reeled. There had to be a way to take advantage of this. But if there was, Duke Vedet couldn't see it. And that lack of vision was what hurt the most.

Dropship **Titanslayer**
Nadir Jump Point, Westover
Free Worlds League

Bernard brooded in his stateroom as the JumpShip to which his DropShip was attached slowly recharged. There was nothing to do anymore, no more plans to make, no more reports to read. *The moment I turned my back on the Broken Swords, I became a fugitive— for the rest of my life.* He rubbed the cool metal of his former rank insignia with his fingertips, pressing in turn on each of the four points of the star. It already had taken on the importance of a talisman.

His dreams were gone. Aside from the handful of loyal men who had left the battlefield with him, Loki had discovered and rooted out all his other comrades in the LCAF. He didn't want to think what was happening to them at this moment. Things could be worse—Loki might apprehend him.

I have to find a chance to prove that I'm as good as I know I am. If that meant siding with former enemies, then so be it. Being a mercenary is not the worst profession a former general could choose. From now on he swore he would make his own circumstances, he would seize and hold the initiative.

Duke Vedet, Trillian Steiner and even Roderick Steiner would not be able to stop him—not in the future.

For now, the first order of business was survival. If Bernard Nordhoff was anything, he was a survivor.

Epilogue

Diplomat Corps HQ
Tharkad, Lyran Commonwealth
30 March 3138

Klaus Wehner carefully folded the paper and put it in the envelope, pressure-sealing it shut. Loki was highly sophisticated in the way it monitored communications, but there were ways around their devices and systems. Resorting to something so low-tech as a handwritten cipher delivered by a commercial merchant to a third party to pass on—that was hard to detect.

His report to his SAFE handlers in the Marik-Stewart Commonwealth would outline the updated targets of the Lyran Commonwealth, just as he had done with the first wave of attacks. The information that he provided the Marik-Stewart forces had been invaluable. They had been able to position elements of the Silver Hawk Irregulars, train the locals, prepare defensives and generally make any attacks by the Lyran Commonwealth highly contested, bloody affairs.

He had failed in some respects. Trillian Steiner was a genius, he had to admit. True, she did not know that he was a deep undercover SAFE plant for the Marik-Stewart Commonwealth. But that lack of knowledge was more a testimony to SAFE's skills than to her oversights. No, where she had outfoxed him was in the involvement of Clan Wolf against his government. She had kept it a secret, even from him, her trusted aide-de-camp. As a result, despite all his successes, Klaus felt as if he had failed.

He studied his monitor. Serving a ranking diplomat—and a member of the archon's family—had given him access to information that had preserved much of the Marik-Stewart Commonwealth. He knew that the Lyrans considered SAFE a joke, regardless of which Free Worlds state they worked for. Klaus had proven them wrong.

He felt some level of guilt: he liked Trillian Steiner personally. She was not only attractive but also brilliant. *It's a pity that we are on opposite sides.* Even at her lowest point, living homeless in the streets of Zanzibar, Trillian had been a dynamo. When that policeman had assaulted her, she had killed him with her bare hands. *She is a Steiner through and through.* He even felt a little guilty that he had shared her actions with his handlers, though he knew their intelligence people would only leverage that information at the right time.

His other pang of guilt was over the fate of the Duchy of Tamarind-Abbey. The Free Worlds League was not like the Lyran Commonwealth. Each member of the League stood alone. While *he* knew they had been doomed in this campaign, it was up to his handlers to pass that information on. It had been difficult to watch a fellow member-state collapse. Fontaine Marik had been crafty enough to hold together the handful of worlds he had, but in the end Klaus had been forced to watch silently as the Duchy suffered the brunt of the Lyran assault.

Wehner looked at the monitor and chuckled out loud. He scanned the Loki reports and admired how Bernard Nordhoff had managed to remain at large. He found it ironic that he had spread the rumor that

Nordhoff might be planning a coup on Hesperus II when, in fact, the former Lyran general actually had been planning something along those lines. In trying to further divide the Lyrans, he had actually exposed a real threat.

Nordhoff was missing along with four other officers. Loki hadn't found him yet, but it made sense to assume he would try to sell his services to the highest bidder: a rogue general gone mercenary. He had included both the news and his speculation in the message to his handlers.

Finding him and perhaps enlisting him . . . that would be another coup.

Klaus Wehner turned off his monitor. It was time to leave for the evening. He would go back to his apartment, leaving the envelope at a drop point on the way. The next morning he was scheduled to meet with Trillian Steiner for breakfast.

Another day deep in the belly of the beast.

About the Author

Blaine Lee Pardoe is the author of numerous science fiction novels, as well as military history and business management books. He is a graduate of Central Michigan University and works at Ernst & Young LLP as an associate director in information technology. Blaine has written ten of the MechWarrior and BattleTech novels. He can be reached at bpardoe870@aol.com.